KT-119-537

VENDETTA

Out searching for one of her dogs, Georgina Casey discovers semi-conscious Jack Riley, an escapee from Dartmoor Prison. Without really knowing why she's doing it. Georgina rescues Jack and nurses him back to health. There is an undeniable chemistry between them but there are more urgent matters at hand. The net is closing in and Jack needs to find his cousin, Clint Baxter — the man whose place in prison Jack took. But convoluted family ties and old wounds trap him in the middle of a deadly plot. Now Jack must hold his nerve if he is to save the day — and get the girl.

Books by Glenis Wilson
Published by The House of Ulverscroft:

BLOOD ON THE TURF
PHOTO FINISH
WEB OF EVASION
LOVE IN LAGANAS
THE HONEY TREE
ANGEL HARVEST

GLENIS WILSON

◆

VENDETTA

Complete and Unabridged

ULVERSCROFT
Leicester

First published in Great Britain in 2012

First Large Print Edition
published 2012

The moral right of the author has been asserted

Copyright © 2011 by Glenis Wilson

All rights reserved

British Library CIP Data

Wilson, Glenis.
  Vendetta.
  1. Escaped prisoners- -Fiction.
  2. Assassination- -Prevention- -Fiction.
  3. Suspense fiction.
  4. Large type books.
  I. Title
  823.9'2–dc23

  ISBN 978–1–4448–1007–3

Published by
F. A. Thorpe (Publishing)
Anstey, Leicestershire

Set by Words & Graphics Ltd.
Anstey, Leicestershire
Printed and bound in Great Britain by
T. J. International Ltd., Padstow, Cornwall

This book is printed on acid-free paper

ROTHERHAM LIBRARY &
INFORMATION SERVICES

B52003538 2
OES452499

B52 003 538 2

SPECIAL MESSAGE TO READERS

This book is published under the auspices of

THE ULVERSCROFT FOUNDATION

(registered charity No. 264873 UK)

Established in 1972 to provide funds for

res

ROTHERHAM LIBRARY & INFORMATION SERVICE

SWINTON 23 JUN 2014 KIMBERWORTH ASTON
- 9 JUL 2012

08 MAY 2018

11 APR 2016
21 SEP 2012 30 SEP 2016
WICKERSLEY

Gr

9102 130 L -
- 1 AUG 2013 - 7 OCT 2016

13 AUG 2019

Yo
29 OCT 2016
by Thorpe - 3 SEP 2019

c RAWMARSH

15 APR 2023

This book must be returned by the date specified at the time of issue as
the DATE DUE FOR RETURN.
The loan may be extended (personally, by post, telephone or online) for
a further period if the book is not required by another reader, by quoting
the above number / author / title.

Enquiries: 01709 336774
www.rotherham.gov.uk/libraries

c/

94-98 Chalmers Street, Surry Hills,
N.S.W. 2010, Australia

Prologue

The Sierra's steering wheel felt slippery beneath O'Malley's palms. A trickle of sweat ran down his face. It found its way between his neck and the white dog-collar. His heart was beating violently.

He'd answered his mobile in the hotel. Michael, his brother, swept aside Matthew's greeting.

'I've read in the newspaper you're going to Allington Hall for a party tonight.'

'Yes, my Goddaughter, Belinda's eighteenth birthday party, but I'm also going for lunch.'

'No you're not. Your housekeeper's just told me you intend going. Now I'm telling you, back off.'

'What's wrong, what's happened?'

'Nothing, yet. But it will. When the next car to drive up to the Hall passes the mailbox.'

Apprehension moved through O'Malley.

'I didn't build up O'Malley's Quarrying Company so the bloody Duke of Allington could take over and enjoy the profits. He's ruined me, man! But today I get even.'

'Michael, I beg you, don't do it.'

'Too late. Ironic, isn't it, he finished my explosives and now my explosives will finish him.'

Matthew's face blanched. It was no idle threat. Michael had a history of violence. He was also an explosives expert.

'So, keep away. If you go, it's your neck — and mine.'

'I can't stand by . . . '

'And you can't dish your own brother. So back off.'

The words stayed in O'Malley's brain, back off, back off. There was no way he could. He had to try and prevent the blast. But Michael had been right. Blood ties were too strong to break. No way could he betray his younger brother.

Now Allington Hall was two minutes away. He caught sight of it before the lane curved and it was lost to view. He remembered the tree-lined drive with the mailbox a short way up from the entrance. The explosive must be hidden inside it.

The car swung round the last bend. O'Malley saw the entrance up ahead. A massive sigh of relief welled up in him. All was peaceful, no pall of smoke, no broken trees. He was in time.

The bright sunshine reflected a sharp glare

2

across his eyes. A white car was travelling very fast down the drive towards the entrance. Belinda was driving.

A scream tore from his throat as he hit the accelerator knowing that he was powerless to prevent the tragedy.

A piercing blast from a car horn dragged his attention back to the lane. A red Yaris hurtled towards him, filling his windscreen. Inside were two terrified women, faces contorted with screams.

He wrenched the wheel and the car bucketed past the entrance. The Yaris plunged wildly and entered the driveway but the angle was too sharp and there was nowhere to go. Even as O'Malley hit his brakes there was a terrific crash and the Yaris embedded itself deeply into one of the big trees. The front end crumpled like an eggshell. And in horror, he saw the white car draw level with the mailbox. An ear-shattering blast knocked him sideways, the Sierra rocking from the force. The air was filled with pieces of metal, twigs and a myriad of leaves kaleidoscopically whirling in a smoke darkened sky.

Sitting up gingerly, Father O'Malley crossed himself. An eerie silence had fallen, nothing moved. There was a terrible finality about it.

Shaken to the core, he knew that no-one

could possibly have survived, knew there was nothing he could do. Except for one thing, the only thing. Father O'Malley found his trembling lips forming the words of the prayer for absolution.

1

The ground came up and hit Jack Riley with a thwack, knocking every last vestige of breath from his body. Cold, mist-licked grass filled his mouth as he lay gasping, completely winded and exhausted beyond belief.

For a second, stunned by the fall, he imagined himself spread-eagled on the tussocks of some racecourse, the pounding in his head possibly the hooves of the horse thundering away following the rest of the pack towards the next fence. But only a second, he'd been running not riding.

How many hours had passed whilst he'd run, dogtrotted and finally slogged one dead-weight foot after the other? Too many. Total numbing tiredness caused the stumble over the half-buried tree root and he was past getting up. So he lay where he'd dropped.

As the harsh sawing of his breath gradually eased Jack elbowed himself up on one arm, shaking his head to try and clear the fog inside his brain whilst outside, the fog clung tenaciously to him in heavy droplets. Already being a twice a day shaver, the stubble was sprouting vigorously on his face and the moisture insidiously found its way between the bristles and clothed him with uncomfortable wet coldness.

A couple of hours back it would also have been clinging to the dark, pencil moustache but, fording one of the peaty streams that dissected the moor, he'd shaved it off using a disposable razor, cold water and the stream as a mirror. The razor was now buried deeply in the stream bed secured from water movement by a couple of large stones. They'd never find it, not even using the dogs. Air and water certainly came free on the moor but not food or shelter and right now they were both needed — and fast.

The thin, blue striped, prison shirt was soaked with both sweat and fog, his jeans not much better. Only his feet were dry. But they were freezing cold and extremely sore. Wellingtons were definitely not made for running in.

Pulling himself into a sitting position, he eased the rubber boots off, first one, no problem — the second had him yelping. He swore and tentatively fingered his left ankle. Certainly sprained, possibly fractured. That was all he needed.

Levering himself upright, he gingerly put the foot down on the grass and tried some weight on it. A sharp red-hot pain shot high

6

up his calf, the leg buckling beneath him. He wasn't going anywhere, and he knew it. That was when the first of the shakes started.

He'd picked up malaria in India a few years back while winter racing over there. Thankfully, it had only surfaced a couple of times since and each time the attacks had been mild but they were sufficient to incapacitate until the fever had run its course. Although it took nothing to spark off another bout the total exhaustion coupled with exposure had certainly weakened his resistance.

Running shaky fingers through dark hair, he gave a despairing groan realising bitterly it was now only a matter of time before they found him.

★ ★ ★

Inside the prison the air quivered with electric expectancy, like a finely taut violin string: the word was already round. At the long table in the dining room was an empty chair. Above the clatter of cutlery on plates comments passed up and down, behind the words, the grudging envy thinly veiled.

'Baxter's away.'

'Never make it, silly sod.'

'In this fog? Sooner him than me.'

Wells, his cell mate, said in an aggrieved

tone, 'Never said a bleeding word ... come to think about it, he's been damned funny last few weeks. Hardly spoke at all ... ' Still shaking his head he dug into a pile of mashed potatoes.

There was silence in the prison governor's room, as Hickson himself flicked through the file.

'Clint Baxter, aged 32, 6 Calgary Street, Nottingham. Quite a long way from home.' He halted at the fingerprint record, scrutinising the photographs of the full face and both profiles. A dark, curly-haired thin-faced man stared insolently back. A partial smile hung about his lips, turning the thin moustache upwards slightly at one corner. 'Baxter's a typical recidivist.' Hickson tapped the file with his pencil. 'His third term of imprisonment. Five years for burglary.'

'Yes, sir.' Officer Conway said stolidly. A worm of uneasiness crawled low down in his belly. He'd been Duty Officer on the outside working party — his first time, and he'd lost one. His now the unenviable task of reporting to the Governor there was 'one away.'

'Not been with us long ... A former trustee at Bristol a couple of years back, I see.'

'Yes, sir.'

Hickson slapped the file closed and

appeared to lose interest. 'Alert the local police, usual procedure, even in this pea soup it's merely a matter of time.'

'Don't know why they bother, sir.' Conway said, his courage seeping back now the interview was at an end.

'Because, Conway, they're prisoners — you're not. Never forget that.'

'Yes, sir,' he said, suitably chastened.

'And, Conway,' the Officer halted on his way to the door, 'as soon as he's back, I want to know.'

'Yes, sir.' Conway made himself scarce.

★   ★   ★

The six o'clock news on the local radio announced a convict had absconded from the prison earlier and was still at large. His description was given as slimly built, dark, with a pencil moustache. The only distinguishing mark was a scar down the centre of the right thumb. The newsreader finished with the words, 'He is not thought to be dangerous.'

Georgina Casey rose from the table, stretched weary limbs and switched off the radio. 'The last time I came home on holiday there was one away,' she remarked out loud to the black and white collie. 'Two days he lasted.' Jess lay still but the long tail thumped against the rug.

Recalling that previous holiday she winced, thrust the memory away, and took the single plate from the table. Moving across to two feeding bowls in a corner of the cosy kitchen, she scraped half the remains into each. Jess lay watching; a drop of saliva dripped onto her front paw.

'Come on then.' Georgina tapped one of the bowls. In an instant the collie had snuffled a rubbery, wet nose at the extra titbit so soon after her usual feed. The girl watched as the collie licked the bowl clean and then cast covetous eyes on the second bowl. The girl shook her head and with resignation Jess returned to the rug beside the warm Aga.

'Good girl,' Georgina praised. 'Still, I wonder where young Jasper's got to? I bet it's the Thompsons' bitch over Egton Hill. It's about the only thing that would keep him from his dinner.' She consulted her watch. 'We'll give him another half hour then we'll have to go and find him.'

When the dog didn't show up, Georgina, sighing with exasperation, shrugged on a duffel jacket and, flicking her fingers to Jess, left the comfort of the warm kitchen and stepped out into the unfriendly fog. Unerringly, she crossed the stack yard and skirted the big barn. 'OK, Jess, find Jasper.'

The torch beam bobbed along following the waving plume as the collie darted from side to side trying to pick up the trail. The wetness of the evening hampered her but a minute or two later her ears flattened and she took off. Georgina hurried after the animal and sure enough the scent led upwards in the direction of Egton Hill.

After twenty minutes, panting with exertion, Georgina halted to catch her breath. The enveloping fog reduced her immediate world to a few feet. She put up a mittened hand to push a damp strand of auburn hair back inside the duffel hood. Annoyance was rising when the clogging silence was shattered. A crescendo of barks ripped through the fog but whether it was Jess or the younger dog, she couldn't make out.

'Jess, Jess, come here.' Georgina called again twice, but the dog didn't appear. The barking simply went on and on.

Cursing, Georgina began to run in the direction of the sound.

★ ★ ★

The white German Shepherd gave a deep, rumbling growl and stiff-legged its way to the door.

11

'Max.' The man behind the desk said the name softly yet with an edge of warning. The huge dog halted, another growl vibrating low in his throat. A knock sounded on the door. The man laid down his gold fountain pen, leaned his elbows on the burgundy leather desktop and made a pyramid of his fingertips. 'Enter.' His cold, dark eyes watched the door open. A thin man dressed in a crumpled, fawn raincoat entered. He edged nervously around the animal, thinking not for the first time it was more like a wolf than a dog. He approached the desk and the imposing man with silver tipped black hair sitting behind it.

'Mornin', Mr Blake.'

'Any news on Baxter?'

'I guess so.'

'Well? Come on, Palmer, did he manage to do the job or not?'

Palmer dipped into his raincoat pocket and withdrew a heavy linen bag. Loosening the drawstring top, he gently tipped the contents out onto the desktop. The dark red leather showed off the opals beautifully. 'It should make the papers tonight.'

A slow smile spread over Blake's face. 'I take it Baxter left no traces?'

'None. It went off as smooth as silk.'

'Good.'

'Beautiful to watch it was. The way Baxter

persuaded that safe to open, it was wonderful.' The obvious admiration in Palmer's voice came across clearly.

'It would seem to settle the matter then, wouldn't you agree.'

'Baxter's definitely your man, Mr Blake. He's certain to pull the job off.'

'On last night's showing, yes. But this little lot,' Blake stirred the opal necklace with a neatly manicured finger, 'is merely the hors d'oeuvre. What about his nerve, could he go through with the big one?'

'I'd say so. Dead cool he was. No hesitation at all, straight down to work and a quick exit.'

Blake nodded slowly continuing to run a finger through the gems. 'Let's test his nerve a little further then, shall we?'

He scooped up the opals and returned them to the linen bag. 'Give this back to Baxter. I want it returned, intact to where he found it. By now Lady Crewton must be extremely annoyed by its disappearance. She's due to wear it in two days time at her birthday party and I want you to make sure she can.'

Palmer's eyes widened. 'That's a tall one, Mr Blake.'

'Exactly. If Baxter manages it . . . he's definitely the right man for the job. But, of course, we have to be dead sure.'

'What if he jibs?'

Blake rose from his chair, crossed to the door and opened it. 'It's your job to make sure he goes through with it. Oh, and do try not to get caught, either of you. Because in that unhappy situation, I don't know you, I've never met you.'

'Yes, Mr Blake.'

'And Palmer, don't bother to report back. Baxter's got just two days. I shall know if he's succeeded if Lady Crewton wears the necklace on Saturday evening. I've been invited to the party.'

★   ★   ★

Clint Baxter tip-toed into the little bedroom. He soft footed in professional style over to the baby's cot and leaned his forearms along the top rail. A wide proud smile on his face, he remained there motionless savouring the sight of the miracle of new life lying there. Mine, he thought, my very own child.

The new-born baby girl lay peacefully sleeping unaware of the adoration and love beaming down upon her. Baxter raised his finger and wagged it at her. 'Nearly a month old already young lady,' he whispered, 'and no name. Can't be done.'

He was still leaning over the cot in a happy

daydream when Anne Baxter came into the room dressed in a cotton dressing gown and fluffy slippers.

'I can see she's going to be spoilt rotten.'

Baxter came back to the present with a jump. 'Hello, love.' He unhitched himself from the rail and swept Anne into his arms. 'God, she's wonderful, all ours.' He hugged her tightly. 'I still can't take it in. She's so perfect. A human being in miniature.'

Anne laughed. 'You're prejudiced. You're a daddy for the first time — and on top of that, it's a baby girl. You know what they say about being Daddy's girl.'

'Don't spoil it love, it's bloody marvellous to be here with both of you. All the while I was banged up in that bloody prison just the thought of you kept me going.'

'Yes,' Anne said soberly, 'we've a lot to thank Jack for. Without him you'd still be in there.' She shivered and Baxter protectively crushed her close to him.

'Don't think about it, eh? Jack owed me one. OK, by now I probably owe him again but you can't expect me to give myself up now, not now.'

'That was the deal, Clint.'

'Sure it was but life's tough, Anne, if you get a chance bloody well grab it — and hang on to it.' He ran his fingers through her long blonde hair, still damp from bathroom steam, and tipped her head back, kissing her hungrily. 'It's been so long,' he groaned.

There was a loud, demanding wail. The infant had woken up.

'Shame,' she laughed. 'It's time for her feed.'

A second later the telephone shrilled in opposition and Baxter dragged himself away to answer it.

On the way down the hall he looked at his watch, six o'clock. It didn't need guesswork to know who was calling. He'd been waiting all day for this one. 'Yes?'

A man's voice said in a flat, unemotional tone, 'Give your password.'

Baxter swallowed hard. 'Party piece.'

'The Red Cow on Dolman Street. Meet me in the gents at exactly six-thirty. Come in through the saloon bar. I shall already have entered from the lounge. Right?'

'Right . . . er . . . was he . . . was the boss pleased?'

There was a click and the phone went dead.

Baxter swallowed again. He had a feeling that somehow, this time, he was way out of his depth — and still diving.

★　★　★

16

Jack, acknowledging his inevitable capture, lay back on the wet grass and closed his eyes. He was all sorts of a fool to have offered this chance to Clint on the strength of a promise, but he'd trusted him. It had never occurred to him that Clint would break his word and do a runner. It was a million years away from the world they'd shared together as youngsters on the farm in Ireland when a promise was a promise.

He started to shake violently again whilst the heat of the increasing fever made his face burn as though he were seated in front of a roaring fire instead of alone on a cold, fog shrouded moor. The pain in his foot was intense, painful jabs piercing the continuous throbbing. The left Wellington lay useless because the foot had swelled up so much it was impossible to put it back on.

Jack allowed himself to drift off into semi-consciousness, the exhaustion he'd kept at bay sweeping in like a tidal wave and washing him away. He slept for nearly an hour and whilst he slept dusk fell.

A barn owl floated low overhead, just a shadow in the gloom. It hooted eerily as it softly flapped past, but lost in a wild, disorientated dream, Jack never heard it. In the dream he was being pinned down and water was pouring over his face. Struggling in fear against the threatening suffocation, Jack awoke, sweating. Relief at finding it was only a dream was so great he let out a deep sigh. Then he gave a cry of real fear and threw up an arm to shield himself. With a sharp bark the dog which had been slobbering over him jumped away in alarm, her tail waving uncertainly.

Rubbing his eyes and trying to focus, Jack struggled to sit up, half made it and dropped back again. He put out a hand towards the collie. She barked excitedly.

A short way off he heard a voice calling and let his hand drop in resigned defeat. Well, they'd found him. His freedom could be measured in minutes now.

He closed his eyes and lay waiting for his captors to reach him.

2

Alexander Blake returned to his desk, and as the German Shepherd pressed affectionately against his legs, absently lowered his hand, stroking the dog's ears. He dropped heavily into his swivel chair, which swung a little and left him facing the photograph on the desktop.

The two women smiled at him from where they sat under the canopied garden seat with the late daffodils nodding golden heads in the background. Their faces were very alike, one simply a younger version of the older. He gave a loud sigh and picked up the photograph, holding it in both hands, remembering the words he'd written on the back, pain creasing his forehead.

For long minutes he sat motionless, back in time six months to the moment he had snapped the photograph of his wife and daughter. Gloria had only given him the one child. Blake had been denied an heir because of her very necessary hysterectomy but it had been a source of distress to her. Despite Blake's constant reassurances that as long as he had her for a wife he could ask the Gods for no more, it left Gloria with a sense of guilt. In vain he had gently reminded her that Patricia was just as precious to him as a son would have been. And as the years passed Patricia had half-jokingly said to him that a grandson would be just as good as a son and she'd produce one for him one day.

A spasm of pain gripped him and he closed his eyes against the sight of her face laughing up at him from the 7″ × 5″ gold frame.

Max gave a quick, excited wuff and jumped up. A young man came in, his eyes going immediately to the photograph Blake was still holding. Striding over, he took it from Blake's hand. 'The grieving time is over, Dad.' The Irish brogue was thick. Sean Rooney replaced the photo on the desk.

Blake gave his son-in-law a tight, bleak smile. 'Quite right. Revenge will be very sweet.'

'What did Palmer say?'

'Baxter pulled it off expertly enough.'

'And now?'

'Let's see if he can put it back just as expertly.'

It was Rooney's turn to smile. 'You do think them up, don't you, you old bastard.' He gripped Blake's shoulder in a quick gesture of warmth.

'We have to be sure. There's a lot at stake.'

'Where you're concerned Alex, what other way is there to live?'

Blake inclined his head. 'You have to concede, without a little danger, life is merely animated sleep.'

'And who wants to sleep their life away? Plenty of time for that when the Reaper calls.'

'Some would not agree.'

'You're referring to old Magda, I suppose. You've not been over to Ireland to see that old witch again, surely?' Rooney hunched his shoulders in irritation and walked to the window, staring out moodily at the spread of smooth turf and glittering lake.

'Old she may be, but a witch? No. She's a woman of deep wisdom.'

'A charlatan, like the rest of her kind.'

Blake rose and went to stand behind the younger man. Resting his hand on Rooney's arm he said softly, 'You are a young man, Sean. When your wounds have faded to scars, you will start to look around again, find another woman to spend your life with.'

'Never!' Rooney grated out the words, his muscles tensing beneath the sweatshirt.

'Oh yes, my son. However much you try to deceive yourself, you know in your heart my words are the truth. Celibacy is all very well for priests but a normal man . . . ' He felt Rooney's shoulders slump and went on gently. 'For myself, I am not an old man, not yet, but I'm probably too old for a further marriage, certainly for more children. And no, I have not been to ask Magda to act as a channel again. There's no need, once was sufficient. Allow me my comfort from that first and only time, boy. It is enough to keep me going.'

Rooney swung away and headed for the door. Pausing, he said, 'And supposing, just supposing, Magda Casey got it right. You know how that makes me feel, do you, Alex? It makes me want to put myself in front of a sniper's bullet and take a quick one-way ticket straight to Patricia.'

He went out slamming the door behind him.

Blake returned to his desk and readjusted the photo. He ran a gentle fingertip down the line of his wife's cheek, sighed and said aloud, 'Oh Gloria, at least at my age the skin's been toughened by years and experience but the young . . . they feel the razor cut so much more sharply.'

The phone rang. 'Yes, Strachan . . . in tonight's papers, right.' He nodded vehemently, 'Yes, yes, keep up the surveillance. Use the helicopter. Dartmoor's a hell of a big place, and we need to find him first. Keep me informed.'

He frowned. Time to accomplish what he'd set out to do after the double tragedy had been swept under the carpet by the authorities. Justice, as he saw it, had to be done, would be done. Riley's escape was a complication. However, if Riley could be found before he had a chance to talk . . .

Blake stood up, motioned the dog to heel and went to the door. What he needed was a breath of fresh air. A walk round the lake would clear his thinking.

Leaving by the rear door he walked out across the soft springy turf breathing the fresh Yorkshire air. A fierce determination rose up inside, he was going to pull it off, nothing and nobody was going to stop him, certainly not Jack Riley. If anyone could find the man, Strachan could.

Blake bent down, picked up a piece of broken branch and hurled it high and wide. Barking excitedly, the dog lunged after it.

★ ★ ★

Gil Thomas, down wind of the collie bitch, eased the weight of the dead pheasant in his left hand and watched the scene below him. He'd noted the man's laboured progress up the hillside, noted the give-away prison clothing and knew there was some money

23

waiting for his knowledge. From the look of him the man was just about done for. All Gil needed to do was melt away through the fog, find his ancient bike hidden under the culvert and head for the nearby hamlet of Paxton.

Amongst the scattering of cottages was P.C. Bruce Attewell's. Bruce was ever willing to pay an informer's price for information that would put him in a good light with his superiors. But sometimes it paid better to approach the other party.

Whilst Gil was determining which way to jump, the collie had put in an appearance. He knew very well whose animal it was. There was nothing around this neck of the woods he did not make it his business to know. Jess belonged to Farmer Casey. But he was away at the horse sales for a few days. His daughter, Georgina Casey, had come back to look after things. He'd known her since she was a babbie. Poor girl, life had certainly kicked her in the teeth. Gil had no wish to involve her in anything unpleasant and so he hesitated. And was lost.

He eased himself down on to the wet grass, grimacing as the wetness penetrated the knees of his old cord trousers but, for the sake of concealment, remained where he was. It would never do to be seen just now. He waited, eyes straining to see through the fog.

A small, hooded figure became visible and shouted a command to the excited animal. Reluctantly, the collie obeyed the order to heel.

Gil felt a rise of concern as he watched Georgina approach the recumbent figure. The man appeared all in but he was still an escaped convict — a potentially dangerous character. Gil felt his muscles tense in readiness for action and waited apprehensively to see what happened.

★　★　★

Clint Baxter walked down Dolman Street and came to the entrance to the Red Cow. A painting of a benign Hereford gazed thoughtfully down at him from above the door. He hesitated, cast a quick glance at his watch and noted it was six twenty-five. Five minutes before he was due to meet Palmer. He pressed open the heavy glass panelled door and entered the warm, smoky interior.

'Double whisky, mate.' He shoved the money across the bar and took the chunky glass. He lowered it halfway with one swallow. The liquid burned its way down. Baxter ordered another double. He was a fool to let himself feel intimidated, the job had gone off beautifully. He remembered the moment

25

when the safe door had swung open. It took skill to do that — he had it. He squared his shoulders. No doubt about it, he was a master safe cracker. Let Palmer wait. He ordered a third whisky.

At quarter to seven he went to the gents. Letting the outer door close behind him, he leaned back nonchalantly against it. The urinal stalls were all empty. But farther down were two cubicles. One had the door closed whilst the other stood ajar.

'Palmer? You in there?' His whisper sounded hollowly around the tiled walls. 'Palmer?' He raised his voice. 'It's me, Baxter.' A toilet flushed suddenly making him jump. 'OK, no need to rush.' Baxter chuckled as he walked down and stood beside the closed door. 'No rush at all, I can wait.'

'But I can't,' said a totally unexpected voice behind him. And as an arm encircled his throat cutting off his breath, Baxter was dragged backwards into the open cubicle. Clawing at his assailant's arm, Baxter gasped desperately for air. Palmer had the advantage and he was wiry and strong.

The blood sang in Baxter's ears and his chest felt as though it would burst. Sheer fright lent him strength and the two men rocked back and forth staggering and bouncing off the toilet walls. But his senses were going and a red mist swam in front of his vision.

Palmer let go. 'Don't ever do that again,' he panted, 'because next time will be the last, got it?'

Baxter was beyond speaking. He slumped against the toilet bowl retching and sobbing. Palmer eyed him with disgust. 'If I tell the boss about you pulling this stunt, you'll be out.'

'I got held up,' Baxter croaked.

'Sure you did.' Palmer caught hold of Baxter's hair and jerked his head back. 'By a bottle of bloody whisky.'

'I needed a drink.'

'Dutch courage, eh. Well if you need a drink before you can do anything you're no use to us.' Palmer pushed Baxter roughly away.

'No, no, I don't, I swear it . . . please . . . just give me another job, any job. I'll prove it to you.' Baxter dragged himself up. 'I pulled the first one off all right, didn't I?'

Palmer eyed him. 'That was only half the job.'

'So, tell me what you want me to do. Just give me a chance. Tell me what you want.'

Palmer, smiling nastily, told him.

'You're not serious?' Baxter's face was a study. 'Put the necklace back? Are you crazy?'

'Do the job and you're in. Botch it and you, the wife and the baby are all out in the street.'

'For God's sake . . . '

'He doesn't come into it. The accommodation was conditional with the job.'

Palmer pulled the linen bag containing the opal necklace from an inside pocket and swung it gently back and forth. Baxter's eyes followed it like a mesmerised rabbit.

'I'll be banged up for years next time.' He licked bone-dry lips.

'Then don't get caught.' Palmer tossed the bag at him. 'You've got just two days to do it.'

★ ★ ★

Georgina Casey, keeping her eyes on the recumbent man's face, reached for Jess's collar and clutched it tight. A finger of fear traced itself down her spine. She moved a pace or two nearer.

His clothes bore out that he was a convict and with the dark hair and thin face there was no doubt in her mind that he was the one described in the radio news bulletin. Still, she was bothered by the absence of a moustache and at the angle he lay, there was no chance of checking for the identifying scar on his right thumb. Looking down at him, at the closed eyes, the vulnerability, she was incongruously filled with an impossible hope that the scar was absent and he wasn't the wanted man. Her gaze took in the abandoned Wellington boot and the ashen look on his face, with head lolling to one side. Nerving herself, she took another step forward.

'Are you badly hurt?' The question came out a tight, little whisper. Very slowly he opened his eyes and focused upon her.

'A woman?'

Georgina saw the puzzlement. 'I'm not attached to the authorities, if that's what you think.' He said nothing but lay watching her. 'And you? You are Clint Baxter, aren't you?'

Wearily, he moved his head in a gesture of denial. 'No.'

'No?' Georgina peered down at him. Despite the prison clothing and how ill he looked, she had the ridiculous feeling of having met him briefly somewhere before. 'Who are you?'

Before he could make a reply his body was seized with a terrible ague. Without hesitation, the girl pulled off her duffel coat and dropping on her knees, tucked it around his shaking body. 'You need a doctor. I'll go and fetch some help.'

'No.' His teeth were chattering and he

could barely get the words out. 'For God's sake, no.'

'But you can't stay here, not on the moor, in this dankness. You look as though you're suffering from exposure now.'

'Wrong . . . malaria . . . ' The man was barely conscious.

Georgina bent over him and re-tucked the thick coat more tightly about his still body. 'Jess, here girl.' She patted the grass. 'Lie down.' The collie looked at her questioningly. 'Lie down.' Georgina repeated firmly and she obeyed. Pushing the warm, furry body closely against him, Georgina held the palm of her hand down in front of Jess's nose and ordered, 'Stay.' Jess dropped her head across the man's chest and sighed deeply.

The girl hurried away and Jess whimpered forlornly, her eyes following the small figure until the fog swallowed up all trace.

Georgina was shivering with cold and beaded with droplets of moisture as she neared the farm. Covering the last few yards to the barn, she failed to see the black shadow that appeared and angled straight towards her. With a rush, it flung itself upon her. She gave a cry of fear as she staggered backwards, but a split second later her alarmed cry turned to one of relief as she tried to withstand the exuberant welcome of Jasper, the young collie.

'You young devil!' she scolded whilst rubbing the furry ears hard.

The dog pranced delightedly after her as she opened the kitchen door. He hungrily began gulping down his delayed dinner whilst Georgina ran upstairs and ransacked her father's wardrobe. Choosing a strong trench coat, she took it back to the kitchen. Snatching up a kitchen chair she carried it through to the beamed living room of the farmhouse. Scrambling up, she removed the curtain and rings from the two windows and took down the mahogany poles. They were perfect for what she needed.

Calling Jasper to heel, full-fed and obedient now, she went across the yard to the stables. In minutes, Chester, the hunter, was tacked up and led back to the kitchen door. With several false starts and a few colourful expletives, she succeeded eventually in strapping each of the long poles to either stirrup iron.

Chester rolled his eyes and stamped apprehensively but with much encouragement and honeyed tones, she urged the big horse to start the long toil back to where the injured man lay. Despite the cold, perspiration was standing out on her forehead and

31

she tried desperately to ignore the shaky feeling in the calves of her legs where there should have been solid muscle. If the idea proved unworkable, God alone knew how she would bring him back to the farmhouse without reporting his discovery to anyone else.

She pulled a few horse nuts from her pocket and rubbed them against the velvety lips. Involuntarily, the horse started chewing them. 'Come on boy, you can do it.' He began walking with ears laid back showing his rank disapproval in every stride. Her words were as much an encouragement to herself as to the big animal.

Although the descent to the farm had taken a long time, retracing her steps seemed interminable. The capricious fog was lifting now in thin patches and Georgina prayed it would provide sufficient cover until she brought the man safely back. Just why she wanted to fall in with the man's pleas for secrecy she couldn't explain even to herself.

He had said he wasn't Clint Baxter. If he had lied he was the most accomplished con man in the business. The ring of truth in his words had penetrated deeply and struck a chord inside her.

Her thoughts ranged on further still whilst her gumboots and Chester's hooves trekked inexorably onwards: allowing that this man was not Clint Baxter, just who was he? There was something about him that seemed familiar which of course couldn't possibly be true. Just why she didn't call a halt right now and get back to the safety of the house and phone the police she couldn't say; the possibility of danger was very real, not something to be played with.

For a moment the thought halted her. Both she and the horse stood stock still, the fog wreathing about them. Then, resolutely, she forced her legs to begin walking again. A fellow being was injured, helpless right now, she could not abandon him.

A welcoming bark sounded through the now rapidly thinning fog as they toiled upwards and Georgina realised it was too late to back away.

She reached the spot where the man lay. He was still there, exactly in the same position. Her heart somersaulted. Oh God, was he dead? Hastily she hitched Chester's reins around the branch of the nearest bush and ran across to the man. His face was ghastly but a vein in his neck was throbbing. Relief flooded her. The side of the man's body where Jess had been lying was cosily warm. She rubbed Jess's ears hard. 'Good girl, well done.'

Pulling a silver flask from her pocket, Georgina tipped a few drops of whisky between the man's lips. One or two trickled down off his chin but most ran down inside his mouth. The effect was quite spectacular. With much coughing and gasping the man's eyes flew open and focused on her.

'You came back.' He smiled slightly and closed his eyes again.

'Wait, don't you dare go out cold on me now.'

'It wouldn't be the chivalrous thing to do, would it?' he said with eyes still closed.

'If I'm to get you back to civilisation, I'll need your help.' Georgina pushed the lip of the flask to his mouth. 'Have some more, you're going to need it.'

Half an hour later Georgina, panting with exertion, said, 'Now all we have to do is to drag you back without you falling off.'

She walked round to the horse's head, unhooked the reins and stood looking down at the man where he lay, lashed to the makeshift stretcher made from the buttoned up trench coat with the two poles slipped through, their ends resting on the wet grass.

'Put theory into practice then, girl.' He half managed a feeble grin, releasing both the steely control he'd forced upon himself and his consciousness at the same time.

Clicking to the horse, Georgina started the long haul back, the two collies circling around the strange entourage. With a rush of compassion Georgina realised the effort it had taken him and also that it was up to her now, she was on her own.

So engrossed was she that it was only Jess that heard the far off high-pitched whine. The dog halted, one paw held up, ears pricked but, seeing nothing, she ran on after the horse.

And far away in the sky, like a mechanical dragonfly, the helicopter methodically covered the area, the pilot catching what glimpses he could through the wispy, intermittent curtains of patchy fog.

3

Gil Thomas found himself releasing a huge sigh of relief as he watched Georgina take the horse's reins and begin to lead the big animal away. Now, he struggled awkwardly up from the wet grass, both trouser legs sopping from the knee down. 'Eh, it'll do me rheumatics a power of good will that,' he said tetchily, bending down and squeezing ineffectually at the dragging corduroy.

Straightening up and taking a last look at the little group going slowly down the moor, he noticed Jess hesitate, noted the raised paw and questing nose before she leaped forward to catch up. 'Something up, eh, little lady?'

Gil moved slowly round within his circle of concealing undergrowth. He took a lot of his indirect instruction from the local fauna. And quite often it paid dividends. Like now.

He could hear the notes of an engine some way off and it was getting closer all the time. Gil stayed stock-still. Georgina and the horse could no longer be seen. A contrary grey curtain of fog had swept across and obliterated their progress. But conversely, above him the sky was reasonably clear and all at once he could make out the bulbous nose and thin rear of a helicopter whining away overhead.

'Would you look at that? The lass got out just in time.' He frowned. 'Suppose it is from the authorities? Old man Blake's chopper looks just like that 'un. P'raps I might try and catch Strachan, see if they're interested in this little set up.'

He bent and rubbed a knee that was playing up. 'One thing I knows, they'd pay more'n young Attewell would.'

Picking up the dead pheasant, he walked stiffly away in the direction of the culvert where he'd hidden his old rattletrap of a bike.

★   ★   ★

The whine of the engine sounded like a gigantic bee as Strachan took her up swiftly allowing for the height of Egton Hill. Dusk was coming up too quickly for his liking. Before he'd been able to take off he'd spent a fruitless two hours checking the shepherds' huts in the immediate vicinity of the prison and had come to the conclusion that Riley had made better progress than he'd credited him for.

Failure in any form irked him. His track record working for Blake had been pretty good up to now and he didn't intend to let Riley slip past him.

Circling slowly, Strachan dipped down and began checking the slope of the hill through binoculars. Although the fog had more or less lifted, patches rolled in now and then obscuring visibility and driving him to take the helicopter above for safety's sake.

Scanning the sweep of the hill, Strachan saw what looked like a black dog come over the skyline from the direction of the Thompson farm. He let the helicopter idle as he tracked the animal on its downhill run. If anybody were lurking about down that side of Egton Hill the dog would doubtless pick up the scent. He kept the binoculars trained on the tiny, black speck but swore with annoyance as it entered some undergrowth and was lost from sight.

Taking the helicopter down as low as he dared and swivelling the powerful glasses in a wide arc, he picked up the dog again as it re-appeared. His exclamation of satisfaction was cut off as the helicopter hit a particularly dense patch of fog. Fear clutched at his stomach as the machine appeared to be flying blindly into a solid wall but automatic reaction took over and he pulled it up hastily, praying that the fog patch would not extend to any great extent.

Within seconds the helicopter was above and out of it. But Strachan was reluctant to take a second chance and swung away leaving the dog to run on unobserved.

He took the machine round in a big swinging circle and headed back towards the prison. Although flying over the moor was his own personal best bet for finding Riley, at ground level were many more eyes and he was confident that a sufficient backhand would ensure that if Riley were spotted, he, Strachan, would be the first to know. And once informed, he'd be on the phone immediately to Blake.

Down in Paxton village, Barbara, barmaid at the Russet Fox, jammed a whisky glass beneath the optic and watched as the glowing amber drained in. She flicked a beer mat with a practiced fingernail and set the glass down.

'That'll be one pound seventy-five, please, Mr Attewell.'

'Thanks, Barbara, keep the change.' He sneezed loudly. 'I need this for medicinal purposes as well as pleasure.' He took a gulp. 'Reckon I've caught the wife's 'flu.'

'Poor you,' commiserated Barbara. 'Has he been caught then, this Baxter fella?'

'Up until the time I finished at the station it hadn't been reported, no.'

'Makes you think, doesn't it? Must be

really desperate to leg it in this weather. Could catch his death of cold.'

'If they weren't desperate they wouldn't try it on. That's all it is you know, a try on.' Attewell took another swallow of whisky and smacked his lips appreciatively. 'They know there's no hope of getting off the moor. And besides,' he smiled knowingly, 'there's too many eyes watching. Someone's bound to report seeing him soon. I mean, let's face it, the man's got to eat. What's to eat up on the moor?'

Barbara pursed her lips. 'Not a thing, Mr Attewell.'

'Precisely. He's got to come within spitting distance of someone's cottage trying to find food.'

She nodded sagely. 'You're right, y'know. I never thought of it like that.'

'And as soon as he does — bingo — we'll have him.' He drained his whisky triumphantly.

Barbara, seeing a chance of baiting the policeman, couldn't resist it. 'But just at the moment no-one has seen him, have they?' she said innocently.

At that moment, Gil Thomas walked in.

Gil, dressed now in his second best trousers and minus the pheasant, was looking forward to a pint of bitter. He checked slightly when he saw Attewell propping up the bar. Gil had already relegated him to a second or even a third option and had decidedly no intention of giving anything away.

'A pint is it, Gil?' Barbara anticipating his affirmation had a hand on the pump.

'Yes, m'love and have one y'self.'

She grinned, leaned forward and patted his stubbly cheek. 'I'll save it for later, OK?'

Gil noisily slurped his way down the pint.

'Same again?'

Gil nodded. 'Mr Strachan not in tonight?'

''Fraid not. He was on the phone earlier and then said he had to go out.'

'D'you reckon he'll be back afore closing?'

'Oh, I couldn't say. He's the boss, he doesn't bother telling me.'

Barbara excused herself and moved down the bar to serve another customer.

Attewell joined the old man. 'Caught anything interesting lately?'

'I could always ask you the same question.' Gil took the head off his second pint.

'Meaning?'

'Not meaning nothing.'

Attewell changed tack. 'Look,' he glanced at his watch and lowered his voice, 'I'm here for about another half-hour, after that. If you've anything interesting to tell me, I'll be waiting out by the far corner of the car park.

Gil grunted, 'Shouldn't bother if I were you.'

Attewell scowled, not wanting to alienate Gil, yet ruffled by the tone. 'Why's that?'

'Because when I've downed this here beer, I'm agoing straight home.'

'I see.' The policeman stiffened. 'Someone else paying you better I take it.'

Gil gulped his beer. 'Don't know what you're talking about I'm sure. Anyways, I'm off. G'night to you.' He left the policeman and cycled ponderously away from the Russet Fox taking the turning that led to his own cottage.

However a quarter of a mile down the lane, he dismounted. With surprising agility for his age, Gil lifted the disreputable old bike over a stile set in the hedgerow and followed it himself. Concealing the bike under the bottom of the hedge, he went on up the grassy slope.

Gil reached the top and looked down on the Caseys' farm set in the hollow away to his right.

The fog had completely gone and he could clearly see a golden puddle of light spilling out from one of the windows where it shone on the expanse of yard. It looked to be coming from the kitchen. Gathering his breath, the old man began the descent.

When he reached the yard, he headed quietly for Chester's stable. Stopping to listen intently outside, he heard the soft movement of a well-bedded down horse changing leg position. So they'd made it back. The question now being was the man in the house with young Georgina? Gil stealthily crept around the perimeter of the yard using the deep shadows to conceal his movements until he rounded the house corner and saw the uncurtained kitchen window.

He could see Georgina pouring boiling water into two mugs and stirring them vigorously. She set them on a tray and carried them from the kitchen, out of his angle of vision.

Waiting in the shadows, he was rewarded when a soft light was switched on in the upstairs window.

'Well,' he muttered, 'unless yon lass has taken a lover, and that's out for sure, it's got to be that bloke off the moor she's got in bed.'

Gil continued to wait for the best part of an hour but neither the girl nor anyone else reappeared.

★　★　★

The Audi snaked its way down the green, twisting lanes of Co. Offaly. Peter Casey hummed gently, tapping the leather covered steering wheel. His heavy gold ring added a beat to the Irish tune. He still wore the wedding ring despite the lonely fifteen years on his own since Ruth had walked out. On his own on one level for he had been forced into single parenthood with Georgina to look after. His thoughts right now were centred on horses. The bringing together at Ballykenny Stud Farm of Glory Boy and Peach Blossom equalled one superb yearling. And today at Goff's sales, he'd bought the colt. From that bloodline it had been a give away at eleven hundred guineas. In four years the horse would be novice chasing.

His thoughts ranged over the blueprint and found it a pleasing prospect. With the right pilot on board the sky was the limit. Of course, the big challenges were a few years into the future and the leading jockeys in today's scene were possibly going to be superseded by the up and comings.

What he needed was a jockey old enough to have the experience yet not too far past the thirty mark right now. Chasing wasn't the flat. If it were, the jockey could still be racing at fifty. But chasing meant falls — regularly. And falls meant injuries, injuries that progressively took longer to heal the older the jockey. Not many of them went on after turning thirty-five.

Grant Gibson was a damn fine jockey and Casey had used him often along with Dick Jackson and Ciggie Butt. But would they still be at the game several years hence? He'd be better to look to a younger man. Possibly someone like . . . Jack Riley, for instance.

Casey pondered the possibility. He'd put Riley up only a couple of times in the past when his usual choices had been booked, but Riley had done a good job. And his age was OK. He'd still be around when the bay colt was ready. Yes, Jack Riley could well be the jockey to put up.

Swinging the big car adroitly round the sharp corner past Murphy's pub, Casey cruised gently down the narrow lane and a quarter of a mile farther on turned off right into what was virtually a cart track, barely wide enough for one vehicle. Dust flew high as the Audi wheels spun along in the dry dirt. He marvelled again, as he did each time he returned, that time had stood so still here.

The track was exactly as it had been when he'd lived here as a boy forty years ago. The same twisting, overhanging oak tree at the bend and then . . . he negotiated the car round slowly . . . there it was. The white-washed cottage sitting basking in the brilliant sunshine. Home, his boyhood home.

The sound of the approaching motor had brought Mary Casey to the door. At the sight of Peter a smile of pure delight lit up her face and she held wide her arms for his embrace. 'Come in lad, I am glad to see you.' She drew him out of the brightness of the sunshine into the dim interior.

'How're you keeping, Ma? You OK?' Peter caught her face between his palms and kissed her forehead.

'Sure and I'm just fine.'

'And Grandma Magda?'

There was a faint, throaty chuckle from by the ingle-nook. 'And why shouldn't I be all right? Do you not know lad, I'm indestructible?'

'Aye, I do that.' Peter hastened to her side and gave her a crushing hug. She looked up at him roguishly from vivid blue eyes. The one white streak in her long, jet black hair falling back from the centre widow's peak whilst the rest framed her heart-shaped face.

'You're as ravishing as ever,' he joked, privately dismayed at the fragile thinness beneath the voluminous black dress. Magda Casey must be at least eighty-five, could easily be more. He deliberately stopped his thoughts going any further. Magda had more senses than the customary five and picking up on others' thoughts was one of them.

She looked sideways at him and chuckled again. 'Away with you and tip the bottle.'

Casey went over to the carved oak sideboard and began pouring the Jameson's.

'And for you, Ma?'

'Not for me, Peter but you join your grandma.'

'And you can bring me the crystal . . . ' Magda cleared a space on the low table beside her rocker.

Casey, hiding his grin, picked up the ball which was covered by a square of white silk and ceremoniously placed it on the table with exaggerated care.

Choosy about whom she used her powers for, Magda always took a look, as she called it, when a visiting member of the family arrived at the cottage.

Taking a gulp from her whisky, she began to stroke the crystal with the silk square. 'Come now, put your hands around the crystal — and yourself inside it.'

Initially, it was as cold as ice but as Peter directed his thoughts and gaze upon it, he could see the tiny reflection of himself staring back and felt his fingertips begin to tingle and get hot.

Magda gave a low cackle of laughter as though she knew exactly what he was experiencing. 'The energies, lad, accept them in, they're replenishing you.'

Casey felt the need to draw breath in deeply and as he did so, a blissful feeling of peace and tranquillity filled his whole being. He closed his eyes.

Magda wasn't laughing any more. She placed her hands over his and gently drew them away from the crystal. 'Enough my young one. We don't want you going too high.' Casey opened his eyes and looked into her face questioningly. She traced a thin finger across his forehead.

'You are not the son of the son of Magda for nothing.' She dropped her gaze to the crystal and her eyes became blank.

Mary left her chair and knelt beside her son and squeezed his hand. He squeezed it in return. Neither said a word and it was very quiet and still beside the peat fire, the three generations totally in tune with each other. The silent moment drew into minutes.

Suddenly, abruptly, Magda began to speak. 'You will return to Ireland, you will not be alone. Georgina will be here. It will be soon . . . very soon. Emerald fields I see . . . and through the fields, a river winding, almost alongside the road. A fine boat is coming down, lots of people on deck . . . fading, fading now . . . ' A pause. 'I see a church. Flowers are everywhere inside, masses and masses, beautiful blooms. The fragrance, ah, I can smell the fragrance.' Magda's nostrils tightened and she tipped her head back as if to take in even more of the lovely perfume. Her attention came back to the crystal once more, her face altered, became very grave as she appeared to watch intently what only she could see. 'Mary, Mother of God! Not in a church, dear Lord, no . . . ' in agitation, she passed a hand over the crystal.

Mother and son leaned forward, neither speaking but each willing Magda to say what she'd seen.

'It's all over the lilies,' she whispered, 'the blood, it's spattered all over the flowers, crimson on white.'

Casey felt his mother's hand gripping tightly. She turned wide, frightened eyes to him. Slipping a reassuring arm around her shoulders, he gave his attention to Magda. But already the old woman had flicked the white silk back over the crystal ball, covering it completely. Her face was impassive, giving no indication of what she was thinking.

'Magda, what happened inside the church, what else did you see?'

'What church? I don't remember. You

should know better than to ask. You forget, I don't hold the memory once the ball is covered. I remember nothing.' She took up her glass and drank the remains of the whisky straight off. Holding out the empty glass to Casey, she said, 'I'd like another, all this idle chatter makes me dry.'

Casey took the proffered glass but he noticed, despite her dismissal, she couldn't conceal the fact that her hand was trembling violently.

4

Baxter sat in the gents for a long time after Palmer had gone. His whole body was one big, sore bruise that had him drawing breath in sharply each time he tried moving. His fingers explored each rib gingerly but with relief he acknowledged that the injuries must be superficial because none grated or pierced as he touched them. Not only his body had taken a beating, his self-confidence had received one too.

The bodily pain was bad but it wasn't enough to take his mind away from the situation now facing him and, ultimately, the threatened security of his family. He groaned aloud as his fingers circled around the bag Palmer had left behind. Just how in hell was he going to do the nigh impossible and replace the opals without getting caught?

Security would be on red alert now at Lady Crewton's place. Two lousy days. No time at all to sound out when they might be away from the property. If he were caught this time . . . Clenching his teeth against the on rush of pain, Baxter rose to his feet, pushed the draw-string bag into his inside jacket pocket and carefully unbolted the toilet door. He moved as fast as the bruised ribs allowed and let himself out a side door.

It was well after eight o'clock when he reached home and Anne was sitting in the lounge gently rocking the fractious baby.

'Colic,' murmured Anne, without looking up. She laid the infant down very gently on to the settee and packed it round securely with several cushions. 'There, I think she's finally off.' She looked up at him smiling. The smile died on her face. 'Good God! What's happened? Clint, your poor face . . . '

'That bad, is it?' He put up a tentative hand and felt the crust of dry blood.

'Sit down. I'll fetch a warm sponge.' Anne hastily headed for the bathroom.

'Don't panic,' Baxter said crossly, 'it's only surface, nothing broken.' He drew the bag from his pocket and let the gems slide back and forth between his fingers. Over on the settee the infant stirred in sleep and emitted a tiny cry. 'Don't you worry.' Baxter held the bag up. 'I'll put these little beauties back, just you wait and see.' Hearing Anne coming back, he hastily stuffed them in the nearest pocket.

'A fight was it?' She dabbed away gently at his face.

'Something like that.'

'It does look better without the blood,' she said grudgingly. 'But for our sakes, baby's and mine, stay away from any more.'

He jerked roughly away from her. 'Leave off, will you? I don't need any lectures.' Snatching the sponge from her, his voice rising in anger and frustration he shouted, 'Get off my back, I'm going for a bath.'

The lounge door slammed shut behind him and the baby awoke with a start and began to scream.

★   ★   ★

Blake came back mentally and physically refreshed from his walk around the perimeter of the lake. He whistled Max. Obediently the dog dropped the piece of wood he was carrying and came to heel.

Blake went into his office and picked up the 'phone and dialled Ireland. Work was a great solace. It had been the one thing that had preserved and kept him going after losing Gloria and Patricia in the car crash.

At the other end of the line a man picked up the 'phone and announced. 'Ballykenny Stud.'

'Blake here. Is Rosamund around?'

'She's been down the stable block but I can see her approaching the office right now.'

'Fair enough, I'll hold on.'

After a few seconds delay a familiar voice said, 'Alex?'

'Hello, Rosamund. All going well?'

'One of the brood mares had a severe bout of colic earlier. I've just been to check on her and the drench seems to have worked well. She's showing no signs of wanting to go down and is cool now, no more sweating so I think we've won.'

'Good, no other problems?'

'None at all.'

'And sales?'

'The Glory Boy colt went at Goff's for eleven hundred guineas. Sold to a Mr Casey, an Irishman actually, who farms over there down in Devon.'

Blake's eyes narrowed. 'Casey? Any relation to old Magda Casey from Clonmore?'

'I wouldn't know. I'll find out if you like.'

'Yes, yes do; check it out, Rosamund. I'd be interested to know. That colt was one of the best ones this season. Casey must have an eye for a horse.'

'Certainly looks that way.'

'Right then, leave it with you. Fax me any information as soon as you get it, O.K?'

'Of course. By the way, the pigeon that left the loft, did it fulfil its purpose?'

Blake chuckled. 'Beautifully, so far. Your

recommendation was a great help.'

It was the woman's turn to laugh. 'I couldn't be more pleased.'

'Rosamund, forgive me for asking, but do you have a personal axe to grind in this?'

'Me? What on earth makes you think that, Alex?' Her voice was guileless. 'I simply want to see justice done.'

'As we all do . . . and we shall. Believe it, Rosamund, we shall.'

'I've every faith in you, Alex.' Her voice was soft. 'It won't be long now.'

But after Blake replaced the 'phone, there was a hard, thoughtful look on his face as his fingertips drummed hard on the leather desktop. Rosamund's innocent tone wasn't entirely convincing. He was quite sure she was hiding something. Impulsively, Blake reached across the desk for Gloria's photograph. Even his beautiful wife had kept something hidden, something he would very much like to find out. The knowledge of a secret withheld had kept him awake many nights following the funeral.

Turning the photograph face down, he worked swiftly easing away the catches until the photograph and the frame parted company. On the exposed reverse were four words . . . words that no one else, not even Sean, especially Sean, had read. He'd written them the morning of the funeral. They leapt up at him from the back of the photograph still having the power to make him wince and mourn for what might have been, would have been.

Blake lifted up a small rectangular white card from where it lay, tucked inside the back of the gold frame. The words written in black ink upon the card he could recite by heart. 'Rosemary, that's for remembrance . . . pray you, love, remember.' Shakespeare, of course. And underneath the quote the words 'The long ago regrets go deep.' The card itself was unsigned.

His mind did a time-slip and he was back enduring the double funeral, standing immobile, a marble-like statue, between the two gaping holes in the green turf of the cemetery. As in a dream he heard the parson intoning the supposedly comforting words of the burial service but they made no sense to him. Not by a fraction did they ease the agony within. The undertaker's hand gently touching him, discreetly prompting the casting down of a scatter of earth was the first thing that penetrated his frozen numbness.

No doubt, if he had been fully in control, he'd have caught sight of the man, it had to be a man, who a few minutes before had placed the wreath of red roses. But he hadn't observed anything and when he stumbled along the line of wreaths, it was too late. But there it lay, the last one, a bright red among all the other discreet, pale-hued blooms.

He'd halted, focussing his eyes with an effort. One green spray of rosemary entwined lovingly within the sweet soft petals. Reading the words written in black ink upon the plain white card, Blake felt anger roar through him. It burned through his very loins, surged up and engulfed his heart and roared on through him, blowing his mind with a fury he could not contain.

Snatching the rosemary he wrenched it from where it lay innocently amidst the red roses and snapped it into tiny shreds. With superhuman effort he controlled himself from stamping on the vile red wreath.

Shaking with passion, he thrust the white card into his pocket and left the cemetery. He'd paced up and down the lane outside for a long time before he finally submitted and allowed himself to be driven home by the anxious undertaker.

In the long, long night that followed, Blake had promised himself that one day he'd find the man who had written the card. He was possibly involved in the deaths of Gloria and Patricia. Certainly he'd made it his business to know just where and when the private funeral was taking place.

But even as Blake promised himself revenge, a cold ball of ice formed in his stomach at what the discovery might tell him. Gloria had always said he was the only man she'd ever loved. Torturing himself, yet still swearing revenge, Blake knew, only too well, he could find out she was a liar.

★ ★ ★

Georgina eased the bedroom door open and angled the tea tray through. The man's face was peaceful in sleep, the tension lines smoothed away, a childlike vulnerability about him.

She felt a swift rush of protectiveness, a basic maternal instinct. Perhaps that explained why she'd brought the injured man home. It hadn't been a sensible thing to do, bringing the escaped convict back to the farm. But, irrationally, even as the thought crossed her mind, it wasn't fear for herself that clutched suddenly at her stomach but fear for him — whoever he was.

Downstairs in the kitchen was the one Wellington she'd pulled off which meant that way up on the moor the other one must still be lying in the wet grass. A damning piece of factual evidence that stated not only that he'd been there but that he had a leg injury and with only one boot still on, would not be able to get very far. If the police were to find it, they would begin a house-to-house search of the vicinity immediately. She knew from past experience they'd be doing that anyway very soon. Well, there was nothing she could do right now, the boot would have to be left where it was until daylight tomorrow. She'd set the alarm clock for a daybreak start.

Georgina moved across and placed the tray on the bedside cabinet. The china mugs chinked as she set it down and the man's eyes flew open, wary, defensive.

'Don't worry, I'm by myself.' What on earth was she saying? Her face must have mirrored the thought because he gave a tiny smile.

'You're quite safe with me. And I can't keep calling you girl. Would you tell me your name?'

Only for a second she hesitated then reassured, smiled back.

'Can you sit up? I've brought a hot drink. I'm Georgina.'

He eased himself up and took the mug from her. 'You know something?' He sipped appreciatively at the steaming liquid. 'You're one very brave lady.' He indicated the prison shirt, which she'd tossed over the back of a chair. 'It convicts me without words.'

'You can't leave here wearing it.'

'Since I have nothing else, I think you could call that Hobson's.'

Georgina shook her head. 'Don't be silly. You wouldn't get two yards down the road before they picked you up. I'll look out some old clothes of Father's. They probably need the buttons altering but apart from that, I think they'll do.'

'I'm in no position to argue with a heaven-sent angel, am I?' His face softened as he looked at her. 'Thanks, Georgina. It's totally inadequate, but thanks.' He made to take another drink from the mug, but a wave of ague shook his body and his teeth rattled against the china.

Georgina swiftly took it from his hand. 'Lay back and rest. It's what you need more than anything right now.' But even as she spoke, his eyes had fluttered and closed.

Georgina took her mug of tea back to her own room. Whoever he was, whatever he'd done, was irrelevant right now. Quite simply, he was a human being who needed caring for. And she intended to do just that. She ignored the little voice inside which said, 'Why?'

★　★　★

It was a comforting thought, Baxter acknowledged, that Lady Crewton didn't go in for guard dogs at Roster Hall. All in all, relieving her of the opals had been moderately easy. But the returning of them was something else. The element of surprise, which had greatly facilitated the heist, was now missing. Just what safety factors had been implemented · following the loss was anybody's guess. And Baxter couldn't afford to guess. Which was why, still wincing from the previous night's injuries, the morning found him stretched out full-length at the bottom of the boundary hedge scanning the front entrance of Roster Hall with a pair of binoculars.

There was little to see. Nothing moved at all. After giving it twenty minutes scrutiny, Baxter crawled cautiously along the hedgerow and reached the rear of the Hall undetected. A flicker of excitement ran through him as he edged along because down by the servants' entrance a white van was parked up. A dark smudge of lettering ran down the side and Baxter trained the glasses upon it. The blue letters sprang into focus and read 'Securehelp Security Services, High Street, Holmington.' Baxter lowered the glasses and laid back full length to consider the implications.

Security was being tightened up. It was a

sure bet the actual safe would be in the spotlight, perhaps Lady Crewton was even having a completely new safe installed.

A slow smile spread over his face. All it need was a bit of nerve, well, a lot of nerve really but then, he'd got it, hadn't he? It only amounted to confidence. Walk in bold as brass and make it look natural. The job was as good as done.

Scrambling to his feet, filled with urgent excitement, Baxter retraced his steps back to the main road. Walking smartly the half-mile east to the nearest lay-by, he noted with relief the stolen white Fiesta was still parked up. The irony of it struck him and he laughed out loud as he swung into the driver's seat and slammed the door shut; he'd been hoping no one had stolen it.

Driving well within the limits, Baxter nosed the car back into a side street on the outskirts of Holmington and left it, keys still in the ignition. With a bit of luck, some kid would take a joyride and get caught. Which would let him off the hook very nicely.

A couple of streets further on Baxter found a pub with a smallish car park and just the right set of wheels he needed. Standing inconspicuously by the pub wall, he lit a cigarette and guardedly scanned the two or three people crossing the car park. He took a draw on the cigarette and studied the glowing tip whilst two of the cars reversed and drove away.

Baxter flicked the cigarette away and walked purposefully over to the motorbike. It was a Honda 600 c.c. propped on its stand. Releasing the helmet from the safety lock, he put it on. It was a full-face model, exactly what he needed. Leaning across the motorbike he fiddled with the steering wheel lock. Within seconds, the ignition fired.

As he roared away, visor down, Baxter was confident no one would be able to recognise him. He rode the bike through the twisting back streets until they led on to the main streets of the town. Cruising with the traffic flow, he scanned the names of the shops and businesses until, slowing down at one set of traffic lights, he spotted a board which read 'Securehelp Security Services'.

He drove around the block again to get his bearings and chose an unrestricted street to dump the Honda. With helmet still on, he sauntered back and entered the offices of the security firm.

The girl on reception was young, impressionable.

He played up the body language of virile male, legs aggressively apart, hands on hips and knew it would draw attention away from the helmet.

She simpered up at him, 'How can I help you?'

Baxter fought down the obvious reply and asked what services they supplied for private house protection. She began to rattle off parrot fashion all the superb ways her firm could assist. Then he held up a hand. 'Just a moment, do you have some literature I could take away?'

'Oh, of course.' She scooped up some leaflets from the desk.

'Thanks.' Baxter took them from her and pretended to run over the details. 'Some of the systems look a bit complex. Do you have a rep who could call to discuss them at the house?' She certainly had. Their Mr Fox would be delighted to give him a call. 'And could I have his business card? I'll give him a ring to arrange a convenient time.' She handed over the pasteboard without hesitation. 'Just one other thing. Your workmen, are they employed directly by your firm or sub-contracted?' Baxter was delighted to learn they were sub-contracted.

A few yards away from Securehelp's offices down the street, he thankfully pulled off the heavy helmet and wiped the sweat from his forehead with the back of his hand. So far so good, dead easy in fact.

Well pleased, Baxter returned to the motorbike, placed the helmet on the seat and swiftly walked away. Glancing at his watch he noted it was nearly twelve o'clock. Lunchtime in town.

He headed for a more affluent area and checked out several of the pricey watering holes of the business world. Hotel Major certainly qualified and in the adjoining car park was an outside gents. Baxter unobtrusively strolled across and went in.

Several class cars pulled in and parked but he waited. It wouldn't do to roll up in a Merc. And then a black B.M.W. swung in. The owner locked it and strode off into the side entrance of the hotel.

Baxter gave him five minutes and then came out of the gents and walked smartly over to the car, opened the door with surprising swiftness with a small, neat tool, before driving slowly away with the minimum of noise. By the time the city gent had downed his luncheon, the job would be well in hand. No problem.

Twisting and turning down every junction that presented itself, Baxter finally drew up outside the property where he was living with Anne and the baby. First, before he could even consider going any further, he had to change. The one good suit he possessed would have to do.

'That you, love?' called Anne as she heard the front door open and close.

'And who else would you be expecting?' He ran lightly up the stairs and met her coming down.

'What's the rush?' She slipped both arms around his neck. 'Don't I even get a kiss?'

He kissed her quickly and loosened her arms. 'Got to see a man about a dog, my love. I'll make it up to you when I get back. Should only take about an hour or so.'

Alone in the bedroom, Baxter found a clean shirt, wet-combed his black hair and put on his charcoal grey suit. With black highly polished shoes completing the outfit, he looked exactly like a successful company executive.

Feeling in the jacket pocket he checked the business card for Mr D. Fox was safely awaiting its presentation and, into his trouser pocket, he slipped the linen bag containing the opal necklace. He couldn't wait to tell Palmer that it had been returned. Buttoning the jacket over the top entirely hid the slight bulge that the necklace made.

Baxter stepped back from the mirror, twitched the jacket once more and nodded with satisfaction. He was ready. Adrenalin pumping now, he ran quickly downstairs, shouted goodbye to Anne and went to the car.

Switching on the engine he revved up, did a 'U' turn and headed out for Roster Hall.

5

Shortly after daybreak Gil Thomas, still in his old slippers, stumped down the weed-choked garden path carrying the feed bucket. Fumbling with the henhouse door, he grunted as a twinge of rheumatism assaulted his knee. 'Come on then.' The grain rattled against the baked earth. Sleepy hens ruffled and shook the dust from their feathers. Gil bent down and felt beneath warm feathers in the nest box. With satisfaction, he withdrew a freshly laid egg and rubbed away the wisps of hay still sticking to it. These young Wyndotts were doing well.

Inside the cottage, Gil put the frying pan on the stove and slapped in a couple of rashers. He gave it a minute or two then cracked the fresh egg on the side of the pan and let the contents slip in beside the sizzling bacon. Sniffing appraisingly, he spooned hot bacon fat over to close its eye before tipping the pan out onto his waiting plate. Usually, after washing his breakfast down with a mug of strong sweet tea, he'd lean back in the chair for a smoke but not this morning. As soon as he'd drunk the tea, Gil laced on his boots and taking his gnarled walking stick, he left the cottage and set off for Egton Hill.

The pearly start to the morning had given way to bright sunshine by the time Gil reached the actual spot where he'd stood and watched the escaped convict last night. Satisfaction ran through him as he saw the cast off Wellington boot was still there. He approached it and hooked his stick inside, flicking the boot up and over. A terrified shrew shot out and disappeared into the grass tussocks.

Gil bent and picked up the boot. He crammed it down into the capacious pocket of his old mac. As irrefutable evidence, it had distinct possibilities, not least of which was that of a bargaining factor. It was going home with him now.

★　★　★

Across the Irish Sea it was also a perfect morning. The sun shone warmly down on the Presbytery making the enclosed courtyard a delightful suntrap. The heat bounced up from the concrete slabs and Father O'Malley loosened his collar as he sat outside drinking his first coffee of the day.

His mind dwelt for a moment on the coming visit. If it were a morning such as this it would crown the day. For the river trip it would make such a difference if the sun were shining, almost as if God himself approved.

His thought was interrupted as Mrs. Rooney, his housekeeper, came through the doorway set in the creeper-clad wall. She carried a breakfast tray and an appetizing aroma drifted across to where Father O'Malley sat at the white painted table.

He beamed. 'Sure, and it smells like my favourite today.'

'And so it is, Father.

He said grace, crossed himself and dug a fork into the juicy, steaming kipper.

'I've brought out the mail as well.' Mrs. Rooney laid several letters down on the table and placed the paper knife on top.

'You're a treasure, Sylvia, so you are. I'm very lucky to have your services.'

'Now you know it's quite the other way round.' She busied herself pouring another hot coffee. 'Will that be all, Father?'

'Indeed it will, thank you.'

Munching a slice of wholemeal bread, thinly spread with creamery butter, Father O'Malley reached for the letters. He stopped in mid-chew, his attention caught by the coat of arms on the thick cream envelope — a letter from the Duke. Hastily, he slit the envelope and drew out a single sheet. It was confirmation of Sunday the 29th October for the peace service. He read the rest of the letter.

The Duke reiterated the need for a symbolic gesture of peace and committed himself to take it in the hope that it would, by example, give cause for reflection.

Father O'Malley swallowed his bread and butter in an involuntary gulp. His mouth suddenly dry, he took a drink of coffee, nervous at the enormity of the whole event. Supposing anything were to happen to his Lordship . . . the repercussions . . . he hastily swallowed more coffee trying to get a grip on himself. Nothing was going to happen. It would be a beautiful occasion to be recorded in the annals of the history of the parish. Determinedly, he raised his voice and called to Mrs. Rooney.

'Yes, Father?' She popped her head through the kitchen door questioningly.

'It's the 29th, Sylvia. The Duke's just written and confirmed the date.'

'Oh very good.' She came across the court-yard. 'Everything can go ahead now then.'

'Yes indeed. A momentous occasion for all of us.'

'As you say, Father, a momentous occasion.'

He smiled. 'We two have seen more than

one momentous occasion, have we not?'

'Please, Father. We agreed. No talk of before. It is the only way I can stay here without starting gossip.'

'But we are alone, Sylvia. No-one can hear what we say.'

'If we talk freely now, we may forget ourselves one day and someone may over-hear. We cannot risk it.'

He sighed a little. 'You are probably right. But sometimes one gets a little lonely for human closeness.'

She drew back abruptly.

'Oh, now, don't get me wrong. I didn't mean bodily closeness, merely a closeness of mind, you understand.'

The woman relaxed. 'I do understand, Matthew, yes, really I do. But what happened between us, well, it was such a long time ago. Sean is a man now, twenty-six next birthday. Time doesn't wait, it goes past very quickly.'

Father O'Malley said softly, 'He is still my son.'

'Hush.' Her eyes widened. 'If anyone should hear . . . '

'Which they won't.'

'I appreciate your kindness, Matthew, taking me in after Patrick died, but I think perhaps I ought to look for another living-in position.'

'Come now, put such thinking out of your

head, woman.' Matthew O'Malley had risen to his feet. 'The things of the past were done in the passion of youth and the moment. Don't fret yourself so . . . all that sort of thing is behind us now. I need a housekeeper and now your husband has gone, you need a job and a home. It is all very simple. Away with you and fetch me some more fresh coffee.' He put his hand on her shoulder, squeezed it reassuringly and smiled gently at her. 'Off you go.'

She pressed her lips together warding off the threatening tears, touched by the warmth of compassion in his voice. There had been little or no warmth in the long years of marriage to Patrick Rooney. A marriage that had saved both her and O'Malley from shame. But it had been a loveless marriage and her very soul had cried out for the feel of Matthew's arms about her, his lips so tender upon hers, and yet for his sake, she had stuck it out. Her delight was in having a son, Matthew's son. That was something his other woman never had.

She put up her hand and allowed herself to touch his cheek softly, He must never, ever, know how deep her true feelings for him were still. 'You are quite right, as ever, Matthew, I do need a job and a home. Thank you for offering me both.'

O'Malley covered her hand with his and pressed her palm firmly against his face. 'God bless you, Sylvia, and may He now grant you a little peace.'

★ ★ ★

The strong sunlight slanted across the pillow and woke Georgina up. She had overslept. Dragging on jeans and a working shirt, she tiptoed across the landing and took a look at the injured man. If anything, he looked worse than the night before. Georgina felt a tremor of anxiety. How on earth would she be able to look after him without medical help?

Bringing in a doctor would be tantamount to handing him back to the prison authorities. She went over to the bedside and placed a palm on his forehead. It was clammily cold but sweat stood out glistening against the pallor of his skin.

Fetching a warm wet flannel, she gently freshened his face, bathing away the clinging sweat. He moved restlessly but didn't wake. Georgina arranging his covers, stared down at him and was filled again with a sense of having met or seen him somewhere before. When he regained consciousness she determined to ask him point blank just who he was. But right now there was nothing else she could do for him.

Going down to the kitchen, she was met by two exuberant collies. She put a handful of biscuits in each dish, renewed the water bowl whilst the electric kettle came to the boil and grabbed herself a quick cup of coffee.

Down in his stable, Chester was already stamping and snorting, letting her know she was behind time with his horse nuts.

'It's going to be a quick job this morning,' she informed the big chestnut as she skipped out and checked his legs. Fishing in a pocket, she came up with a mint and the horse whinnied and mouthed it off her outstretched palm. She patted the firm neck. 'I'll have you out for a canter later. We may have to go into Tavistock.'

Georgina went down to the field to check the others out at grass. Heads swung up at the sight of her and they trotted across snorting in anticipation. If all the horses had been attended to when the two farm workers arrived, they could immediately begin milking the dairy herd. The less people around the farmhouse at the moment the better.

Georgina had just finished as the men turned up for work. 'Morning both,' she called across the yard. 'All stock OK.'

They both raised a hand in acknowledgement before disappearing into the barn.

Sighing with relief, she turned and headed indoors, kicking off her boots at the kitchen door and running lightly upstairs.

The prisoner's eyes met her own as she eased open the door. 'Thank goodness you've come round. I was beginning to get worried.' She went over to him. He'd ceased sweating now although his face was still very pale.

'Don't fret yourself over me, Georgina. I'll survive, depend on it.'

'The way you looked earlier, I wouldn't have bet on it.'

A smile twisted his lips. 'A betting lady are you then?'

'Oh, it's been known.'

'That's my line of country.'

'And just exactly what line would that be?'

A guarded look came over his face. 'I think perhaps I've said a little too much already.'

'Now look here,' Georgina stuck hands on hips, 'I'm sticking my neck out for you. And why, I don't know. It's time you gave me some answers. First of all, who are you, what's your name?'

'Don't badger an injured man, girl, you don't want me to have a relapse now do you?'

'Why don't you want me to know, what are you hiding?'

'Not what, more like who.'

'O.K. So you're not telling me in order to protect someone else. Is that it?'

He sighed tiredly. 'Something like that.'

Georgina shrugged. 'Well, have it your own way, but just ask yourself if she's worth it.'

Jack shook his head slowly. 'You're wrong, girl, it's not a she.'

'I thought at the very least she was your wife,' she said rather flippantly and wondered why her pulse beat quickened as she waited for his reply. But his eyelids were beginning to close wearily. His lips framed an answer and she just caught the murmured words as he drifted back into sleep.

'Married to the job . . . '

Biting her bottom lip in frustration, Georgina went back downstairs. Despite her stomach forcefully reminding her it was breakfast time, she slipped on boots and coat.

'Come on you two,' she flicked her fingers at the two collies, 'you've got work to do.'

Opening the back door she prayed that the two men in the barn wouldn't notice and started off for the hill.

★ ★ ★

Gil reached his cottage. He retrieved the newspaper from the letterbox and went in.

He took the Wellington boot from inside his mac, pondered a moment and then opened the cupboard under the sink. Reaching inside he put the boot right at the back out of sight behind a yellow plastic bucket.

Switching on the kettle, he sat down heavily in the kitchen chair and opened the newspaper. The write up was on page 9. Clint Baxter, Gil noted the name, had escaped from an outside working party the previous day and was still at large. The police said although he was not thought to be dangerous, they advised the public not to approach him but to report any sightings immediately.

Gil gave a throaty chuckle. They'd not hear anything from him. In four days time Farmer Casey was due back from Ireland and would doubtless have purchased any new horses at a much-reduced price. The recession had slammed racing very hard. Gil was quite sure there'd be plenty left in the farmer's wallet, enough to purchase a Wellington boot in order to keep his daughter's name from being linked with helping an escaped convict. Where children were concerned, there seemed no end to the things parents would do to protect them.

However, Gil decided, he'd just have to play it dumb when he went in the Russet Fox. If Strachan or Constable Attewell happened to be in the bar, they'd quiz him for sure. Being an informer sometimes had its disadvantages . . .

★   ★   ★

In the private living quarters at the rear of the Russet Fox Strachan dialled Blake's number. His eyes swept over the newspaper open at page 9. A muscle twitched in his cheek as he clenched his jaw in frustration. The ringing tone ceased abruptly.

'Blake here.'

'Strachan, Mr. Blake.'

'Any joy?'

The face muscle twitched again. 'None. For all the signs I've seen, he could be on the moon.'

Blake said softly, 'I pay you to get results.' The ice in the voice chilled Strachan.

'He's got to surface, he can't avoid it. It's just a question of time.'

'It's imperative to get him before anyone else does.'

'If it is possible to get him, Mr. Blake, believe me, I'll be the first.'

'You'd better be.'

Strachan stood glaring at the dead 'phone. 'I'd like to see you do any bloody better,' he said viciously and crashed the receiver down.

PC Bruce Attewell slipped on the jacket of his uniform. With a prisoner loose roadblocks were already in operation and he knew it was possibly only a matter of hours before reinforcements were drafted in and a full house to house initiated. And that meant a personal appearance by the Divisional Commander.

A burst of racking coughs brought his thoughts back and he went over to the side of the double bed where his wife lay, a victim of the prevalent 'flu bug going around.

'Want another dose of cough stuff, love?'

She smiled wanly. 'Please.'

He poured a measure. 'Not much left.'

Mrs. Attewell tipped her head back and let the thick, soothing liquid slip comfortingly down her raw throat. 'Could you bring me another bottle back with you?'

Attewell looked at the price label. 'It's from Boots. Shouldn't think the local shop'll sell it.'

'No,' she said hoarsely, 'you'll have to go over to Tavistock.'

'Well, that's out for sure this morning. It'll have to be lunch break. I'll go before I start back this afternoon.' He reached across and took an antiseptic lozenge from the bedside cabinet. 'I'll get off now, then.' He popped the lozenge into his mouth. 'Give the germs a bit of competition, eh?'

★　★　★

Georgina, uncomfortably warm from hurrying, unbuttoned her jacket as the sun beat down. There was danger in every minute the injured man was alone at the farm but until the boot was safely recovered that in itself was a danger.

Pinpointing the place she'd found the wounded man, she whistled up the dogs. The grass was still bruised and the bush she'd fastened Chester's reins to still showed a fresh break on one of its lower branches. Both collies circled around, noses to the ground. No doubt at all this was the right spot.

The man had taken his boot off his injured foot and left it behind so it should still be here. Georgina searched the whole area but with a sinking feeling knew she wasn't going to find it. The boot had vanished. And it couldn't have disappeared by itself.

Fear traced its finger down her spine. Someone had got here first.

6

Roster House, home of Lady Crewton, glowed a warm red in the mid-day sunshine. Baxter, driving the stolen BMW, changed down as he approached through the main entrance gates. Following the drive round, he bypassed the impressive oak front doors and drove to the yard at the rear.

The white security van was still parked up. The double rear doors were wide open letting in the warm sunshine and inside two engineers were munching sandwiches. Right now they were watching him with curiosity.

Cutting the engine, Baxter took a deep steadying breath, took hold of the car owner's briefcase that he'd found on the back seat, and got out. Closing the car door almost contemptuously with a flick of his hand, he swung the briefcase in an authoritative manner. It provided just the little touch of authenticity he needed.

Baxter strode to the van. He took the firm's business card in the name of Fox from his wallet. Placing a thumb strategically after the last letter of Fox, he flashed it at the man.

'Foxton,' he said abruptly, 'security spot check.'

The two men looked at him blankly, hands clamped around mugs of tea. The older man frowned. 'Nobody told us to expect you.'

Baxter gave a short laugh. 'Well, they wouldn't, would they? It would hardly be a spot check if you knew I was coming.'

'Suppose not,' the workman conceded grudgingly.

'We've never been checked up on before,' the youth said belligerently.

'Head office ruling, I'm afraid.' Baxter gave him a penetrating look. 'I believe the safe's in the library, isn't it?'

'Yeah.' The youth lost interest and raised his mug.

'Suppose you'll be wanting to have a look then?' The older man reluctantly got to his feet and put down his unfinished tea.

Baxter consolidated his status. 'I understand from Head Office it's located on the second floor.'

'That's right. I'll take you up the back stairs, unless you want to speak to her ladyship?'

'Not necessary,' Baxter said slickly, 'all my findings are reported straight back to the office.'

'Right then, it's up here, second on the left

at the top of the stairs.'

Baxter could have told the workman where it was but he allowed himself to be led upstairs.

Inside the library three walls were lined solidly with books but on the fourth there was an ornate marquetry fire screen set in front of the Adam style fireplace. Leaned against the wall was the huge brass plaque taken down from its pride of place above the fireplace.

Baxter stepped forward and scrutinized the now exposed wall safe. 'What amendments are you carrying out?'

'Wiring it to ring an alarm bell if the door is opened whilst the alarm is set.'

Baxter nodded, lips pursed. 'Any other modifications?'

'Well, we're wiring the outside of the house as well.'

'Uh huh . . . are there any valuables in the safe at the moment?'

'No jewellery, nothing of that sort, but there's quite a few papers.'

'I see.' Baxter made a show of inspecting the safe combination. 'Do you think you could fetch me a torch, I want some more light on this?'

'Sure, we've got one in the van. I'll get it.' The man headed for the door.

'Is the alarm set at the moment?' Baxter

asked nonchalantly.

'No, we've not finished fixing the wiring yet.'

'O.K., well, if you'd just fetch me the torch . . .'

'Right.' The man disappeared through the door.

With nimble fingers it took just seconds before Baxter had the safe door open. He glanced inside. Three or four bundles of documents and a box file lay inside. Taking the bag of opals from an inside pocket, Baxter opened the lid of the box file and placed the necklace inside. With difficulty he held down the laughter which bubbled up inside him. 'Eat your heart out, Palmer,' he said under his breath, closing the safe door. 'One up to me, I think.'

Running lightly down the stairs he met the workman on his way back up again complete with torch.

'Carry on,' Baxter said. 'I'm just going to the car to pick up a diagram. I'll be with you in a minute or two.'

'Righto.'

Once downstairs, Baxter strode across to his car and got in. The youth in the security van appeared to have fallen asleep, head lolling back, eyes shut.

Baxter eased the car forward and drove

down to the gates leading to the main road. The car picked up speed and, as he drove smoothly away, he was laughing like a drain.

★ ★ ★

Upstairs at the farmhouse, Georgina set the lunch tray down on the bedside table. 'Smells good, yes?'

He smiled weakly. 'Sure does.'

'Do you think you could manage a little?'

'I'm willing to give it a go.'

She pressed a further pillow behind him. 'Have you had many attacks before?'

'Just a couple of times.' He dipped a spoon into the piping hot minestrone and sipped a little. Georgina joined him and started her own. Between spoonfuls she said, 'What did you take for it? You know, what medication?'

'It's a dormant strain, not very bad. Quinine usually helped.'

'Hmmm. I'd thought of that actually.'

They drank the soup in companionable silence until the man tiredly let his spoon sink in the bowl. 'Beaten I'm afraid.'

Georgina reached behind him and removed the supporting pillow. He sank back gratefully, eyelids already closing. Then, with a great effort, he forced them open and looked up at her.

'If it wasn't for the pain in my foot, I'd think for sure I was in heaven, because you're nothing short of an angel. Bless you . . . '

The effort of speaking was too much. Sleep claimed him.

Down in the kitchen Georgina put on her riding jacket and boots and went out locking the door behind her.

In the stable Chester whickered and stamped impatiently throwing his head high making tacking up difficult. 'If you'd keep steady, you'd get out for a canter quicker.'

Leading the big horse into the bright sunshine, she shortened the left rein and swung up into the saddle. Checking the length of the leathers, Georgina squeezed her calves against the chestnut sides.

The horse obediently moved into an extended trot out of the yard and up the farm track onto the moor. Feeling the turf, he jig-jogged and Georgina loosened the reins and gave him his head. They covered ground rapidly, cantering smoothly, effortlessly, heading west in the direction of Tavistock.

When the town came in sight Georgina slowed the horse to a walk allowing him time to cool down. Up ahead she could see the small copse where she had once before tied him up whilst she'd walked into the town. She had briefly considered taking the Land

Rover today instead but by now roadblocks would have been set up.

Leaving him secured, Georgina walked down into the main thoroughfare and went straight to Boots.

There was a customer at the pharmacy counter and Georgina took her place behind and waited. Behind her, a man's voice said, 'Having a trip into town?'

She froze and turned slowly. P.C. Attewell, in full uniform, was smiling down at her from his full six foot two. 'Er, yes, just a quick visit.'

'Next.'

'Sorry . . . ' Georgina turned back to the counter. She lowered her voice, 'Could I have a bottle of quinine tablets, please?'

The young woman in the white coat held out her hand. 'The prescription, please.'

'Prescription? I don't have one.' With a sinking feeling she felt her face begin to burn. If only the policeman wasn't listening. Giving a swift sideways glance she saw him frown slightly. Georgina decided to brazen it out. 'Surely I don't need a prescription.'

'I'm afraid quinine tablets are only available on prescription, madam.'

'Look, I need them to bring down a fever, that's all.'

'I'm sorry,' the assistant shook her head, 'But if it's for a temperature, paracetamol will be quite adequate.'

'O.K. I'll take some.' Anything, she thought, to get out of the shop and away from the man's puzzled scrutiny. Handing over the correct money, Georgina clutched the paper bag the assistant handed her and thankfully left the chemist.

Without his original freshness, Chester was less willing to move faster than a trot. 'Come on, boy,' she urged, 'I must get back.'

Catching a little of the tension in her, the big animal gave in and cantered in ground-swallowing strides over the moor. Normally, Georgina wouldn't have worked him so hard but anxiety drove her on. He was sweating profusely by the time she slowed him but it wasn't far to the farm now and he needed to be cooled before she stabled him up.

As they drew nearer, Georgina scanned the sweep of the yard by the farmhouse. 'Thank God,' she murmured. There was no one in sight.

★ ★ ★

Alex Blake, face impassive, listened to Palmer's account of the handing over of the opals at the Red Cow the previous evening.

'You told him the time limit for putting them back?'

'Yes, Mr Blake.'

'He couldn't have a better incentive. The woman and baby are precious to him.'

'It fell right into our hands, did that,' Palmer agreed. 'Finding them somewhere to live has Baxter eating right out of your hand.'

Blake pursed his lips. 'Thursday today. Saturday I'm over at Roster Hall in my capacity of horse breeder. If Lady Crewton appears wearing the opals, Baxter's for the Allington heist.' He smiled coldly. 'And, as a steward of the Jockey Club, guess who else is invited to the bash?'

'Who?'

'Our quarry, Palmer, that's who.'

'You mean, the Duke of Allington?'

'Exactly.'

★ ★ ★

The 'phone shrilled almost at the same moment as Georgina entered the farmhouse.

'Dad,' she smiled with pleasure at the sound of Peter Casey's voice. 'Everything going all right over there in Ireland?'

She listened indulgently to the man's enthusiastic description of the new colt he'd bought at Goffs.

'He certainly sounds a beauty, but you're looking very long term. Couldn't you have bought a two year old?'

She nodded as her father explained he wanted a green youngster, one that had not picked up any vices from rough treatment and whose dam had an equable temperament.

'And I suppose you've already got its future all laid out in your mind, even down to which jockey to put up?'

Casey replied in the affirmative. Georgina laughed. 'Stand by, Jack Riley, eh?'

She listened for a moment.

'So you'll be back earlier? I'll expect you on Saturday afternoon, then. Give my love to Grandmother and Magda. Love you, Dad, bye.'

Replacing the receiver, a frown on her face, she realised, not for the first time the enormity of what she'd done.

No way could she let the unknown man stay here after Saturday morning at the latest. He had to be out before her father arrived home.

★   ★   ★

Inside the prison at Princetown an incident room had been set up in the reception office. Already with the minimum time lapse, roadblocks had been positioned around the moor and the whole community was aware of the prisoner's escape. The Divisional Commander looked up from Baxter's file where it lay open on the desk.

'The additional men are being drafted in.' He cleared his throat. 'We should start house to house inquiries this afternoon. Usual procedure, fan out from the point of escape.'

The Duty Inspector nodded. He'd been here before, knew the routine backwards for setting the machinery working, knew it to be pretty well infallible. He could have voiced the same words used by the Governor, 'merely a matter of time', but prudently thought better of it. Instead, he said, 'The Nottingham home address is under a 24 hour surveillance, sir. Obviously too soon for him to show up there yet, assuming he's done the impossible and got off the moor.'

'Unlikely, I grant, but the rules require it, Inspector.'

'Yes, sir.'

'And take apart all the vehicles going through the blocks. Particularly farm vehicles, tradesmen's vehicles, horseboxes, that type of thing.' He gave a short, derisive snort. 'And that includes hearses transporting coffins. I want the whole area stitched up so tight a tick couldn't get out.'

The Duty Inspector was just as keen as the

Divisional Commander to keep his job. 'I'll make sure the men are fully briefed, sir.'

'As soon as the reports come in, they're on my desk, straight away, O.K.? I want this business wrapping up as quickly as possible.'

'Yes, sir,' the Duty Inspector replied but couldn't help wondering privately just how much of this zeal was application to the job and how much was due to the fact that the Divisional Commander was due to fly to the Seychelles for his annual holidays the following week.

* * *

Strachan's temper had grown worse. He'd spent a fruitless day scouring the moor for any signs of Jack Riley.

His own survival instinct told him that Riley would be seeking habitation if he hadn't already found it. And that meant someone knew of his whereabouts or was sheltering him. Either way, someone knew something. And the eyes and ears of the district was undoubtedly Gil Thomas.

In a belligerent mood, Strachan headed back to the Russet Fox.

* * *

Father O'Malley stepped wearily through the door into the presbytery and closed it behind him shutting out the darkness of the October evening. He hadn't eaten since lunch and it was now well after nine o'clock. He knew Sylvia would have left some food ready but the call of duty tonight had effectively stifled his appetite.

O'Malley walked into the living room and poured himself a Jameson's. Death came to each and all but when it came at the age of three . . . He took a swallow of the whisky and flung himself down into the armchair beside the peat fire.

One didn't question God's ways but the look in the mother's eyes as the child died would stay with him for a long time. As he'd murmured the prayer for absolution, it had brought back the memory of an English country lane last springtime.

He'd whispered that prayer then and he knew it to have touched the very core of his being. That time it was for three women but in his deep heart he knew, to his shame, for two of them it had come very close to being just lip service. And this despite one of them being Belinda, his God-child. In the last seconds of the lives of the two women in the Yaris, he'd recognised one as Gloria. The only woman he had ever truly loved or ever would. The intervening twenty-seven years since they had been lovers was wiped away in an instant. And when he'd prayed, doing the last and only service for her he could, his very heart had bled with grief.

He supposed, as he sat thinking back on this evening's death, that as the child lost its fragile hold on life, he'd identified with the consuming grief in the mother's eyes.

Suddenly, realising that he was in danger of becoming too emotionally involved, Father O'Malley reached out to the bookcase which ran along beside the fireplace and took down a much read slim volume of Shakespeare. It contained just one of the bard's plays — Hamlet. It was his favourite, the one that gained him examination success in English literature at the Public School in England. It had gained one for his best friend too, Anthony Ashley, now Duke of Allington. He pushed the thought of Belinda's father firmly away. Right now he desperately needed to forget, to recapture serenity of mind. Without emotional detachment he was of no use to anybody.

Taking out the bookmark, he began to read, letting the beautiful words fill his mind and taking his thoughts away from the painful memories. It was a very effective solace. Until he came to the few telling words, underlined by his own hand way back in March, which began, 'Rosemary . . . that's for . . . ' He jerked as though struck. Each word seemed to bore into him.

Dropping the book onto the floor, he pressed the palms of both hands against his eyes as if they could blot out the stark message. It was impossible. The words appeared within his mind's eye. And with the words came the picture of the oak coffin bearing Gloria's body out of this world. A coffin surrounded by wreaths, one of which he'd sent.

Composed totally of red roses with just one fragrant green spray of rosemary, a final act of love, a self-sympathy indulgence, and attached, unsigned, the white card. On the card he'd written those same words, 'Rosemary . . . that's for remembrance. Pray you, love, remember.' And he also remembered how the pain of grief within had made him add, 'The long ago regrets go deep.'

7

Miss Maureen Kingston, personal secretary to the Duke of Allington heard the thud of mail through the Allington Hall letterbox.

Flipping quickly through them, she noted the one with the Irish postmark. Maureen walked back up the hall and tapped on the Duke's office door.

She entered without waiting, the familiarity of years acting as his right hand allowing her the privilege. Her eyes softened just a shade too much as she looked at the dark head bent over the desk.

'The mail, sir.' She handed it to him. 'There's one from Ireland.'

'Thanks.' Reading swiftly, he glanced up at her, smiling. 'Father O'Malley is delighted I've confirmed the Irish visit in writing. He says it makes it a reality to him and not simply a dream he's had.'

'But it doesn't commit you. If you want to change your mind you can.' The concern in her voice came across strongly.

The Duke looked at her with a platonic fondness in his gaze. 'Of course I could. But you know I won't.'

'But the possible danger . . . ' she murmured unhappily.

'It's something I must do.' There was a crisp note now in his voice. 'The consequences of it could be of great importance.'

'It's just that, we've lost Belinda . . . I can't bear the thought of losing . . . '

'My dear Maureen, it seems I'm not safe even in my own grounds.' A shadow darkened his face at the hurtful memory.

As his forehead creased quickly with pain, she longed to reach out and smooth her fingers across his brow but that would be over-stepping the dividing line between closeness and intimacy.

'I have to exorcise any possible bitterness. You understand, don't you?'

'I think if you held any bitterness in your heart,' she said unsteadily, 'you wouldn't be attempting such a magnificent gesture.'

'The rest of the world will no doubt see it as my forgiveness of Belinda's murderer, which of course it is, but there's so much more to it than just a service of forgiveness or a peace mission.

'It's not a magnificent gesture, not at all, it's a very selfish one. I have to go to Ireland, Maureen. I have to go — to let go.'

* * *

98

Sean Rooney stepped out from under the hot shower and towelled vigorously. He shrugged on a towelling robe and padded downstairs.

The mail had just arrived. They were all for Blake, except one. It was addressed to himself and had an Irish postmark. His conscience nudged him as he recognised his mother's handwriting. Neither he nor Blake were being fair with her since she was totally innocent of the importance of the information she was giving them. The only thing he could do was keep the knowledge from her until the last moment.

Rooney decided after it was all over, he'd invite her back to England, win her round again. He knew he could.

What was going to happen was justice as far as he and his father-in-law were concerned. As near to justice as they could get with Michael O'Malley banged up in jail for the murder of Belinda Ashley. Gloria and Patricia's death might never have happened for all the action the authorities had taken. Accidental death had been the Coroner's verdict.

Squaring his shoulders, he went through into the kitchen. Blake was just finishing breakfast. 'That the post?'

'Yes, and you're welcome to it. Except for this one.'

'Your mother?'

'Let's see what she has to tell us.' Rooney ripped open the envelope and skimmed down the letter. 'So,' he released a sigh and raised his eyes to Blake, 'it's confirmed. The Duke will be there on the 29th.'

The two men smiled with satisfaction at each other but there was no warmth, just calculated cold triumph.

'And no doubt,' said Rooney very sarcastically, 'seeing that it's practically All Souls Day, he will be wanting to leave a November offering on the altar for his dead.'

'Just one dead.' Blake slammed down his cup, splashing most of the remaining coffee into the saucer. 'And he is weak enough to forgive, can afford to forgive now he is avenged with that swine O'Malley rotting in jail. We have lost two, two — and I will never forgive!'

Rooney looked at him and saw raw, naked hatred blaze from Blake's eyes.

★　★　★

Baxter watched the baby as she splashed in the bath. 'Beats me how much energy she's got.'

Anne laughed. 'Grab the towel, Clint and wrap it around her.'

Baxter tenderly cuddled the sweet smelling

100

infant and waltzed around, humming gently. The baby managed to free one tiny hand from the enveloping towel and reached up to his face. He bent his head and kissed the minute fingers. A feeling of blissful contentment filled him. A strident noise broke the peace as the telephone rang.

Holding the baby, he walked down the hall and answered it. 'Yes?'

Palmer's voice said, 'Give your password.'

'Party piece.'

'O.K. Tomorrow night, Saturday. Be ready.'

'Ready for what, for God's sake?'

'If you did your job and the, let's say, party piece is on show, then we'll need your services.'

'I can tell you now, I did do the job.'

But the phone had gone dead.

Baxter slammed the receiver down hard, frustrated and angry. If it weren't for Anne and the baby, he'd tell them all where to go. The baby picked up his tension and began to cry. He felt a warm wetness seep through the towel and run down his trousers. Swearing under his breath, he went in search of Anne.

★ ★ ★

Jack Riley came awake with a start. He lay for a second or two before opening his eyes. The bedside clock said just after ten. The last fourteen hours were a complete oblivion, helped by four paracetamols but they had done a good job. The fever had gone.

Sitting up slowly he swung both legs out of bed. The injured foot had lost most of the swelling but even putting a little weight on it brought back pain. Making use of the bedroom furniture for support, he managed to reach the adjacent bathroom.

Riley turned on the shower. Lifting his face up to the hot needles, he savoured the refreshing cascade. Water had never felt so good. He heard someone come into the bedroom and give an exclamation of alarm.

Opening the bathroom door a little awkwardly and leaning against it he said, 'Looking for me?'

Relief flooded Georgina's face. 'You're better, thank God for that.' The smell of grilled fish emanating from the tray she held made the saliva flood his mouth.

'You've cooked breakfast for me?'

'I hoped you might manage to eat some. You haven't had anything for at least two days.' She put the food down and slipped a supportive arm around him. Despite his shakiness, the muscles felt hard and strong.

'I'd say you were a very fit man,' she panted as they both managed to cross the room and collapse onto the side of the bed.

'Not just a compassionate lady but intelligent as well.' He looked intently at her. They were sitting very close together, their faces only inches apart.

Swallowing hard, aware of a sudden chemistry between them, she said, 'Won't you tell me your name? It's not Baxter, is it?'

He shook his head slowly, eyes holding hers. Putting his right hand over hers, he gave it a quick shake, 'Jack Riley, as ever was.'

'You're joking!'

Whatever reaction he'd expected it certainly wasn't incredulity. The surprise in her eyes was genuine enough.

'Now I wonder why that should faze you?'

Without answering, she turned his hand palm upwards and studied it.

'And I suppose,' he said, 'that has fazed you too, hasn't it?'

A frown wrinkled her forehead. 'Your thumb, it's scarred exactly as the radio description said.'

He nodded, a slight smile playing around his lips. 'Baxter's got one too.'

'I don't get it.'

'You will, eventually. Right now, I've no intentions of letting food get cold.'

Georgina, still bewildered by his words reached for the coffee pot. 'Do you mind if I join you? I put two cups out ready.' Riley, munching hungrily, waved an acceptance. Georgina poured out the coffee. 'What about sugar, do you take it?'

'No sugar, just a spoonful of honey.' His eyes twinkled at her discomfort. 'What, no honey? Now you are slipping.'

'Oh no you don't.' She jumped up. 'You're not getting another one up on me.'

He tried unsuccessfully to stop himself laughing as she shot out the room and thudded down the stairs, returning moments later triumphantly holding a jar of honey. 'One spoonful, I think that's what you said.'

'I am getting you housetrained, aren't I?'

'Don't worry, it won't last. As soon as you're better, you're on your own.'

'Story of my life,' he drawled.

'Talking of not lasting,' she said, serious now, 'you have to be out by tomorrow lunchtime at the latest.'

'OK.' He accepted it unquestioningly, eating the last forkful.

'Not because I want you out,' Georgina hastened on, 'it's just that Dad will be back in the afternoon.'

'I see.'

'Well, if he sees you, we've had it.'

He went very still, 'Now why would that be?'

'You said you were Jack Riley . . . '

'Yes.'

'I was talking to Dad on the 'phone yesterday, he's in Ireland, at the moment. He actually mentioned your name.'

Riley's eyes narrowed. 'How come.'

'Because you're a jockey. Jumps.'

He thought for a moment. 'Peter Casey? Owner of Egton Pride?'

She nodded. 'Was, Dad sold him last year.'

'And I rode him in the Candis Stakes.'

'You came second.'

'Regretfully.'

They smiled at each other, memories coming back.

'I knew I'd seen you before. But I couldn't put my finger on it.'

'Looking at myself in your bathroom mirror, I hardly recognise myself.'

'No, not just now, when I found you out on the moor.'

'I've got to admit it's all a bit hazy, don't really remember much at all. One thing I can remember is doing my ankle in, thought it might be broken. I took my boot off to check it and couldn't get it back on again . . . ' his voice trailed off.

'I went back for it, yesterday.'

His face relaxed. 'A girl who thinks of everything.'

'The bad news is, I couldn't find it. Someone had got there first.'

They looked at each other, silent now, very aware of the implications.

Riley spoke first. 'I wonder how long we've got?'

Georgina shivered. 'What are we going to do?'

'Get the hell out of here.'

'But you can't walk.'

'There is that,' he acknowledged, grittily.

'You're going to need transport and all we have at the moment is the Land Rover.'

He shook his head. 'There'll be road blocks.'

'And another thing, with that ankle you won't be able to drive.'

He swore under his breath.

'So,' she continued taking a deep breath, 'I'll have to drive.'

'You will not! I've involved you far too much already.'

'I see. You're going to crawl on your hands and knees down the lane then. See reason, Riley, without me, you're stuck.'

He was silent for long moments and then a slow smile spread across his face. 'Not so, girl. There is another way.'

'Oh yes?'

'Hmmm. I'm sure one of your best friends

106

will be willing to give me a lift.'

'Have you flipped? If you tell anybody, you're dead meat.'

'I think not, in fact, I'm quite sure.'

Georgina shook her head in disbelief. 'Go on, surprise me.'

'Well, you see, girl, he's already done me one hell of a favour. I'm sure he'll do me another.'

'In one second I'm going to pour this coffee over your head, you infuriating man.'

'You would too, wouldn't you?' He laughed teasingly at her. 'I'm talking about your horse, of course, Chester.'

'Oh,' she said nonplussed. 'But you can't get very far on him.'

'No, but he'll take me away from you and this farm before your father gets back.'

'So,' Georgina sprang from the bed, 'all you'll be doing is saving my skin, what about you?'

'Once I'm off the premises, I'm not your problem.'

'After all I've done for you, Riley . . . '

'That's just it, Georgina.' He levered himself up with surprising swiftness and stood gripping her shoulders. 'After all you've done, my dear girl, I'm eternally in your debt, don't you understand that?'

But the only thing she understood right at

that moment was the explosion of chemistry between them as they stood, faces very close and eyes holding each other's gaze. She drew in a sharp breath to try and break the almost primeval force between them. 'If you get yourself caught, my efforts will be a total write off. I might just as well have told the police in the first place.'

'I don't intend to get caught. I've some unfinished business with a certain gentleman.' His face darkened.

'Are you talking about Clint Baxter?'

'I am.' His voice was very cold

'He means a lot to you, doesn't he? If he didn't, it wouldn't matter.'

'Let's just say we go back a long, long way.'

A memory picture flashed across his mind of the two of them, both in short trousers, running across the vivid green field. Running so fast when they reached the oak wood, neither could stand upright but were bent double gasping for breath.

Throwing himself down on the springy turf, Clint had drawn the big clasp knife from the clip secured to his waistband and forced open the long blade. Riley could see it all again so clearly, with the sunshine catching the bright steel of the blade as Clint angled it this way and that. And how a few seconds later, the scarlet drops of blood ran down the sharp blade and dripped away into the grass.

'Come back.' The girl's words brought Riley up short. 'You were miles away.'

'Not just miles either, girl, years as well.'

'Want to tell me?'

'Maybe, not now though.'

'So, where do we go from here?'

'I want you to get hold of a large scale map of the area.'

'No problem. Dad has one downstairs in his desk.'

'Go get it then, girl, oh, and how about a fresh jug of coffee?'

'You are feeling better, aren't you?'

'Don't let it fool you. I need a gallon of coffee to sharpen up my brain. To every problem there is a solution and I need to solve this one.'

* * *

'Looks like that's all the cottages checked out. Farms next, eh?' Constable Kenny, drafted in to assist in the house to house, closed the last garden gate and looked inquiringly at Constable Attewell.

'Yeah, looks like Paxton's clear. I reckon we'll have a go at Casey's for a start. It's right at the bottom of Egton Hill, it would be an ideal choice for anybody coming down from the moor. Casey himself is away in Ireland right now but his daughter's there.' He frowned. 'That reminds me, I must ask if either of the two farm workers are running a temperature.'

Kenny raised both eyebrows but Attewell didn't enlighten him.

★ ★ ★

The previous evening Strachan had landed the Robinson helicopter faultlessly close to the huge disused barn. Cutting the controls, he'd jumped down and walked over to the waiting Land Rover. A few minutes later, Strachan had released the hand brake on the 4-wheel drive and was burning rubber back to the Russet Fox.

Gil Thomas, however, prudently keeping a low profile, had decided to give his nightly tipple the go-by for once and Strachan had spent a fruitless and frustrating evening behind the bar. When Barbara had finally called time, his exasperation was at danger level.

Friday morning found him pulling the Land Rover to a halt outside Gil's stone cottage. Gil himself was on the way back up the path with a yellow plastic bucket in his hand and a dozen or more freshly laid eggs

110

resting on a screw of straw on the bottom. With misgivings, he acknowledged Strachan. 'Don't usually see you about at this hour.'

'You weren't in the pub last night.' Strachan's jaw jutted forward. 'Wouldn't be keeping out of my way by any chance?'

'Now why should I be awantin' to do that?'

'Could be you know something.'

''Bout what?'

'You try telling me.' By this time Strachan had taken the lead and walked through the open doorway into the kitchen.

Gil had no choice but to follow. The yellow bucket was suddenly snatched from his hand and three eggs were hurled at the far wall in quick succession. The sticky yolks burst their transparent membranes and dribbled down the pale blue walls making a yellow mural. Gil cried out in alarm, 'Eh up, eh up, what y'doing?'

Strachan whirled round on him. 'O.K., Granddad. I know you're hiding something. So let's have it.' He clenched his right fist and drew back his arm.

Gil cringed. 'I'm not I tell 'ee.'

Strachan's eyes glittered with suppressed rage as he dropped his fist, well aware if he piled on too much pressure he wouldn't get the information — someone else would.

'I tell 'ee, I don't know a thing,' Gil repeated.

'Oh you don't . . . then why break a habit and duck the pub last night? You're running scared, Thomas, now give!' He held the bucket up high in preparation to smashing all the remaining eggs out onto the stone floor.

Gil's eyes darted swiftly to the sink unit. He'd made a big mistake after taking out the yellow bucket by leaving the unit door swinging open.

Strachan's eyes narrowed and he reached over and pushed the door wide open. Amidst the jumble and odds and ends inside, the Wellington boot lay on its side exposed to full view. He stretched a hand inside the cupboard and scattered a wide sweep of clutter out onto the kitchen floor, including the boot. Peering into the empty cupboard, Strachan rasped, 'What're you hiding?'

Emboldened by Strachan's indifference to the Wellington, Gil's courage oozed back a little. 'Me? I'm not hiding anything.'

'Don't give me that.'

'It's true Mester Strachan, honest, I've nothing hidden.' The truth shone out brightly from his words and even Strachan could not but accept he was being told the truth. He slammed the bucket hard onto the kitchen floor. Most of the remaining eggs broke, shells mixing with contents into an unusable mess.

'O.K. so, what do you know about a certain escaped prisoner by the name of Baxter?'

Gil looked down at the bucket, at the gluey mess with pieces of straw coated in yolk and his throat constricted in anger at the unforgivable waste. His precious hens had worked hard to produce those eggs and now, in a split second, it had been for nothing. 'It was your helicopter then, t'other afternoon. Thought it might be. You was out looking for him, this Baxter chap.'

'You're a regular Sherlock Holmes, aren't you?'

'But you didn't find him, did you? If you've come asking questions, stands to reason.'

'There's others asking questions not just me. You know well enough about playing that game, don't you, Thomas? O.K. How much?'

'I'll have t'cost of yon eggs for a start.'

'I'm not talking peanuts, man.' Strachan gripped Gil's shoulders. 'You know something, I'm willing to pay for information.'

'When I know anything, I'll bear that in mind.'

With a snort of disgust, Strachan let his hands drop from the other's shoulders. He strode to the door. 'Think about it. Get the other man's price — and I'll top it.'

Gil watched him go with great relief. But he would be back. And if he didn't get the information, there'd be more than eggs broken.

8

Jack unfolded the large-scale Ordnance Survey map and pinpointed the position of Casey's farm. A narrow twisting track joined the farm to the nearby village of Paxton and it was surrounded by the expanse of moor.

Paxton itself had just one main road running virtually straight through the centre. A criss-cross of tiny lanes linked some of the more distant cottages with the main village.

One lane ran off from the junction by the Russet Fox. It snaked its way across the moor to the south and led eventually to the adjacent village of Pointon. About a third of the way along it was joined by little more than a cart track, which terminated at an old disused farm. Jack pointed to the main roads out of Paxton. 'Useless to consider these, of course. They'll be sealed off tight. And this one,' he indicated Pointon, 'that's a dead duck, I need to go north not south.'

'But that's simply back across the moor. You aren't going to get far on horseback.'

'True.' He pursed his lips. 'I suppose there's the railway station but it's too far.'

'Pity you can't fly an aeroplane,' Georgina

115

quipped. 'We could just do with one right now.'

'Is there a private air field anywhere around here?'

'I was only joking.'

'Yes, but I'm not.'

'Joking or not, it doesn't make any difference. There isn't an active one.'

'Pity. I hold a pilot's licence to fly a helicopter.'

'Do you?' Georgina's eyes widened.

'Uh uh. Learned how to fly through travelling that way to the racecourses. O.K. I did a training course as well and was granted a licence. Could be useful you see if my racing days are suddenly halted.' Georgina began to smile. 'You think it's funny?'

'No, no but I just happen to know where there's a helicopter.'

'One that's useable?'

'Definitely. In fact,' she began to laugh, 'it's been flying over looking for you.'

'You don't say.' Now Riley was smiling too. 'Point me to it.'

So she did. 'You see that cart track leading off the lane to Pointon?' She traced it on the map with a fingernail. 'It's housed in an old barn at a disused farm.'

'Who owns it?'

'The manager of the Russet Fox was using

116

it but everybody knows the helicopter's not his and he's not king-pin. The local grapevine has it that the pub is owned by a business man from up north.'

'Any idea what his name is?'

'Afraid not, but if you believe the rumours, he's a horse breeder. I can't comment because I don't get down here to the farm very often.'

'Where do you normally live?'

'North Yorkshire.'

'Snap.' He grinned. 'Ilkley, actually.'

'And is that where you're going, if you hijack the helicopter?'

'If the fuel tank holds out.'

'Won't the police be staked out waiting for you?'

'No. They're too busy keeping their eyes peeled on Baxter's house on Calgary Street, Nottingham. As Jack Riley, I don't mean a thing to them. Well, not unless they catch up with me before I get that helicopter off the ground.'

'I don't follow.'

Riley patiently spelled it out to her. 'If they get their hands on me in the next few hours, it will be back to prison and the full routine, including finger-printing. We're cousins actually, my mother and his were twins, which probably accounts for it. But however much we resemble each other, our fingerprints are unique. Even true twins have a different set of prints.'

'I'm still in the dark.'

'If they check my prints they'll know I'm not Baxter.'

Georgina shook her head in bewilderment. 'I don't get it.'

'Simple, girl. Clint Baxter commits a crime for which he gets banged up in Princetown. Whilst he was working his sentence, I swapped places. We engineered it whilst he was on an outside party, exactly like I escaped, using fog as cover. No-one noticed a thing. He got away and I took his place.'

'My God! You're mad. Doing time for another man.'

'Not really. I owed him. But it was only supposed to be for a short time. You see Anne, Clint's wife, had a miscarriage a couple of years ago and she was expecting again. The birth was imminent and he desperately wanted to be with her. The deal was that after the birth he was supposed to bail me out and finish his sentence.'

'And he's done a runner instead?'

'Exactly.'

'Why don't you just go to the police and tell them?'

'Because, my dear girl, they'd throw the

book at me and both of us would end up inside. Since I don't consider I've committed a crime there's no way I'm going back.'

'But if the authorities catch you . . . '

'I'll have no choice. It will all have to come out.'

'What do you think has happened to Baxter?'

His face hardened. 'That's what I intend to find out.'

★ ★ ★

Gil eyed the sink unit contents strewn about the kitchen floor, bent down sighing heavily and scooped them all back into the cupboard. The Wellington boot he stood upright in a corner of the kitchen beside his own pairs of boots. 'Hide a tree in a wood,' he muttered to himself and took the yellow bucket outside. Swilling it round with hot water, he threw the glutinous contents away down the drain and left the bucket upside down to drain off.

Minutes later, he was pedalling away down the lane leading to Casey's farm.

As he cycled along, Gil pondered what story he could tell young Georgina. It would probably be best to stick partly to the truth and say all his eggs had been broken when the bucket had fallen onto the floor.

As he concentrated on what to tell her, two interesting things happened, the implications of which didn't fully register at the time but which he subconsciously noted.

He was almost at the farm when he remembered about the escaped convict holed up inside the farmhouse. In agitation he began to peddle fast as he could. To add to his discomfort, it began to spot with rain.

★　★　★

Strachan seethed with frustration as he drove the Land Rover away from Gil's cottage. He was annoyed with himself at the way he'd handled the situation. It should have proved so easy to intimidate the old man. Instead, the round had definitely gone to Gil. But something Gil had said which he couldn't quite recall kept niggling away at the back of his mind like a maggot in an apple.

He reached the Russet Fox and helped himself to a measure of whisky. The old man had undoubtedly been speaking the truth about not having anything hidden but after the eggs were smashed his composure had certainly slipped.

It was when he'd been talking about the helicopter, Strachan thought, that Gil had given something away. He tried recalling the exact words and the maggot popped out of the apple. 'It was your helicopter then, going over Egton Hill . . . ' Gil had given away the location by pinpointing where he had actually seen the helicopter. And suppose, just suppose, that the old man had been watching the escaped convict at the time he'd spotted the helicopter.

Strachan tossed back the rest of the whisky and went through to his bedroom. He unlocked the writing desk, pulled out a Walther and made for the door.

The quickest way of covering ground and checking was to get the helicopter airborne and take a look. He intended to do just that.

★   ★   ★

Constable Kenny slipped into the passenger seat of the Escort beside Bruce Attewell and belted up. 'Drop of good tea that, you make a real good brew, thanks.'

'Well, reckon we'd earned a tea break. Anyway, with the missus ill in bed, she needed one making too.'

'Nipping home for a cuppa is one of the perks of working a patch like this.' The envy was evident and Constable Attewell grinned at his mate.

'I reckon Casey's farm wasn't going

anywhere for half an hour.'

'Couldn't agree with you more,' Kenny nodded.

Attewell turned the panda car around. 'O.K. Let's go and sound them out.'

★ ★ ★

Georgina came into the bedroom and dumped an armful of clothes onto the bed. 'There you go. Dad doesn't often use these. I've altered the buttons a bit so they shouldn't be too bad a fit.'

'If I'm ever on the run again, I'll know where to come.' Riley smiled at her.

'For both our sakes, I hope they catch Baxter pretty quickly.'

Riley shook his head. 'I don't see it. One thing's sure, he's nowhere around these parts.'

'How can you be so sure?'

'One decent thing he did was to send me a card when the baby arrived. He didn't sign it, just wrote, 'Mother and baby girl doing fine.' Actually, I believe he was still going to stick to his side of the bargain at that time.'

'So what's changed his mind?'

'Wish I knew. It could just be the attraction of the little one but somehow I don't go for that. Whatever the reason, it's got some clout.

122

One thing I do know is that the baby was born in Nottingham and the card was postmarked Nottingham as well.'

'Up North . . . ' Georgina murmured. 'You said you needed to go North.'

'That's right. But I've no intention of ditching the helicopter anywhere near Nottingham. It would be too much of a coincidence. No, I think if the chopper will make it somewhere on the moors might be best. Yorkshire, I mean.'

'Then what?'

'I make my way home and pick up the Porsche.'

'And drive down to Nottingham?'

'Dead right, girl.'

'And then?'

'Ha, good question. Play it as it comes.'

'But if you do track him down,' Georgina persisted.

'I guess I kind of persuade him to have a chat to the nearest policeman.'

'I think you'll be lucky.'

'Sarcasm, girl, doesn't become you.'

Georgina went over to the door laughing. 'I'll leave you to try the gear on, give me a shout when you've finished and I'll bring some coffee up.'

★ ★ ★

Strachan felt the rise of excitement within him as he thrashed the Land Rover down the lane to Pointon. Coming to the turning, he spun the wheel and drove over the cracked concrete to the old barn. Working at speed on the levers, he brought the ground handling wheels into play and rolled out the Robinson R22 helicopter. Climbing into the cockpit he switched on and ran through the control checks, swore softly as the fuel gauge showed less than a quarter full. It was far too low for safety. He must have flown over a lot more ground than expected.

He taxied over to the pump and as the tank filled, he noticed the sky had progressively become more and more overcast. As he fitted the fuel cap back into position a curtain of rain spread across and the first spots fell. Visibility was going to be seriously curtailed.

Strachan climbed into the cockpit and hesitated. Unless Riley had found food by now the man would be climbing the walls. There was no way he'd still be hanging around up on Egton Hill or the surrounding moor. Food was non-existent up there. And if he wasn't still loose on the moor, he had to be holed up in some habitation. The only house anywhere near Egton Hill was Casey's farmhouse.

It would be pointless getting airborne in

the helicopter, far better to simply take the Land Rover and drive over to Casey's.

Impulsively, he abandoned the helicopter and ran back to the Land Rover. If Riley was at Casey's farmhouse or in one of the outbuildings, he intended to be the first to pick him up.

★ ★ ★

Georgina set a pan of vegetable soup on the stove and cut some sandwiches whilst the coffee heated. Jack could have either or both, whichever he liked. With the loss of two days' food intake and the malaria attack, he needed feeding up.

The music from the radio on the worktop close by faded out and was replaced by a time check and news bulletin. The prisoner's escape was given only the merest mention to the effect that the police were still searching the area. Georgina, still stirring the soup, reached across and took the local newspaper from the kitchen table and scanned it.

A short warning bark outside caused her to look up sharply. In the doorway stood Gil. He put his hand down and patted Jasper before taking off his cap.

'Mornin', Miss Georgina.'

'Hello, Gil.'

'I was just coming to see if I could buy a few eggs from you.'

'I thought you always had plenty from your own hens,' Georgina said brightly, whilst inside her stomach fluttered with nerves. One of the last people she'd have wished to visit the farm right now was Gil.

'Aye, you're right, 'cept I've had a bit of an accident like and er . . . they've all got broke.' He was kneading the old cap with both hands and Georgina realized he was equally as nervous as she was.

'What's the matter, Gil? Is there something else?'

It was the icebreaker he needed. 'I've known you since you was born,' he blurted out, 'and nobody was sorrier'n I was 'bout what happened to your husband.'

Georgina stiffened. Whatever she'd expected him to say it had certainly not been that.

'You've had enough trouble. I'd not like to think you were headed for a lot more.'

She felt suddenly cold inside. Did he guess she might know the whereabouts of Jack Riley?

'I was just coming for me eggs, but I think I'd best warn you. You've got company coming, two lots. I don't think they saw me but I spotted 'em both.'

'Who?' Georgina let the newspaper fall onto the worktop, her fingers shaking. The fear now running through her was not for herself but for the injured man upstairs.

'Strachan,' Gil almost spat the man's name out, 'and right behind him there's t'local bobby and his mate, doing a house to house for this 'ere escaped bloke.' The silence left by his words was cut through by a voice calling from the bedroom.

'Georgina, I'm quite decent, you can come up. Your dad's clothes fit me a treat.'

Gil's eyes met Georgina's and neither needed to say a word.

'Georgina? Are you there?' Riley called again.

'Yes, yes, I'm here.' Her eyes had not left Gil's and the old man ceased kneading his cap and clutched her arm.

'Best get him out quick. If they catch you harbouring, phew . . . ' He blew gustily between pursed lips.

'You knew!'

'Aye, that I did. But you'm wasting time.' He gave her arm a little jerk. 'You'll have to be quick. Them two'll be here pretty soon.'

She flashed him a look of extreme gratitude. 'Thanks.'

'I'll go outside and keep Strachan talking, give you chance to slip out t'other way.'

Georgina didn't wait to hear his words. She was already racing up the stairs.

Strachan drove the Land Rover into the farmyard and screeched to a halt. He jumped out ignoring the two collies that set up a cacophony of barking as they circled the vehicle.

He ran over to the main barn and gave it a cursory check. There was very little scope for concealment and he wasted no time in going across to the stables.

Chester whickered and turned a head over withers to look at him. Strachan backed away from the big horse and climbed the ladder to the hayloft. The hay was spread thinly and the only possible hiding place was a large loose pile mounded up in the far corner. Seizing a large pronged fork, Strachan viciously dug at it, repeatedly thrusting in the sharp prongs. No one could have remained hidden and escaped injury.

Swearing with disgust, he threw down the hayfork, spun around and clambered back down the ladder. The dogs pranced around him barking excitedly as he ran from the stables across the yard to the farmhouse. Their barks changed to warning growls as he approached the kitchen door and he kicked out at Jasper, missing by a fraction as the dog leapt nimbly aside before rushing at him.

'Now then, steady.' Gil appeared from the kitchen door and the collie dropped back.

'Get these bloody dogs off.'

'Only doin' their job,' Gil said evenly, but he ordered both to lie down. 'Was it me you wanted?'

'No, I've no time to waste on you. Besides, you told me all I needed to know.'

'I never told you nothin'.' Gil desperately tried to remember just what he had said earlier to Strachan.

'Egton Hill, you said, and we all know there's only one house anywhere near — this one.'

'So? I didn't say I'd seen that convict feller, did I?'

'You didn't have to. Get out of my way.' Strachan made to move forward.

Gil stood his ground but simultaneously both men heard the sound of a vehicle driving into the yard. It was a police car and it drew up as close as possible to where the two men were standing. Gil motioned the dogs to stay as the two constables got out.

'Is Miss Casey in?' Attewell addressed his question to Strachan.

'Don't ask me. I've only just got here.'

He turned to Gil. 'Well?'

'She was, earlier on.'

'And now?'

129

'Ah well, I couldn't say officer.'

'O.K. Gil, that's enough. Out of the way.' Attewell moved round him and banged on the already open door. There was no answer. He knocked again, calling out her name but no one answered. 'I guess I'll go take a look inside. Stay here Constable Kenny and I'd be obliged if you two gentlemen would remain here as well.'

Attewell went into the kitchen. He looked around, taking in the freshly cut pile of sandwiches, the soup bubbling away on the stove, the radio playing to itself and the open newspaper lying on the worktop. He also took in one lone Wellington boot standing near to the Aga. Bending down he took a closer look.

'Prison issue, I presume,' he said, straightening up and looking at the three men waiting in the doorway. They stayed silent and as they did so, a horse whinnied. They all heard the sound of heavy hoof beats setting off from the farm.

As one, they rushed from the kitchen out into the yard. A horse with two figures astride was already galloping rapidly away across the moor.

Attewell dropped the boot and the two policemen scrambled for the police car. Whilst Attewell went through the gears, Constable Kenny was contacting the incident room at Princetown on the radio.

Strachan, in the Land Rover took off after them. Gil, abandoning all hope of his eggs, climbed stiffly back on his bike and cycled away.

Inside the farmhouse kitchen, the newspaper had fluttered across the worktop with the draught from the doorway. The flames from the gas ring licked up, hungrily consumed and surged afresh as the newspaper finally fell onto the rush mat covering the floor.

In seconds the mat was blazing merrily.

9

Father Matthew O'Malley had deliberated a long time before writing to his brother. Michael's violently aggressive temper had landed him in an Irish jail for physical assault twice before. In an English prison now, he supposed Michael did have access to newspapers, so would be aware of the Duke's coming visit to Ireland. However, there was a slight chance Michael might still be ignorant of the fact. But purposely setting down in black and white the date and details of the service of forgiveness made Matthew uneasy in the extreme.

Michael, albeit the major share holder, had a lot of sympathisers among his business associates: they were nearly all part owners in the same racing syndicate which had crashed heavily last year.

Matthew hesitated, pen poised over the paper, seeing again the number 5 horse, Buttercross Boy coming home in a driving finish to win by a short head from Linear Walkway. The race, The Candis Stakes, had been televised and was the cause of much controversy following the Steward's verdict of

132

interference, which resulted in the placings being reversed. It had lost Buttercross Boy the valuable addition to his pedigree and the prize money, which itself was in the five figure bracket. But Matthew knew his brother had been swaggeringly confident of the horse's ability and had urged the other members to place sizeable bets. Two or three of his own work force, the ones who could least afford to lose, had taken his advice, backed heavily and subsequently lost heavily.

The resentment and bitterness was aimed at the officiating Stewards. The Senior Steward that day had been the Duke of Allington. He had also been the Senior Steward in a similar situation involving the same horse at Kelso the previous season. However, an appeal to the disciplinary Committee of the Jockey Club was not upheld. The outraged members of the syndicate were left seething with impotent frustration.

Financially, Michael's business had been left teetering and when it finally crashed, having been taken over by a conglomerate of which the Duke of Allington was Chairman, the fires which had begun to die down were fanned fiercely. Jobs were lost, livelihoods were now on the line. And whilst none was involved in Michael's final vindictive action, a lot secretly applauded his try to even the score. Simply being locked away in jail put Michael on a pedestal to quite a few. And they were not in jail.

If the service was seen as a thumb to the nose, reprisals in any form against the Duke during the visit could not be ruled out.

Matthew signed his name at the bottom of the letter, folded it and slid the single sheet into the envelope. It was done. Everything was in God's hands. And despite all the sorrow and suffering that came his way Matthew's faith beamed out strong and unquenchable.

Scanning the list of Dublin's florists — only the best for the Duke — he lifted the telephone.

'Good morning, Father O'Malley from Kileverton, County Kildare. I need a special display of flowers for decorating the church. I'll need them in place and all arranged in time for a special service to be held on Sunday 29th October, that's a week on Sunday.

'I'll leave it to your firm to choose but I would especially like some white blooms. Purity and peace, you understand. Lilies I think, yes, definitely, we'll have some lilies.'

★ ★ ★

'You won't forget you have a luncheon date in Newmarket, with the Jockey Club Stewards, will you?' Maureen Kingston, keeping an index finger at Friday's page, let the black leather covered appointments diary close.

Anthony Ashley, Duke of Allington, pushed a cuff back and looked at his watch. 'Hmmm, yes I suppose I'd better get going. Have George bring the car round in about ten minutes please, Maureen.'

'Very good.'

'And tomorrow? What time am I due at Lady Crewton's?'

Maureen flipped over the page. 'Seven-thirty for eight.'

'Remind George as well, would you? Oh, and could you slip into Holmington and choose a present for her Ladyship.' He flashed a smile. 'I'll leave it entirely to your feminine intuition. I'm no good at that sort of thing.'

Maureen gave him a warm smile but Ashley didn't realize just what a glow his casual acknowledgment of her femininity had affected within her.

He walked up the wide imposing staircase and went into his bedroom. A dressing room led off, one wall of which housed a closet full of clothes. He stripped off jacket and shirt in front of the mirror above the small hand-basin. He reached across and pressed a small, concealed catch under the base of the mirror and it swung forward revealing a narrow recessed wall safe.

There was very little inside; several pairs of cufflinks, mostly plain gold but a couple of pearl and onyx, matching tiepins and a Cartier gold wristwatch. The safe also contained one other item, a ladies' dark blue velvet jewellery box. It had belonged to his daughter, Belinda. He lifted it out and opened the lid. Inside resting on pale blue silk, lay a heavy gold cross and chain.

As always, Ashley murmured the short prayer, 'Safe in your loving hands, Father,' as he carefully fastened the chain around his neck and adjusted the cross so that it lay absolutely central. It seemed to nestle down among the dark hairs on his chest and he stood for a moment or two looking at the reflection in the mirror.

'God bless, my darling, wherever you are,' he said softly touching the cross lightly with a fingertip. It gleamed brightly, seeming to hold an intangible part of Belinda's personality and bring her a little closer to him.

Slipping on a fresh white shirt, he buttoned it over the top concealing the cross. No one in the whole world knew he now wore it on all his official engagements, would always continue to whilst ever he lived. He had left Belinda once before and had come home to emptiness. Now, he would always take a tiny part of her with him — and bring her back.

It had been a decision made from selfishness not to place the cross and chain inside Belinda's coffin but his need was greater, his own personal fragmentation no less. Belinda was in safer care than he could provide, had provided; she would not begrudge him a self-indulgence that brought him a tiny crumb of comfort.

Father O'Malley had dropped a hand on the Duke's shoulder and blessed the tough decision. It was almost like a miracle in itself, the fact that Belinda had not been wearing it on the day she died. If she had, he would not even have had this small comfort.

It had been Father O'Malley's gift to Belinda on her Christening ceremony, nearly 18 years ago. After the funeral last March at the small Yorkshire church, he had returned home to the presbytery in Ireland and had spoken of the cross and chain to Sylvia Rooney, confiding that the Duke now kept it secure within his personal safe as a keepsake. Of how much guilt and regret that confidence was to cause him later, he was mercifully unaware.

The Duke was still very aware he was wearing the heavy chain by the coldness of the metal around his neck. However, by the time he'd knotted a tie and shrugged into the smart dark jacket, it had warmed to body heat and become part of him, comfortably unnoticeable yet unbreakably solid when touched, as unbreakable as the love bond between Belinda and himself.

★　★　★

The Connemara pony trotted down the Co. Offaly lane, throwing up small puffs of dust from its hooves and the following trap creaked in its harness as the pony drew it steadily along the track to Magda Casey's cottage. Mary, working in the kitchen, saw it approaching. She recognized Kieran Rafferty and felt a quiver of apprehension.

Messages were passed over the bar at Murphy's of an evening when the menfolk from the local cottages slipped in for a jar. Any emergency calls were usually transmitted by the dispatching of Kieran on the assurance of a free Guinness on his return.

She tried to read the man's face as he approached but his expression remained, as normal, stolidly impassive, cheeks creased and pinched beneath the old cap. Catching up a towel, she ran out, drying her hands. 'What brings you, Kieran?'

He halted the trap and climbed stiffly down. 'Best call your Peter, Mary. 'Tis a message for him.'

'From England?'

'To be sure it is.'

She turned and hurried back to the cottage.

A second or two later Peter Casey was outside talking to Kieran.

'Is it bad, Peter?' Mary called from the doorway.

'Not sure. Tell you when I've phoned Devon.'

Rafferty, message delivered and his mind on the waiting Guiness, clicked to the stoic pony and with a jerk the trap set off again down the dusty lane.

★　★　★

Riley and Georgina had watched as Strachan's Land Rover pulled into the yard. Watched as he checked out the barn and stable before going round the corner of the farmhouse towards the kitchen, being challenged and harassed at every step by the two dogs.

Taking advantage of Gil Thomas delaying

Strachan's entry into the farmhouse, they'd made a run for the stable. Georgina had snatched Chester's bridle from the peg whilst Riley threw the cloth and saddle over the horse's withers, cinching up the girth.

Georgina looked through the chink in the partially open stable door.

'There's a police car coming.' Her voice hit a high note, betraying the tension.

'Easy, girl.' Riley's tone was low, controlled and effectively stayed the rise of her nervousness.

She smiled briefly and whispered, 'I'm not a horse.'

'That you're not. I had noticed.' Automatically, he ran two fingers between the horse's warm belly and the webbing of the girth, then satisfied, said, 'Right. Shall we go?'

'We?' For a second Georgina queried him.

'Don't argue. You can't stay now, can you?' And without waiting for her to answer, he clicked to the big animal and led him from the stable, kicking a covering of shavings in front to muffle the ring of shod hooves on concrete.

Georgina held cupped hands for his left boot and Riley sprang up into the saddle. He reached down and caught her up behind him. 'Hold tight.'

The chestnut took the double weight easily.

Riley booted the horse from a canter to a gallop and they took off across the moor.

'We'll cover some ground. Try to lose them.' Georgina squeezed his waist tighter to show she'd heard and pressed her cheek to his broad back for protection against the pouring rain, letting the wind catch her auburn hair and stream it away.

They swung in a wide circle, by-passing the edge of Paxton, before curving in to intercept the approach to the disused farm. Chester was blowing hard now and the man reined back to a trot guiding the horse across the uneven broken concrete.

There was no need to ask if it was the right place. The helicopter stood outside the old barn all ready for use. Riley slid cowboy fashion from the horse. Georgina followed suit.

'He'll make it back on his own from the end of the track, won't he?'

'Oh yes,' she nodded. 'I'll catch the bridle back behind the irons. He'll go straight home across the moor.'

Riley ran across to the waiting helicopter. Looking into the cockpit, he checked for the keys. A rise of satisfaction filled him. They were in place. He pulled on the headset, checked all the control panel, especially the fuel reading. He switched on the engine and the machine throbbed with power, its vibrations ever intensifying as the revolutions increased. He was once more back at the control of the Hughes 300, his instructor's words drumming in his ears, going through the full sequence of safety checks.

Georgina came running back across the concrete, long hair made glossily red by the streaming rain and blown away from her face by the stiff wind.

He increased the power as she reached the helicopter, the rotor now whirring away furiously. Gasping for breath, she pulled herself up and collapsed into the passenger seat. Riley pointed to the passenger headset and motioned her to put it on.

'Somebody up there loves us,' he shouted above the noise of the engine.

'You reckon?'

'Sure do. Look at that fuel gauge.'

She looked. '100% full.'

'Exactly.' He grinned at her with exultation. 'We're going to make it, girl, all the way back to Yorkshire.'

He began lift off and as he did so, a police car followed closely by a Land Rover came bumping down the track.

'You see why I told you not to argue?' He jerked his head sideways. As Georgina followed his prompting, he added, 'Don't wave. You've been kidnapped. OK?'

'I've what? Certainly not! You'll get ten years if they catch you.'

'But you won't. This will get you off the hook for helping me. Nobody else knows I was out for the count on Egton Hill and you aided and abetted of your own free will.'

'Now you're being stupid, putting yourself in a no-win situation.'

'My darling girl,' he drawled taking the helicopter high, the ground falling away rapidly below, 'they aren't going to get within a furlong of me, and besides, I'm not the one they're looking for. Once we've ditched this old bird on the Yorkshire moors, I'm a faceless man. Nothing to do with Mr Clint Baxter. I'm Mr Jack Riley, remember?'

'But you can't stay in Yorkshire. You'll have to go down to Nottingham, try to see Baxter . . . ' She clutched at his sleeve, face suddenly alive. 'That's it, Jack. Don't you see? Why not forget about Baxter? The authorities can't link you to him. You said yourself your fingerprints won't match the set inside the prison.'

She dropped back and relaxed in the confined seat. 'It's all so simple, just forget Baxter.'

Riley turned to look at her, a lazy smile on

his face. 'I'll forget Baxter altogether, it's as simple as that.'

'Absolutely,' she said with satisfaction.

'Except, of course, for one thing, girl.'

'Oh?' she queried, turning to him wide eyed.

'I'm not going to.'

10

Blake's office door opened and Rooney came in carrying a tray of sandwiches and coffee. Max lifted a muzzle and sniffed with interest.

'Tongue with mustard.'

Blake grunted, 'The only thing to commend a working lunch.' He reached for the red-covered books relating to his Leeds Betting Shop and scanned the totals for each of the last three months. 'Thank God the punters never learn. Pour me a black coffee, Sean.'

The two men worked steadily on, the books from the two Halifax betting shops and one from Bradford joined the Leeds one. The telephone rang. Blake answered. 'Any news of Riley, Strachan?' His face hardened. 'So, you and the police let him get away. His tone icy, Blake continued, 'I suggest, Strachan, you take the helicopter up and you don't come down again until you find him.' He crashed down the receiver. 'Just how the hell could they have blown it? Riley was a sitting duck.'

Rooney scowled. 'Fill me in.'

Blake did so.

'Bloody hell fire! And Strachan missed him.'

'The police didn't get him either.'

'If they had we'd be looking round corners now. Just how much does Riley know?'

'Only Baxter can tell us that.'

'I'd say we'd better pull him in and ask him, don't you?'

'Yes, and put details of tomorrow's heist to Baxter. The sweet approach, this time, I think, Sean. All good pals together, eh?'

The two men smiled knowingly at each other.

'I'll get hold of Palmer. Have him fix up the details for this afternoon.'

Blake leaned back in his chair and drained his second coffee. 'Do that, son,' he said. 'Do that.'

★ ★ ★

Anne Baxter tucked the cot blanket around the sleeping infant. 'She'll sleep though to her six o'clock feed.'

'Good.' Clint Baxter slipped an arm around her waist. 'Any interruptions right now I can do without.'

Anne twisted around within the encircling strong arm and leaned back. She looked up into his brown eyes, clearly reading the

146

message being put across. She began to laugh. 'Oh no, Clint. I must get the washing done whilst she's asleep.'

Ignoring her protests, he pulled her to him urgently, lips searching hers. He carried her across the room and lowered her onto the bed. She struggled against his hold, drawing her lips away. 'Don't, Clint. You're much too tempting.'

Laughing down at her as she struggled ineffectually beneath him, he buried his head against the yielding softness of her neck and began kissing her with a deep, consuming hunger.

Anne ceased struggling and allowed herself to enjoy the exquisite pleasure of his love-making. The whole world shrank to the circle of his arms about her, nothing else existed.

His hands traced patterns of delight over her responsive flesh and she made tiny sounds of unchecked excitement. The sounds of pleasure drew an immediate response from the man, increasing his desire for her. For a second or two he could have sworn he even heard bells ring. And then the girl was pushing at him, hands hard against his chest.

'The 'phone, Clint . . . the 'phone . . . '

He swore forcibly and rolled off as the bell gave another strident double ring.

Anne sat up, dissolving into helpless laughter.

Baxter pounded downstairs, frustration and apprehension running neck and neck within him. He had not expected another call so soon, had thought himself free of Blake's demands at least until tomorrow night. He snatched up the receiver as it gave yet another ring. 'Hello, yes?'

'Getting to be a habit, keeping me waiting.' Palmer's voice came silkily, chillingly, down the line raising the hair at the back of Baxter's neck.

He said the first thing that came into his head. 'I was in the shower.'

'Sure you were — in bed more like, with that blonde bird of yours.'

Baxter's frustration overflowed. 'Chance would be a fine thing.'

'You're dead right about that. You'd better get yourself over here straight away. The boss wants me to run it past you about tomorrow's little bit of activity.'

'I thought he was waiting to make sure I'd done my homework first.'

'He's a trusting man, he's taking you at your word.'

'So what's the score?'

'Down by the river, on Dock Street. There're some semi-derelict warehouses.

Fourth one along. Meet me in half an hour. Got it? Half an hour.'

★ ★ ★

As Kieran Rafferty's pony and trap disappeared in a cloud of dust, Peter Casey fished in his pocket for his mobile and dialled first Devon then followed up with a second call. His face darkened at the news.

Mary said anxiously, 'What's happened?'

'There's trouble at the farm. One of the farm hands put a call through to ask me to get back to England. It could have been a lot worse, although it's bad enough.'

Both women listened expectantly.

'There's been a fire at the farm.'

'Holy Mother of God!' Mary crossed herself.

'Don't fret. No one's hurt and the stock's all OK.'

'What of the damage?' Magda leaned forward in her chair, eyes fixed on her grandson.

'I gather the kitchen's a real mess. Fortunately, Jake was fixing a gap in one of the hedges around Home field and saw the smoke. The fire was checked before it really got a hold.'

'And Georgina?'

'She was out at the time, Mother.'

Mary sighed with relief. 'So, are you going back straight away?'

'Yes, immediately. I rang Dublin airport and managed to get a seat on the next flight.'

'It'll not be long before we see you back in Ireland.' Magda lay back in her chair, eyes closed. She said with sad resignation, 'I wish it were not so, but it follows a path.'

Casey and his mother exchanged glances, aware of the inevitability of what she'd said. They knew from Magda's previous predictions there was no point in questioning her words. Nor was there any point in expecting further comments. The old woman's body slackened, her jaw dropped a little and she fell asleep.

★ ★ ★

Strachan slammed down the receiver and swore viciously. If he came clean now and admitted that not only had Riley made off on horseback but had hi-jacked Blake's own helicopter . . . No, it would not be a good idea.

He thought of the scene at the disused farm. How he'd followed the police car in the Land Rover, foot to the floorboards, hope surging afresh as they'd passed the loose horse trotting homewards, knowing Riley must now surely be afoot. The utter disbelief on seeing the rotor whirring away on top of the helicopter. Not for a second had the possibility of Riley being able to fly crossed his mind. He recalled the impotent, helpless fury which had consumed him as the machine lifted above the two vehicles before increasing speed and flying away up country.

If he didn't tell Blake the only way out would be to find Riley. There had to be some way of knowing where the helicopter was heading. He tried to put himself in Riley's place. What would he do? Get even, that was for sure. It was the only lead he could think of. Riley would certainly want to even up the score with Baxter. A long shot but it could be the right one and in any case, what had he to lose now?

He tried to remember Baxter's home address. Blake had mentioned it. He racked his brains. The word had seemed somehow familiar at the time. Yes, that was it, Calgary. It was in Nottingham. The helicopter had been heading northeast. If Riley held that course it could be significant. Nottingham just happened to be north-east. His immediate thought was so did a lot of other places, but he didn't have a lot of choice. In fact, it was Hobson's — no choice at all.

He had really handed Riley the perfect escape route by leaving the keys in the helicopter and he knew Blake would see clearly whose fault it was. His one and only chance was to catch up with Riley — before Blake caught up with him.

Strachan went over to the small bookcase and took down a road atlas. He began to plan the swiftest route. The Land Rover might not be the fastest vehicle but it was reliable and it would certainly get him to Nottingham. Whether it would be a wild goose chase or not, he didn't know. What was for sure, outside the rain was now coming down in torrents. He was going to have a hell of a journey.

★　★　★

Gil Thomas hunched his shoulders against the cold discomfort of the rain and cycled steadfastly away from Casey's farm. He took a back way through one of the bridle paths instead of going directly past the Russet Fox. The last person he wanted to bump into right now was Strachan.

He had seen his ace card ruined by the appearance at the farm of Strachan and the police. No longer was Riley's hideout secret.

But there might be other ways of turning the situation to his advantage. It just needed a bit of thinking about.

He turned into the unsurfaced lane leading to his cottage. The rain was beating down harder than ever now and the tyres of the bicycle swished and splashed through the dimpled puddles. Above, the clouds were low, heavy with more rain to come but as he cast a knowledgeable eye upwards, Gil spotted something else. A familiar shape, dark against the grey sky but still easily recognizable, the distinctive sound of its engine muffled by the falling rain.

He wobbled to a halt, putting one booted foot down unsuspectingly into a waterlogged rut. High overhead, the helicopter flew steadily on, setting a north-eastern course. Gil watched the machine until, dwindling away in the far distance, it disappeared from sight. He wondered where it was heading and just what had caused Strachan to take off. It obviously had to be Strachan, nobody else in the village could fly a helicopter.

Despite the rain, his spirits rose a little. He'd be able to go down for a quiet drink in the pub now.

★ ★ ★

Casey's fire was the sole talk of the Russet Fox. Jake, having left his duties at Casey's farm a full hour since was well on the way to being drunk. He was becoming more expansive with each successive newcomer into the bar. The price of a pint was looked on as very fair to be told the story of how the farm caught fire from the one eyewitness.

Gil sauntered in and Jake waved the almost empty tankard at him.

'Fill me up again, 'tis thirsty work a telling all about t'fire.'

'What fire would that be?'

'Why up at t'farm.'

Gil was instantly alert. 'Casey's?'

'O'course Casey's, where else?'

'Go on then, Barbara give him another and I'll have one as well meself.'

'I'll see you right next round.' Jake beamed toothily at him.

'Yes, and I've heard that before. Just get on wi' telling me about this 'ere fire.'

For the sixth time, Jake obligingly told Gil all the relevant details plus a few more the story had acquired on the way.

'So you actually rang up Ireland?' Gil was incredulous of Jake pulling off such a feat. 'What's happening now then? Is Casey comin' home?'

'Oh aah.' Jake sniffed and looked sadly at the exposed glass bottom of his tankard.

'Fill him up again, Barbara.' Gil reluctantly

tossed some more coins onto the bar.

'You're a good sort, d'you know?' Jake wrapped a chummy arm around Gil's shoulders.

'I must be, buying you two pints. Well, then, when's Casey due back?'

'Ooh, I reckon it'll not be too long now. Said he was coming home straight away. Flyin' you know.' Jake airily waved the now full tankard and an arc of best bitter splashed over Gil's mac.

'You daft old fool! Look what y'doin.' Gil wiped a hand down the trickle of beer.

Another farm worker came in and Jake peered blearily across. 'Now then, Geoff, heard about yon fire, have you?'

Gil drained the rest of his pint and left Jake to it. He'd found the information of Casey's imminent return very interesting. What he needed to do now was to be at the farm to see Casey before the police arrived. But first he had to call in at his own cottage and collect up that Wellington boot.

⋆   ⋆   ⋆

Casey's flight arrived at Plymouth airport. With difficulty, Casey contained his rising impatience at the inevitable time loss as he waited for his luggage. Once through, he picked up a taxi.

'Casey's farm, Paxton,' he instructed the driver.

It was still raining when the vehicle pulled in at the farm gate and the headlights gleamed and reflected on standing pools of water in the yard. Casey alighted from the taxi, paid the man and walked across to the house.

Two canine shapes materialised from the barn and welcomed him joyously. Casey patted the two eager animals. He straightened up aware of water running down his neck. The rain was still bucketing down, meeting and mixing with the puddles of water left by the fire crew. It was a blessing he was grateful for but the overall air of sombreness was even more enhanced by the relentless downpour.

Casey walked to the back door. It was still standing, just. The architrave was blackened and charred, the hinges standing proud with screws protruding. A terrible smell of burning hung in the wet air, it clung to everything, adding to the general desolation. The dogs were silent now, tails held low, keeping close to his heels.

'I agree it's a bit grim.' At the sound of his voice, they looked up. Jess managed a half-hearted wag. Casey braced himself and went inside.

The smell was even worse and the whole

floor was covered in a black wet mess. All the wall units were completely gutted, just a few ribs of useless wood still hanging on the twisted metal brackets. Jess put her muzzle in the air and gave one lone howl, a desolate sound. Casey took a deep breath. 'Come on, let's have you both out.' He swung round and the dogs obediently followed him from the kitchen.

Walking around the corner of the farm-house, his foot caught something long and yielding causing him to stumble and grab for the wall. Jasper gave a quick wuff. The man kicked the obstacle out of the way. It was a single Wellington boot. 'How the hell can you lose one boot?' he muttered.

'Quite easily, I reckon,' a voice answered.

Casey jerked. 'Who's there?'

'Only me, Mester Casey, just wanted a little chat.' The old man flicked fingers at the two fawning dogs.

'Gil Thomas.' Casey relaxed. 'What do you want? I'm not in the mood for chatting right now.'

'I dare say you ain't. Not with the fire coming on top of everything else.'

There was a short silence, then Casey said, 'OK. Out with it. I take it you're not here to hand out condolences.'

'True enough, although I'm sorry it's

happened. The fire were an accident though, sure enough. Young Georgina was only hottin' up a drop o' soup for the man, but she were interrupted. I reckon as how she just left the gas on.'

'What man?' He gripped Gil by the shoulders, 'What are you talking about? Is Georgina all right?'

'Well now, I can't rightly answer that.'

'Oh for God's sake.' Casey gave him a shake. 'Where's my daughter now?'

'She went off, with that man. They left together, riding on yon horse.'

Casey let his arms drop in amazement. Seizing his advantage, Gil fished in his capacious inside pocket and drew out a Wellington boot.

'I reckons as how you'll find this one matches the one you just fell over. They belonged to the man. No, that's not strictly true. He was a wearing of 'em but the boots belong to t'prison authorities.'

Casey drew in his breath with a sharp hiss. 'She went off with an escaped convict?' His voice was incredulous. 'You don't know what you're saying, man. She must have been coerced, abducted . . . '

'Well, 'tis true that's the story I thought would go down better wi' police.'

He pushed the Wellington boot back into

his pocket. ''Course it's not true. He's been here nigh on three days, since he escaped.'

Casey's face was a picture. 'I'm not listening to anymore,' he blustered. 'It's obvious the man forced her to hide him.'

Gil shook his head slowly, 'Won't wash Mester Casey.'

'It bloody well will, how else do you explain Georgina aiding and concealing a criminal, eh?'

'She did it for her own reasons. She must have wanted to.'

'Like hell she did! You don't know what you're talking about.' He started to stride off. Gil caught his jacket sleeve.

'But I do know, you see, I was there, when she found this criminal. Up on Egton Hill it were.'

Fear prickled in Casey's stomach. Suddenly he knew Gil wasn't making it up. 'Go on.'

'No way at all the convict could have made it to the farm. Busted up his leg he had and that weren't all. A shakin' and groanin' he was. Couldn't even crawl.'

'Ha,' Casey seized at the straw. 'So how the hell did Georgina carry him all the way back to the farm?'

'She went back to t'farm and fetched yon horse and a sort of stretcher thing, tied to saddle irons it were. The old horse pulled him back to the farm.'

'My God!' Casey's face whitened. 'You'd better keep quiet about all this. My Georgina could be put inside . . .'

'Aah, I knows that. 'Course, for a consideration, you could have this here Wellington boot. I picked it up where she found him, see. I reckons, evidence like, it's worth a bit.'

'I read you,' Casey's voice was strained. He had aged ten years in less minutes. The shock and tension running through him brought his voice down to almost a whisper. 'All right, Thomas, how much?'

11

By the time Baxter had turned into Dock Street, he was wet through. The pouring rain had saturated his jacket and penetrated through to his shirt, which clung limply across his shoulders.

Baxter walked past two derelict warehouses before turning into an alleyway to avoid a workman dressed in a dark donkey jacket who came tacking down the street dodging the rain.

The fourth warehouse along was in the same very rough state as all the rest, partially boarded up, partially smashed up. Baxter shivered inside his wet jacket and thought for the umpteenth time he must have been mad to get involved. He stepped out from the alleyway. As he did so, a hand dropped hard onto his arm. He spun round. Palmer gave a deprecating snort and left the shadow of the alley behind him.

'You want to try looking behind you as well as in front. That way you'll live longer.'

Baxter, angry with himself for being taken by surprise, snarled, 'I'll still be living when you're long gone.'

Palmer snorted again. 'You'll better toe the line if you want to keep breathing.'

He pushed a hand forward in the right hand pocket of his mac. 'OK. You lead.' Baxter eyed the movement, saw the unmistakable end of a gun barrel pushing at the gabardine and felt a tremor of fear.

'You can put that away,' he blustered, 'I'm not going to run off.'

'How right you are.'

The circle of steel inside the mac pocket jerked upwards a fraction and Baxter swallowed a mouthful of saliva and walked on towards the fourth warehouse.

Another identical alley ran along the side and Palmer motioned him down it. At the far end a stout wooden door allowed them access to a rear yard. Palmer swung the door closed behind them and padlocked it. Fear leapt up afresh in Baxter and he hid it with difficulty.

'Second floor,' Palmer said indicating the metal steps of a fire escape zig-zagging up the side of the brickwork. When they reached the top Baxter hesitated at the door but feeling a quick jab under his ribs from the gun, he stepped through.

Inside, the three long windows no longer held any glass. They were heavily boarded allowing no chinks of light in or out. A bench ran the whole way along one wall and over it hung several fluorescent lights. Most of the floor area was covered in packing cases.

At one end of the room behind a trestle table sat a young man. Incongruously, he was impeccably dressed in a charcoal grey suit. His voice, when he spoke, gave away his nationality immediately.

'To be sure and it's filthy weather out there in the streets, so it is. Would you care for a drop of Jameson's to warm you up now?'

Oh God, a Mick, thought Baxter, his palms beginning to sweat at the possible implications. He nodded. 'Yes, I'll have one.'

Rooney produced a bottle and two glasses from a cupboard under the bench. He poured a liberal amount out and handed the glass to Baxter.

'Now, the reason you're here. In a moment, I'm going to brief you on tomorrow night's . . . work. But first, I want to know how much you told Riley.'

'Nothing, sum total.'

'Ha, come now. You must have spoken with him, given reasons why you needed to break out of Princetown.'

'Because of my wife, she was due to have the baby.'

'Yes, of course.' Rooney topped up the drinks. 'But what else did you tell him?'

'Nothing, I swear nothing.'

163

'I do hope it's the truth you're telling me.' Rooney's voice was silkily smooth. 'We intend to pick Riley up and, er . . . ask . . . him. I'm sure he'll be very willing to tell us.'

'Look, I swear to God I didn't tell him anything.'

'O.K.' Rooney tossed off his whisky, 'I'll take your word for it.' He generously refilled the glass. 'But tell me one thing. Just what made Riley take your rap?'

'Because he's soft,' Baxter said derisively. 'I worked on him, told him his mother would have cut off her right arm for my mother. They were twins you see. They both died from cancer within a few weeks of each other. When I said the baby would have been the first grandchild, he agreed straight off, soft, you see.'

'I doubt it. He's a jump jockey, anything but soft.' Rooney narrowed his eyes. 'Did he have any connection with Ireland, ride any horses over there?'

'Oh yes, quite often.' Baxter opened up, mellowed by the Jameson's. 'A second home really. We spent time over in Kildare as boys. And our mothers knew Rosamund O'Connor. Great friends they were. That was before she took over the Ballykenny Stud. We used to stay at her dad's farm for holidays every year.'

'Really?' Rooney was all attention. 'Do go on.'

'That's about it. When we grew up Jack went in for the horses. He decided to make a living the hard way and work,' Baxter chuckled. 'I found I had a talent for letting other people, and then relieving them of the proceeds.'

'Talking of which,' Rooney reached for a sheet of paper, 'have a good look at this layout of the interior of Allington Hall. The Duke is due at Lady Crewton's at seven-thirty, so he should be safely out of the way by seven.'

Baxter picked up the paper and looked closely at the sketch plan. 'Where's the safe?'

Rooney pointed out the Duke's bedroom.

'This room leading off is the dressing room. The wall safe is hidden behind the back of the mirror.'

'What am I supposed to lift?'

'You probably won't believe this but it's a gold cross and chain.'

Baxter sobered up fast. 'And that's it?'

'That's it.'

'You expect me to stick my bloody neck out for a trinket not worth five bob? Forget it!' He tossed the paper onto the table in disgust.

'You'll do as you're told.' Rooney's voice

was ice now. 'When you've done the job, I want to see you back here with the cross and chain. And I want you here before the Duke leaves Roster Hall. There must be no possibility of him catching you doing the job. Understand?'

'You're nuts. First you get me to lift a pricey opal necklace. OK. I do the job. Then what? You tell me to take the blasted thing back. Well, I go along with it because you've got a big job lined up for a bloke that's got bottle. Or so I thought. Now you tell me to nick something not worth a sneeze.'

Rooney slowly stood up. His eyes never left Baxter's face. 'If you don't bring the cross and chain here tomorrow night, your wife will be drawing the widow's pension.'

Baxter stared at him. 'You don't mean it.'

'Try me.'

'You wouldn't dare . . . '

'You're expendable.'

Baxter felt the sharp pressure of Palmer's gun at the back of his neck.

'No, wait. If you want the cross and chain, all right . . . ' He managed to get the words out although his tongue had dried to sandpaper. 'All right, I'll do it.'

'You'd better.'

'You'll have it, I promise you.'

'Tomorrow night.' There was no mistaking

the menace in Rooney's voice. 'I'll be waiting.'

★ ★ ★

Anthony Ashley, Duke of Allington was feeling distinctly well fed. The luncheon in Newmarket had been remarkably good. He climbed into the waiting car. 'Straight back to Allington Hall if you please, George.'

'Very good, sir.' George adjusted his chauffeur's cap and switched on the Daimler's engine. It purred sweetly into life and he adroitly negotiated the congested main street in Newmarket. The Duke selected a cassette and settled back to listen to Mozart's Concerto No. 21. The journey was smooth and swift, the big car making nonsense of the miles between Newmarket and Allington Hall.

As he climbed out, the Duke said, 'Refuel ready for Saturday's trip over to Roster Hall and then you can take until tomorrow evening off, George. Collect me up at six-thirty.'

'Thank you, sir.' George touched his cap.

Ashley let himself in and went straight upstairs to his room. He opened the door and as usual, the first thing that caught his eye was a large framed photograph of Belinda hanging on the wall opposite. His fingers went involuntarily to the cross resting against his chest.

He went through into the dressing room, shed his jacket and shirt and carefully undid the clasp from around his neck. The gold cross and chain slithered down into his palm and nestled there. For a long moment Ashley gazed at the emotive symbol then briefly placed his lips against the cross.

Opening the safe, he replaced it in the blue velvet box and secured the safe door. Tomorrow he would wear it at Lady Crewton's party.

* * *

On the Friday afternoon the e-mail came through for Blake. He found it on his return from exercising Max. Rosamund had sent it from Ballykenny Stud. He read it through.

They'd had torrential rain in Ireland since the preceding day. The foaling area roof had taken so much and then given up. Necessary repairs would have to be taken.

Since, officially, no foaling was due until after the first of January, hopefully it was not a panic situation, although if the roof was to be repaired and not renewed, a reasonably quick assessment ought to be made.

Blake grimaced and picked up the 'phone. Rosamund was still working in the office and she answered it straight away. 'Having trouble, Rosamund?'

'You could say so Blake.'

'How bad is the roof?'

'It's in pretty poor shape. And, of course, there's several other minor repairs that will be needed shortly.'

'Looks like an expensive time in front.'

'Which is why I'd like you to come over and check it out.'

'If you think it's necessary, OK. But I've too much on just now. I'll send Sean?'

'Whatever you wish.'

'It will have to wait until after the week-end though, we're both busy. I'll send him at the beginning of next week.'

'Fine, look forward to seeing him.'

★   ★   ★

Hickson, Governor of the prison of Princetown looked across at the Police Officers. 'You realize,' he addressed his words to the senior of the two, 'it's doing wonders for all the inmates' moral. One of their own actually getting away, and not just getting away, but off the moor completely. They'll be dining out on this for evermore when they're released.'

'I'm no more happy about this than you are,' the Divisional Commander said sourly.

'Please sir,' the young duty officer came in, 'Constables Attewell and Kenny have just arrived in reception.'

'Well, let's have them in. They're no use to me down there.'

'Yes, sir.' The duty officer escaped and returned a couple of minutes later with the two men.

'You lost Baxter.' The Divisional Commander stared at a point on the far wall just above Attewell's head.

'I'm afraid so, sir.'

'Well, give me the full story, Constable, don't be shy.' The senior officer's gaze dropped and his eyes lazered into Attewell's. 'I want to know how an escaped convict can make a laughing stock of an entire police force, not to mention the drafted in reinforcements.'

Attewell swallowed hard, took a black notebook from his top pocket and flipped it open. He proceeded to update his superior on Baxter's movements.

At the end of Attewell's monologue, the Divisional Commander jumped to his feet. His voice was now very low. 'Of all the methods of transportation an absconder could choose, a helicopter would be at the top of the list. It's just about the fastest, has the most freedom of movement, and is the most difficult to trace. Add to that the odds on the convict being able to fly one . . . ' He slumped back down into the chair. 'Go and interview the helicopter's owner, find out how much fuel it was carrying and how far that would take it before refuelling. And get yourself over to Casey's farm. See what you can find.'

'Yes sir.'

'Go on then, what are you still standing there for?'

Attewell and Kenny went out.

The Divisional Commander addressed the duty officer. 'Better notify the Nottinghamshire Force. Baxter may go home but he's fly. I doubt he'll drop into the net. Still, it's about all we've got to work on right now.'

'Very good, sir.' The duty officer noted the wry expression on his superior's face and found himself sympathising a little. Last year his own holiday in Jersey had gone by the board because of work. This year it seemed to be the Commander's turn. Right now the Seychelles looked like being a dead duck.

★ ★ ★

Rosamund O'Connor put the 'phone down and sighed wearily. She stood up, shovelling receipts, cheque books and ledger into the desk drawer and locking it. Today was nearly over, long and tiring though it had been, the discipline of work had kept her thoughts away from this time last year. But the thoughts were creeping in now.

Locking the office door, Rosamund took an umbrella and walked up through the village to the Church standing on the rise. Tonight, she needed to walk in the cold rain, feel it beat against her heated cheeks and calm her emotions.

It took her a good half hour before she finally stood in front of the heavy studded Church door. Pushing it open, Rosamund stepped inside, genuflected before the altar and chose a candle. As she lit the wick and saw the gold and blue wavering flame grow, she commended her mother's soul into the hands of God.

Setting the lighted candle down, Rosamund knelt before the Blessed Virgin's statue to pray. Engrossed in her prayers, she didn't notice Father O'Malley enter the Church and walk towards her.

The priest genuflected and then stood to one side with bowed head, respectful of her need for privacy. Today's date was 20th of

172

October. A year ago Sheelagh O'Connor had died at the infirmary. He had been summoned by Rosamund to give her mother the last rites. Even before the woman in front rose from her knees, Father O'Malley was forming the right words in his mind to ease her emotional pain.

Rosamund ended her prayer and looked up.

'Bless you, my child.'

Rosamund scrambled to her feet. 'Thank you, Father.'

'We may find the date our loved ones depart a burden to carry but that date was set before they ever came to earth. It was a date decided by God. And in His sight, I have no doubt, it is one for celebration.'

Rosamund bit her lower lip and nodded her head slowly. 'I, too, have no doubts about that Father. But it's hard . . . '

'Let God take the strain, my child, place your grief in His hands.'

Impulsively, Rosamund grasped O'Malley's hand in hers. 'You are such a comfort. How can it be you are so good and yet your brother Michael is so bad?'

'Good and bad are in everyone. It is up to us to choose which way to go.'

'With your example before him, how could Michael have done those terrible things? The physical and emotional pain he has caused to other people, the wrong he did to my dear friend, Maria Baxter, forcing himself upon her, leaving her with child.'

'God undoubtedly wanted Clint to be born. We do not question Him.'

Rosamund, bone weariness and grief combining to expose her vulnerability, was weeping now.

'But I have wished Clint dead many times, Father. Maria didn't just suffer giving him life, she has suffered so much since . . . truly it is a case of like father, like son.'

'The sins of the Father would certainly seem apt,' O'Malley murmured.

'And because of what I have done, I am no better . . .'

Father O'Malley looked at the deep anguish on her face. 'You wish to make a confession, my child?'

'If only I could,' Rosamund whispered the words. 'But because of who you are, you are the last person in the world I could tell.'

'I am a priest.' O'Malley looked at her in puzzlement. 'Nothing is too bad that it cannot be forgiven, provided you are sufficiently contrite.'

'I wish that were true, Father, but you cannot help me.'

Before O'Malley could say anything, Rosamund spun round and ran down the aisle leaving the bewildered priest looking at the solid oak door as it swung closed behind her.

12

Constables Attewell and Kenny heard the grotesque clang of the prison security gate closing behind them as they made their way across the car park to the police car.

Attewell blew his cheeks out. 'Phew, the old man's got a head of steam going.'

'What you could call a bit abrasive,' grinned Kenny.

'It's O.K. for you lot, dragged in, what about us? We live here.'

'Lucky beggars,' said Kenny and carried on grinning. 'I'd swap you any day for my patch.'

'No thanks,' Attewell said shortly, opening the car door.

'Where we headed first, then? That farm?'

'Yes. See if we can catch anybody in.' He headed out of the car park and turned in the direction of Paxton.

'You don't reckon the girl will have come back, do you?'

'Georgina? Shouldn't think so. Can't understand her. Why the dickens did she hide Baxter there in the first place?'

'Could be a straight forward case of coercion.'

'Well, it could be but somehow I don't reckon it was. She was in Tavistock yesterday lunchtime, you know. I didn't tell the old man, he'd have had my guts for not following it up, but I saw her in Boots buying some paracetamol.'

'So what?'

'Nothing odd about that I agree, except before she bought the paracetamol, she actually asked for some quinine tablets.'

'Eh?'

'See what I mean? Now why would she want quinine tablets? They wouldn't be for herself, so they must have been for someone at the farm, and apart from Baxter, there's only the two farm workers.'

'Unless she was running an errand for somebody else.'

'No.' Attewell shook his head decisively. 'I was right behind her when she asked for the quinine. When the assistant wouldn't play ball without a prescription, she got a bit flustered and took the paracetamol instead. If she'd been doing an errand for somebody else, they'd have given her a prescription for them, I reckon.'

'Sounds about right.'

'So. It's the farm workers or Baxter. And if it is Baxter, Georgina Casey was buying them for him of her own free will. There was no gun at her back.'

'Looks like an A. and A. job,' Kenny agreed pursing his lips. 'But for the life of me I can't see why.'

Attewell swung the police car into Casey's farmyard for the second time that day. 'Well someone's home because the light's on,' he said. 'Let's ask them shall we?'

The two men left the car and went across and banged on the front door. Inside a dog barked and a man's voice quietened it. A moment or two later, Peter Casey opened the door.

'Hello, Mr. Casey.'

'Didn't take you long, did it? I've only been home a short while.'

'Just want to ask a few questions, Mr Casey. And have a look round inside the farmhouse if you don't mind.'

Casey shrugged indifferently. 'Help yourself. There's nothing hidden, nothing for you to see.'

'We'd like you to accompany us if you would, sir.'

'Whatever you wish.' Casey shrugged again and led the way upstairs.

The two constables spent a fruitless time going through the contents of the upper rooms. 'It seems you were right, sir. But we'll just check the downstairs.'

'Feel free.'

Once more the two police officers drew blank. 'Have you any idea why your daughter should be helping an escaped convict, sir?'

'Well it's obvious, man, isn't it? She was put in a position where she had no choice.'

'It is possible, but we don't think so.'

'Oh for goodness' sake!'

'Can I just ask you if either of your two farm workers has been ill at all, running a temperature, that sort of thing, in the last two days?'

'Not to my knowledge. Both of them have been working as normal.'

'Thank you, sir.'

'Why on earth should you ask that?'

'Just following a line of enquiry.'

'Well, if you've finished your search and your questions . . .'

'One last question, if you don't mind, Mr. Casey. Have you any idea where your daughter has flown off to with this escaped convict?'

'Flown off?' Casey's face was creased in a frown, 'What the hell are you talking about? She rode off on horseback, didn't she?'

'Initially, yes. But both she and Baxter took off from the old farm near Pointon in Strachan's helicopter.'

'The devil they did!'

'The helicopter flew north-east after take off. Obviously, the convict was a qualified pilot. What we'd like to know is where they were headed for. Any ideas, sir?'

'None whatsoever. I wish to God I had.' Casey slumped down in an armchair. His distress was evident and both constables exchanged glances.

'We'll be off now then, sir. In case you think of anywhere they might have gone, perhaps you'll ring the station?'

Casey nodded.

The two constables showed themselves out.

★　★　★

When they'd gone, Casey went to the sideboard and poured himself a large whisky. The burn of the liquor had him coughing a little but it steadied him. Thank God he'd seen Gil Thomas before the police arrived.

If Gil had decided to offer the second boot to Attewell and told him where and how he'd found it, Georgina's case wouldn't still be in the doubtful category, it would be an open and shut one against her. Casey felt the sweat stand out on his forehead. Just what the hell was going on between Georgina and this convict?

He swallowed the rest of his drink. If

Georgina was hiding the man, she might be headed for the one place she could feel safe, her own home.

Casey sat with his head in his hands and thought it out. It made sense to him. The only trouble was if he'd sat and thought it out, undoubtedly the police would be doing the same thing. However, they would still have the bother of tracing Georgina's address.

He came to a decision. If he could reach her home before the police did and she was there, at least he could tell her Gil had approached him first and the story of coercion would hold water. It was worth a try, anything was worth a try.

But there was a job to be done first. Whistling to the dogs, Casey left the farmhouse and went out past the stables to the muckheap. Taking a hayfork he dug firmly into it, tossing forkful after forkful aside. Buried deeply inside it he eventually unearthed two Wellington boots. He pulled them clear and took them into the barn. With a Stanley knife he set to and systematically cut the boots first into thin strips and finally into tiny pieces, letting them drop into a bucket. The last pieces fell in and he sighed with satisfaction. Any possible fingerprints had been obliterated and no longer could they be identified as prison issue.

Casey picked up the bucket and went out to the slurry pit. Swinging the bucket in a half circle, he scattered the contents over a wide area. The wind caught the fragments spreading them still further before dropping them into the thick evil-smelling mud. For a second or two the pieces of rubber lay on top and then slowly sank below the surface and no trace was left.

Going back to the farmhouse, he wrote a note for Jake saying he had to go away for a few days and asking him to take charge of feeding all the stock including the two dogs.

Then he went upstairs to fetch his suitcase. It was ironic he thought, the suitcase hadn't even been unpacked.

★ ★ ★

It had been a noisy, cramped journey in the helicopter. Conversation had petered out a long time ago, the effort of trying to make themselves heard above the engine proved too self-defeating.

Georgina leaned over close to Riley. 'Do you know exactly where we're headed for?'

'Give or take, yes.'

'Do I get to know?'

'When we start going down,' he grinned at

her. 'The low fuel warning light has already come on and this is what will decide for us.' He pointed to the fuel gauge.

'It looks horrendously low to me.' She pulled a face. 'What do we do when it's all gone, bail out?'

'Oh, I think I can judge it close enough to make a landing.' He grew serious. 'Just where though, that's the problem. Can't land in any built up areas on two counts. First, safety, don't want to wipe anybody out. And second, secrecy. The longer it takes before anyone finds this old bird the better.'

'Right now,' Georgina said, 'I have two counts — coffee . . . and a loo. Not necessarily in that order.'

'I'll have to see what I can do then, won't I?' Riley laughed.

★ ★ ★

Sean Rooney came out of the warehouse, left Dock Street and drove away from Holmington in the direction of Harrogate. He didn't think Baxter would attempt to trail him back but it made sense not to take chances.

From being reasonably co-operative, Baxter had gone hostile and just how far he could be pushed was an unknown quantity. But his story of Riley's mother and his own being twins and their joint long standing holidays at Rosamund O'Connor's in Ireland had been very enlightening. Blake was going to be extremely interested.

Rooney detoured around the outskirts of Harrogate until he was satisfied there was no vehicle tailing him before heading home. He parked up and went straight in to the office. Blake wasn't there.

Rooney swore with frustration.

He checked the computer, noted the e-mail message from Ireland and read it through quickly. It was odds on he'd be going to see Rosamund. He reached for the desk diary. Yes, Blake had pencilled in his name and a provisional date of next Tuesday.

Angrily, he tossed the diary back onto the desk. It hit the red leather inlay and slid across, cannoning into the photograph of Gloria and Patricia. The photograph went spinning and landed with a crash in the wastebasket.

Rooney winced and went to pick it up. By a miracle, the glass was unbroken but the catch on the reverse had sprung open and the back was hanging off. As Rooney fished it out a small white card slipped out and fell to the floor followed by the photograph itself that landed face downwards.

On the back of the photograph were four words written in Blake's handwriting. 'My three in one.' Rooney frowned and picked it up. He had no idea what Blake meant but he intended to ask.

The other small card still lay on the floor and he scooped it up. The frown deepened on reading the cryptic words written in black letters. 'Rosemary, that's for remembrance. Pray you, love, remember.' The Shakespearean quote was followed by 'The long ago regrets go deep.' There was no indication where the card came from but it was obviously the sort that came pinned to flowers. And it had come out of the photograph frame; that probably meant it had been attached to a spray or wreath at the women's funerals. Just who the hell had written it?

Rooney sat down in Blake's chair behind the desk and steeled himself to remember the details of the funeral. One ghastly picture came straight away. The darkness of the gaping hole in the ground seemingly going down forever and which drew him inexorably into its depths as Patricia's coffin was lowered.

How at the last moment, when it seemed he would overbalance and topple in, Blake's steely grip on his arm had held him firm. And how they had almost simultaneously thrown a single red rose each into the cold earth.

Rooney shuddered, re-living the horror. The bile rose up in his mouth tasting rancid and sour. He took deep breaths fighting against the impulse to retch and resolutely pushing the picture of the graveside from his mind.

He recalled lurching away on leaden feet following Blake to where the discreetly unobtrusive undertaker had displayed the floral tributes. Not that he'd taken much in as he passed down the line of wreaths and flowers, apart from noticing the heart-shaped wreath of pink and white carnations with the card bearing his own last message to Patricia. There had been a large display and nothing registered, except for that one last wreath.

Rooney sat bolt upright. Now that one he did remember. The red roses had stood out from all the others, a bold defiant colour on the sombre occasion. And he had stopped and looked closer, wondering who had sent them. The card had been missing.

Now, he knew instinctively that Blake had removed it. Blake had been a few seconds in front, time enough to take it from the red wreath. The point was why? The flowers themselves, red roses, proclaimed their message without words. And in any case, the card was unsigned. But it was undoubtedly a symbol of love.

Rooney's skin prickled. He was assuming it had been sent for Gloria, but supposing it had been meant instead for Patricia. A wave of violent jealousy swept through him. But almost immediately it was gone. Patricia had been his, no other man existed for her. And if that was so the wreath must have been meant for Gloria. But what did that spell out to Blake?

Rooney gave a silent whistle of dismay. He couldn't begin to understand what it must have done to the man, and on the day of the funeral, too.

He replaced the photograph inside the frame. No way now would he ask Blake what the four words written on the back stood for.

But one thing was for sure, he was determined to find out just who had sent the red wreath and more importantly, why.

★ ★ ★

'Well, we've made it.' Riley held the helicopter almost stationary as he scanned the ground below. 'This is Ilkley Moor and we're about out of juice so down we go.'

Georgina shivered. 'It looks a long way from civilization.'

'Which is what I'm aiming for.' He turned to look at her as the helicopter began the descent. 'Sorry about the coffee. As regards your other request, I'll just have to turn my back.'

'I'll survive,' she said watching the moor rushing up to meet them as the Robinson came in to land.

Riley negotiated a ridge and let the machine drop into a gulley. It hit the rough tussocks of grass and juddered to a halt, sinking into the soaked ground, the rotor turning slower and slower and finally coming to a complete stop. After the unrelieved noise of the long journey, the stillness was intense.

'All change.' Riley dragged off his headset and smiled at her, 'You OK?'

'Sure.' Georgina undid the safety belt and pushed open the cockpit door. A blast of cold, wet air rushed in, the wind buffeting the exposed cockpit and lowering the interior temperature in seconds. Riley jumped down and came round the nose of the helicopter to the passenger side.

'Give me your hand.'

Georgina scrambled from her seat and with legs cramped and stiff from sitting, clambered out, falling against Riley as she misjudged the distance to the ground. He caught her easily and set her down on the sodden grass, his arm remaining around her. 'You're quite O.K.?'

'Just stiffened up.' For a few seconds neither moved, held by the invisible electricity that ran between them. Gently he put her from him.

'We'd better get going. It wouldn't do to let anyone catch us near the helicopter.'

'Nobody in their right mind would be out here in this murk.'

Together they climbed the ridge and scanned the desolate expanse of moorland. The rain battered down, reducing visibility to a few yards as it swept across the soggy landscape in a sullen grey curtain assisted by a shroud of mist.

'Any ideas where we are?' Georgina huddled inside her duffel jacket and pulled the collar up as high as it would go.

'On the east side of Ilkley moor, broadly speaking.'

'And where are we headed?'

'Certainly not upwards, we're not equipped to survive spending nights out at this altitude, especially in weather like this. Come on, give me your hand, don't want you tripping and breaking your leg. I don't think I'm up to carrying you yet.'

Beneath the light-hearted banter, Georgina could detect an edge of tiredness. She looked up at his thin profile as he tried to get a bearing with a pocket compass. 'Are you all right?'

'Now why shouldn't I be?'

'Oh, little things, like two days of not eating, a bout of debilitating malaria, a busted up leg, etc.'

'Didn't you know?' He turned, rain streaming down his face, and smiled at her. 'All jockeys are a tough breed.' Before she could move Riley caught her face between his palms and kissed her rain-wet lips. Georgina gasped with the unexpectedness of it. And despite the biting cold rain, she felt a warm tingle run the full length of her body.

Without giving her time to think, Riley caught her hand and set a strong pace downwards over the moor. The rough grass tussocks dragged and snatched at their feet, treacherously slippery, making progress hard work. They were soon both panting with exertion.

The moor seemed to shrink from a wide panorama to an eerie narrow strip of ground which extended only a few feet in front in the rolling mist. Across the uneven ground, each tussock of grass and patch of heather was a duplicate of the one before. And all the while, the chilling rain slanted down, penetrating their clothing and soaking their shoes.

'At least,' Georgina panted as she scrambled along beside Riley, 'all this exercise is warming us up.'

He grunted. 'Best if we don't talk. We're going to need all the breath we've got for hiking. I've got to admit, I'm not sure just where we are.'

A shadow of anxiety touched her. 'We are going to make it make to civilization tonight aren't we?'

'Trust me.'

And they both knew as they continued to slog one foot after another there was nothing else to be done but stick with it. The only indication that they were going in the right direction was to keep walking downhill.

13

Strachan felt his stomach rumble with hunger. The steak pie and chips he'd eaten at a service area on the M5 three hours ago had long since been digested.

The road map was propped up against the dash and he took a swift look at it. The A453 along which he was driving would very shortly be running into Nottingham. Where Calgary Street was situated he couldn't begin to guess. What he needed was a street map of Nottingham.

He looked at his watch. It was getting on, the shops would be closing soon but if he could find a newsagents they'd probably sell local street maps.

He drove on, aware that he was now in a built-up area. Crossing a fly-over he glimpsed water, which was obviously the River Trent. Signs pointed to the City centre and he followed these and negotiated the increased traffic.

Keeping an eye out for a multi-storey car park, he saw the words 'Victoria Centre' followed by a large letter 'P'.

Strachan followed the signs, turning first

into Glasshouse Street and then descending the ramp into the bowels of the massive car park. It was Friday; a traditional shopping day, and the car park was almost full. At last he spotted a vacant space and reversed the Land Rover into it. Getting out, he stretched stiff limbs, relaxing the tedious ache which had held his shoulders in a grip for at least the last hour or so. Making a mental note of the colour zone, he took the lift up to the shopping centre itself. Nobody in the sea of shoppers and commuters paid the slightest attention to him and he melted in with the throng and made his way to the main entrance.

The high, ornate Emett clock burst into a clangour of musical activity as the water fountain hit the decorative wheel turning slowly round. Strachan hesitated a few moments with some of the sight-seers around the edge of the pool of water. As the last tinkling notes died away, the clock chimed the hour.

Six bloody hours, Strachan thought, walking swiftly away. He couldn't afford to waste any time taking in tourist attractions. Walking along Parliament Street he dived into a tiny newspaper shop and bought a street map. He walked on past the Theatre Royal and soon found a small cafe. Placing his order for food and coffee he dropped down tiredly into a seat at the rear where he was obscured from the street and pedestrians.

He sipped the reviving coffee and checked the street map whilst he waited for his meal to be brought. Calgary Street proved to be in the middle of the city with access at both ends providing a connecting link between two more similar streets. It was only a few minutes walk away from the car park.

The waiter brought his plate of steaming hot food and for a few minutes Strachan forgot his urgency and ate with relish, strength creeping back with every mouthful. After a second coffee and a last look at the map, he left the cafe and headed back towards the car park.

Cutting through an adjoining street, he crossed over at a set of traffic lights and turned left leaving behind the shopping areas and entering a maze of small streets all flanked on each side with old terraced houses.

Coming to the end of the row of houses, he turned into Calgary Street. The first number was an odd one. Baxter's home number was 6. Strachan crossed over. It was one painted dark blue. It looked totally deserted, curtains half-pulled across both upstairs and down-stairs windows.

Walking the last few yards to the end of the street, Strachan turned the corner and found that each of the houses boasted a small backyard abutting an alleyway running parallel to Calgary Street. Strachan made his way along to the rear of the dark blue one.

Inside the yard was a small wooden shed, a circular clothes drier and a dustbin. He lifted the lid off the bin. It was empty. Looking casually over into the next door's yard, he saw the bin was crammed.

Strachan went up to the back door and tried it tentatively. To his amazement it opened. Slipping quickly inside he waited, listening. It was deathly quiet. He left the kitchen and went through all the rooms systematically. The house was empty.

It seemed clear that since Baxter had moved out and gone into the rent-free furnished house in Holmington provided by Blake as a safe bolt hole, nobody had been living here at No. 6. It looked like a case of waiting it out for Riley to appear. And if he didn't ... Strachan shrugged the thought away angrily, he had no other lead. Riley would come, of course he would.

But in the meantime, he stood up yawning widely as the sense of urgency abruptly left him and tiredness flooded in. It wouldn't be a bad idea to make a cup of coffee and bring it upstairs to bed and have a stretch out.

He went back downstairs, opened the kitchen door and came face to face with two policemen.

★ ★ ★

Peter Casey's flight was late arriving at Leeds and Bradford airport. The combined appalling weather and low cloud added to the dismal atmosphere.

He shrugged deeper into his puffa jacket and crossed the wet tarmac to the taxi rank. 'Skipton,' he said brusquely to the nearest cab driver. 'I'll direct you when we get there.'

He slumped back in the seat and closed his eyes. It had been a long, tiring day. Too much travelling, too much stress, and it wasn't over yet. If the escaped convict was hiding out with her, Casey knew his temper was likely to snap.

Georgina was all he had left now since Ruth had gone. The father and daughter bond between them had grown stronger over the years, particularly by the support he'd given her over the business with Dave, her husband.

'Skipton coming up,' the taxi driver said over his shoulder. 'Where would you like dropping off?'

Casey rubbed the back of his hand over his eyes and gave the address.

In a few minutes the taxi was pulling up in front of a row of tiny stone-built cottages. Casey jumped out and paid the driver.

'Anytime you want transport, just ring this number, sir.' The man pushed a piece of card into his hand, ran the window up and drove off leaving Casey standing on the pavement, suitcase in hand.

Georgina's was an end of terrace cottage built in large sandstone blocks with diamond leaded windows. It was a pretty little place. He'd only been here a couple of times before, shortly after her wedding. Pity for his daughter ripped through him. What a bloody awful shame it had turned out like it had. Whatever help the girl needed right now, he'd give it willingly.

A door opened in the adjoining cottage and a young woman nursing a fractious toddler on her hip stepped onto the doorstep. 'Hello, Mr. Casey, isn't it?'

'That's right.' Peter smiled back at her.

'Georgina's not here, I'm afraid. I thought she was down in Devon.'

'Yes, yes, she did come down, but we've had a spot of trouble at the farm so she thought it best to make her way home. I take it she's not arrived yet?'

'No, not a sign of her. Anyway, you'll be wanting the key. Just a sec.' The girl took the toddler back indoors and reappeared very quickly holding a bottle of milk and a couple of keys on a ring.

'I'm sure you could do with a cup of tea, so have this on me.'

'That's very good of you, I appreciate it, thanks.'

'Anything else you're short of just pop round.'

'I'm much obliged.' Casey smiled at her and unlocked the front door.

The unwelcoming coldness of an empty house hit him immediately. What he needed to warm him up and take away the stiffness of travelling was a deep hot bath. Testing the water supply, he turned on the boiler and set it for the full works, twenty-four hour hot water and central heating.

He could be facing a long abortive wait but he might as well do so in comfort. And he intended to wait, for however long it took. Sooner or later, Georgina would come back. When she did, he'd be here.

★   ★   ★

'Are you sure we're not just going round in circles?' Georgina said stumbling along

198

beside Riley. 'We seem to have been walking for hours.'

'Don't tell me you live at Skipton and you've never walked over Ilkley moor before, shame on you.'

'Dave and I used to bring a packed lunch up on Sundays occasionally. But only in summer, when the weather was good. We weren't daft enough to walk over the moor in murk like this.'

'Daft or not, it's the only way we'll get off, the alternative is to sit down and freeze.'

'I'd sooner keep walk . . . oh!' her voice tailed off as a large animal with curved horns suddenly loomed up out of the mist in front of them. It gave a loud bleat of fright and lumbered across their path.

Startled, Georgina stepped hastily sideways to avoid the sheep and her feet slithered from under her. She gave a cry of alarm as an unseen, rain-swollen pool dropped away sharply beneath her and she went down on her knees into the freezing dark water. Although it was only about two feet deep, the shock of the cold water made her gasp. In seconds, her thick clothing had soaked up the water like a sponge.

Riley caught her arm and pulled her upright. She staggered out, shivering from head to foot, water pouring off.

'This moor is bloody lethal!' she exploded, squeezing at her saturated clinging jeans.

'Well, you did say all this exercise was warming.' Despite his banter, Riley was concerned. Getting wet with the rain was bad enough but being plunged into icy water fully dressed was another.

'Take your jacket and sweater off. I'll wring them out, my wrists are stronger than yours.'

Georgina did as she was told. Through teeth chattering with cold she managed to say, 'A hot bath would be nice . . . '

Riley finished wringing out the sweater and pulled it back over her head. 'At least it's not dripping, girl, and that's the best I can say.' He turned his attention to the duffel coat and a stream of water ran away through his strong fingers.

'A blazing log fire wouldn't come amiss either.' Her voice broke a little.

'Here, let's get your coat on.' With a great deal of struggling, he managed to pull the wet coat over the arms of her sweater and up over her shoulders. She shuddered as the coat plastered the wet sweater against her skin.

'Oh God, Jack, I'm so bloody cold.'

'Come here,' he undid his own saturated jacket and held out his arms, 'snuggle up against me. Body heat's the only thing we've got. Let's make use of it.'

Georgina moved inside the circle of his arms and nestled against him, her cheek pressed to his chest. He held her very close, their coats forming a protective tent around them, shielding them a little from the downpour. For several minutes they remained in silence, each very aware of the other. But as Georgina slowly stopped shivering Riley whispered, 'You know, girl, given different circumstances, like for instance, in front of a blazing log fire, this could be rather enjoyable.'

'You think so?'

'Hmmm. It has possibilities.'

'You could be right. But we'd have to find the log fire first.'

'So what are we waiting for?' Riley stepped back, 'Come on. Time to get moving.' He fastened her coat and zipped up his jacket.

Taking her hand in his Riley picked his way between the tussocks onto a narrow sheep track leading downwards. Neither spoke, as bent forwards, rain beating against their faces, they weaved an unsteady path to the bottom of the next gulley and up again to the crest of the following heather covered ridge.

Stopping to catch their breath, Riley said, 'Look! Over there, do you see the red flag?' He pointed to a tall post and a flag fluttering gamely in the wet tearing wind. 'Now I know where we are, well, approximately, anyway. It's a warning flag for the T.A. They must be on manoeuvres. We'll have to swing north to avoid the danger area.'

Another half hour of trudging brought them to the last ridge in a featureless landscape and they saw a line of pine trees on the skyline.

'Nearly there now, girl. One last pull, come on.'

'I've nearly had it, Jack. I can't feel my legs at all, they're so cold.'

'You can't give up now. See those big rocks just this side of the pines? They're the famous Cow and Calf. It's the finish of the moor. Down below them is the road into Ilkley.'

He put a supporting arm around her waist and together they stumbled on through the rain and mist of the low cloud.

By the time they reached the Cow and Calf rocks, the fickle mist had almost lifted. Riley was now half-carrying Georgina and with his face close to hers, he could see her lips were blue and pinched with cold. The pain in his own leg had flared up fiercely, aggravated by the rough terrain and taking the strain of the girl's weight. Just how he was going to get them both down the narrow tarmac road into Ilkley itself, he couldn't begin to think. The freezing rain not only numbed the body but seized up brainpower as well.

It was Georgina who first heard voices. Looking in the direction of the huge rocks, they both saw the climbers. Two or three figures dressed in protective clothing and wearing safety harness and ropes, they stood at the lip of the amphitheatre formed by the sheer millstone grit rocks.

'What are we going to do, Jack?'

'One of two things: either we back away before they see us, or we go on and take our chances.'

'But we can't go back.' Desperation made her voice high and sharp.

He took a swift sideways look at her, noted just how close to snapping she was, and decided.

'We go on, brazen it out. We're just a . . .' he looked down at her hands, ' . . . a married couple.' He removed a birthstone ring from her right hand and placed it on the third finger of her left. Then he gently turned the ring around leaving just the simple gold band showing. He raised his eyes to her face and they stared at each other. Slowly the tears welled up, overflowed and trickled down her cheeks.

'Do we have to?' It was the smallest of whispers.

'It bothers you that much?'

She drew in a deep breath and gave a single nod.

'I'm sorry,' he hesitated, 'but if it helps us to get off this moor incognito, then, yes, I think it is necessary.'

Staring down at her left hand she said very quietly, 'If we must . . . all right.'

Riley placed his hand over hers and squeezed it. 'Let's go, girl. See if the natives are friendly.'

They moved on slowly now, through the knee high and dripping rust-coloured bracken. Riley had his arm around her waist giving her what support he could as they covered the last couple of hundred yards.

The climbers were making their way down the far side of the rocks. In the car park a white minibus was parked up on the approach to the narrow road running from Menston to Ilkley.

Riley and Georgina slipped and slithered down the final long run of shallow steps on the south side of the Cow and Calf rocks. All the climbers were down now and busy stowing away gear in the minibus.

'Hi, there, 'Riley raised an arm, 'are you going to Ilkley by any chance?'

One of the men finished loading a coil of rope and came forward to speak to them. 'Passing through? Are you short of a lift?'

'We'd certainly appreciate it. My wife's not feeling too good. She had a slight accident and got a soaking.'

'It doesn't do to take chances up here. You have to respect the moor.'

'So we've found out.'

'I think we can squeeze you in, it's not far to Ilkley. My name's Marriott, by the way, christened Frederick but Fred will do.' He held out a thick, calloused hand.

Riley shook it. 'And ours is Jones.'

'We'll be a few minutes loading up and then it's Ilkley first stop.' He peered down at Georgina. 'If I were you, I'd get the wife inside the bus now. It's not much warmer but it stops the rain. She looks all in.'

'Thanks very much . . . er, Fred.'

'Yes, it's very kind of you,' Georgina managed a wan smile.

The man was right. It wasn't much warmer inside the bus but it cut out the bite of the wind and Georgina sank thankfully down on to a seat and leaned against Riley's shoulder.

'We'll make it look good, shall we?' he murmured and slipping arm around her, gave her a kiss on the cheek.

The rest of the party climbed aboard and finally, Fred swung up into the driver's seat. 'Everybody right?' He switched on the engine and turned the minibus round, headlights cutting golden arcs through the gloom and rain, cleared the car park and headed left on the Ilkley road.

'Just sing out where you want to get off,' he said above the noise of the engine, 'I can drop you at the door.'

Riley was about to say 'my place' but changed in time and said, 'Our place is the other side of Ilkley. Is that O.K.?'

''Course. Anyway, we're going farther on past Skipton.'

Georgina tugged at Riley's sleeve. 'Could we go to my home instead?' she whispered. 'I'm desperate for some dry clothes.'

Riley frowned. 'You're sure you want to? My place is closer and quite isolated. We'd be safer there.'

'Oh, please, Jack, I'd much rather go home.'

'O.K. then, if that's what you want.'

She nodded, 'Please.'

Riley raised his voice. 'Fred, do you mind if we go on with you to Skipton?'

'I thought you said you lived at Ilkley.'

'Well, we do, but . . . the wife wants to stay at her mothers.' Riley improvised in desperation. 'Our heating is on the blink, I'd forgotten. She doesn't fancy a cold house with no hot water.'

'Sensible woman,' replied Fred, 'Skipton, then.'

The minibus rattled on down the winding road leaving Ilkley behind and eating up the miles. Georgina dozed fitfully leaning against Riley's shoulder.

Keeping up the pretence of being married, he tenderly smoothed back the long strands of wet hair from her face and rested his head against hers. It took a lot of will power to prevent himself from dozing off, too.

'We're approaching Skipton now, Mr. Jones.' Fred's voice broke in. 'Whereabouts do you want?'

Riley gently eased his arm from around Georgina and woke her. He said in low voice. 'What address is it?'

She told him and added, 'It's only about half a mile farther on, a turning to the right.'

The driver found it easily and drew up at the row of terrace cottages. 'There you are then. I hope your wife's O.K.'

'Thanks again, you've been a great help.' Riley helped Georgina down the steps and raised a hand in farewell as the minibus lurched forward into the darkness and disappeared.

Taking her arm, Riley turned her to face the cottage. 'I don't want to alarm you, girl, but did you happen to leave some lights on?'

'It's probably only Jenny from next door keeping an eye on things.'

She opened the front door and they both went in. A man came hurrying through from the kitchen. 'Thank God you're home.'

'Dad! What on earth are you doing here?'

'Waiting for you.' The man swung round aggressively, 'And I suppose this is Baxter, is it?'

'Sorry to disappoint you, Mr. Casey. I'm Riley, Jack Riley. Remember me?'

14

Peter Casey narrowed his eyes and stared at Riley. 'Of course. You're a jockey. But what's all this about Baxter?'

'A long story. Right now Georgina needs a hot bath and dry clothes.'

'I'll second that.' She reached up and put her arms around her father and kissed him. 'Lovely to see you.'

'You're absolutely wet through! What on earth have you been doing?'

'Falling into waterlogged holes on Ilkley moor, actually.'

'Well, I should do as Riley suggests and get yourself into a hot bath. The water will be ready soon, I put it on when I got here.'

She frowned. 'But why are you back?'

'I had a call from Jake.'

'From Jake? I don't believe it!'

'He asked me to come back.'

'If Jake managed to phone Ireland there must be something drastically wrong at the farm.'

Her father put hands in pockets and hunched his shoulders, the memory of the black, wrecked kitchen rushing back, momentarily dulling the pleasure of seeing his daughter. 'There was a fire, only a small one, but Jake did right in calling me. It's my farm and it's my place to be there.'

'How bad was it?' Georgina sat with a hand pressed to her mouth.

'Fortunately, only the kitchen was damaged, nothing else. The stock's all right, the horses, both dogs, they're all OK.'

'Thank God,' she released a sigh of relief, getting unsteadily to her feet. 'I'm so sorry, Dad, but it was my fault.'

'Nonsense.' Casey waved a dismissive hand.

'No,' Georgina said stubbornly, 'I was warming soup in the kitchen and I ran off and left it.'

'It was an accident, forget it.'

'If I could butt in,' Riley said, 'if it's anybody's fault, then I take fullest responsibility. She was warming the soup for me and because of me she had to leave the farm unattended. I forced her to come with me.'

'Now hold on, just a minute,' Casey frowned. 'As I understand it, Georgina was hiding the escaped convict.'

'Yes, me.'

'So where does Baxter come in?' 'This is where we came in. And I'll say it again, it's a long story. I vote we hold this conversation after Georgina's got rid of those wet clothes.'

Riley looked ruefully down at his own clothing, 'Mine aren't in too good a shape either.'

Georgina said in a shaky voice, 'You'll find some men's clothing in the spare bedroom, help yourself.' She walked to the door. 'I'll have that hot bath now.'

When she'd left the room both men looked at each other. Riley raised an eyebrow.

'Dave's clothes,' Casey said shortly, answering the unspoken question, 'her husband.'

Riley remained silent, waiting, but Casey abruptly changed the conversation. 'Georgina doesn't drink so I can't offer you a whisky. I'll put the kettle on, I guess you could do with a hot drink, after you've put on dry clothes.' Their eyes met again.

'There's been nothing between us,' Riley said, 'I'm not stepping into another man's shoes, metaphorically speaking anyway, even if I am literally.'

Casey shrugged. 'You heard what Georgina said, help yourself. It's the first door on the left. I'll make some coffee.'

★ ★ ★

Rooney, still gazing at the cryptic wording, hastily pocketed the incriminating card as Blake entered the office.

'What have you to tell me then?'

'About Baxter? A little unexpected eye-opener.'

'Right, let's be having it.'

'I'll give you the story just as Baxter told it. See what you make of it.' Blake's face remained inscrutable whilst Rooney filled him in on the afternoon's disclosures. 'Now that's what you call interesting. Why should Rosamund recommend a supposed friend for a gun job that carries the life sentence?'

'She did know it wasn't just for the safe cracking, didn't she?'

'Oh yes, son. She knew all right.'

'Why don't you ask her straight out?'

His father-in-law gave a throaty chuckle. 'Is that my usual way of doing things?'

Rooney smiled thinly, 'No.'

'She sent an e-mail, by the way, about the brood mares' foaling area. Apparently the roof's had it.'

'Yes, I read it.'

'I told her I'd send you over.'

'Thanks, a lot.'

'When you get to be boss, son, you can do the sending.'

'That makes me feel a great deal better, so it does.'

Blake leaned forward and clapped a hand on Rooney's shoulder. 'While you're in

Ireland, find out all you can, discreetly, of course.'

'Of course.'

'Still, that's next week. Tomorrow's the testing time for Baxter.'

'If he does the job.'

'He'll do it. He has too much to lose.'

'Like his life.'

'We're in this for the end results, I don't care how high the stakes go,' Blake's face was like granite. 'Someone is going to pay for Gloria's death.'

'And for Patricia's,' Rooney added very softly.

'Son, she may have been your wife, but never forget, she was my flesh and blood, my daughter. The only child Gloria gave me. So when I talk of paying for Gloria's death, I also mean Patricia's.'

Rooney put a hand to his eyes, 'Sure, and I'm sorry. I know you included her as well. The nerve's still bloody raw, even after more than six months.'

'And it's the same for me, Sean.'

'But you found a bit of comfort, didn't you? When you went to Ireland and saw old Magda Casey?'

'Yes, I did.'

'Don't you reckon it was just wishful thinking?'

'No, I'm sure it wasn't. The old woman took hold of Gloria's scarf and the things she told me, well, it wasn't possible to disbelieve. They were things Gloria had said to me in private, some of them years ago. Nobody else in the world knew.'

'You're as sure as that?' Rooney hunched forward in his chair, fists clenched.

'I am, son.'

'God, I wish I could be.' '

'If you mean that, it's obvious, isn't it?'

Rooney looked deep into Blake's eyes. 'You're saying I should go to Ireland and see Magda Casey?'

'You're going to Ireland on Tuesday, aren't you'? But, a word of advice, take an article of Patricia's with you. The old woman will need it.'

★ ★ ★

Strachan walked slowly into the kitchen and said, 'Now hold on, officers, what's going on here?'

The tallest of the two Nottinghamshire policemen said, 'That's what we were just about to ask you, sir.'

'I'm checking out these premises. I heard they were empty, available.'

'Where did you hear that, sir?'

214

'Oh, you know, on the local grapevine.'

'And would you mind telling me your name?'

'Brown.'

'And your address?'

'Right now I'm in digs near Trent Bridge. But if I don't find somewhere soon it'll be under Trent Bridge.'

The policeman changed tack. 'Do you know the gentleman who lived here?'

'Baxter you mean?'

'That's right.'

'I can't say I know him, know of him, more like. He's doing time.'

'Was, he's escaped.'

'You don't say?'

'Afraid so. Skipped from a working party on Wednesday. Common knowledge now.'

'They never get off the moor though, do they?'

'He did.'

'Really? I suppose that's why you're staking this place out then.'

'You're certainly wasting your time here. When Baxter comes back, and he will do, we'll pick him up.'

'I wish you luck, then.' He left them to it.

The alley led onto an adjoining street and Strachan walked briskly along to the corner. The last building turned out to be The Black

215

Swan pub and he thankfully pushed open the doors and went through. Inside, at the bar, he ordered a large brandy. When the barmaid set the balloon glass down he said, 'Anywhere round here I can get a room for a night or two?'

'Sure. Right here. B & B only though.'

'Sounds fine to me.'

'You'd like to see the room now?'

'Why not.'

The barmaid cocked her blonde head at the barman. 'Take over a minute, Sid.' She took down a key from beside the optics and led Strachan up the creaky back staircase to the first floor. Unlocking a door, she walked into the bedroom. 'Would this suit?'

Strachan ignored her and crossed to the window. He drew back the grubby net curtain and looked out. The view covered a wide angle. It showed the back yards and alley of the Calgary Street terraces. He let the curtain fall back into place.

'This will do just fine.'

The barmaid handed him the keys and walked out.

Apart from the bed, a side cabinet and wardrobe, the only other piece of furniture was a rickety chair.

Strachan set chair at an angle before the window. It gave him a clear view of the

216

backyards, which glowed orange under streetlights.

He sat and sipped the double brandy and hoped like hell Riley would approach No. 6 Calgary Street from the back entrance.

★　★　★

Riley returned to the kitchen. He'd dressed in some casual slacks, warm shirt and thick pullover. Casey looked up from spooning brown sugar into his coffee.

'You're a very similar build to Dave.'

'They fit pretty well.'

'What did you do with the wet gear?'

'Hung it on a coat hanger in the airing cupboard.'

Casey grunted. 'I'll take it back home with me when I go, after all it is mine.'

'Yes. Sorry about that, but Georgina insisted.'

'She usually does.'

There was a long silence during which Riley went in search of a jar of honey, found it in the tiny pantry and spooned a liberal amount into his scalding coffee.

'So,' Casey settled in the armchair and stretched out his legs, 'Tell me about Baxter.'

Riley stirred his mug. 'He's my cousin and

I wish to God he wasn't. The charge against him was armed robbery. He's been inside before.' Riley took a gulp of coffee. As he recalled the memory, a surge of guilt ran through him but he pushed the thought away. 'Baxter served a sentence in Ireland.'

'You don't say?' Casey was paying rapt attention. 'For what crime?'

'Grievous bodily harm.'

'Sounds nasty.'

'Yes, it was. Rattled the family cage somewhat.'

'What relationship is he to you?'

'Baxter is the illegitimate son of my mother's twin sister, my Aunt Maria.'

'And his father?'

'A very closely kept family skeleton.'

'But you know?'

'Oh I do.'

'But not common knowledge'

'No.'

'And you're not going to tell me?'

'No.'

'Does it have any bearing on how things are at present?'

'My God, I hope not,' Riley took another gulp of coffee, hesitated and then said, 'The family hushed it all up, never pressed charges against the man. You see . . . Maria was raped.'

218

'A vile word for a vile act,' said a woman's voice.

Both men swung round. Georgina stood in the doorway a look of utter distaste on her face. 'How could they have let him get away with it?'

Riley smiled sadly, 'Do you not see, girl, it would hurt Maria less that way.'

'But she conceived because of it. Surely she could have had an abortion?'

'Maria is a Catholic,' Riley's voice was gentle, 'it was never an option.'

'And so she had to go through with it, pay the whole price for something which was not her fault.'

'You are seeing it through a woman's eyes.'

'Damn right I am.'

'Well look at it like this also. Maria was in love with the man, at least, up to the time of the rape she was. He wouldn't marry her and she wasn't prepared to let him make love to her because of her religious beliefs.'

'It does not excuse him in the slightest.'

'Oh I agree, girl. But I'm just telling you the way it was.'

'He could have had no real love for her at all.'

'He's a callous bastard all right. His own skin comes first, that's for sure.'

'And has this callous streak been passed on

through the genes, then?' Casey put in.

'I think you can say he's running true to form, yes.'

'And where's Baxter now?'

Riley shrugged, 'That I don't know.'

'You still haven't explained why you were hiding up at my farm and involving my daughter.'

'No, I haven't.' Riley refilled his own mug and handed one to Georgina. 'Basically, I took his rap. We swapped places. I suppose it was because our mothers were identical twins we two looked so alike. We were often taken for twins as well.'

Casey narrowed his eyes. 'You must have owed Baxter a big one, Riley.'

There was dead silence in the room. Then Riley said in a low voice, 'That's very perceptive of you, Casey. Yes, I did. Just about the biggest.'

Georgina stared at him across the table. 'Will you tell us what it was?

Riley shook his head slowly, 'I think not.'

'So, apart from the obvious reason, why did Baxter want you to swap?'

'The arrangement was only supposed to be for a short time whilst Anne, Baxter's wife, gave birth to their child.'

'And he ran out?'

'Looks like it, but I don't know the reason

why. That's what I'm going to find out.'

'But you said you don't know where he is.'

'And I don't. But I intend to find him.'

'Talking of finding,' Casey set down his empty mug on the table, 'the reason I've come all the way up here is to warn you the police will probably be arriving pretty soon.'

'Here?' Georgina said in dismay.

'I'm afraid so. They've already been to the farm to see me.'

'What on earth are we to do?'

'I suggest you come back to the farm with me.'

'No.' It was said with quiet determination.

'There's no way you'd stand up to all the interrogating without the police knowing everything. You're far too honest, my dear.' He drew up his shoulders in distaste. 'If they get to know how you met Riley on Egton Hill and brought him back to the farm . . . there's no way I can help you avoid prosecution.'

Georgina drew in her breath, eyes wide with alarm. 'But no-one knows.'

'I'm afraid that's not so. Besides the police, I also had another visitor. He was up on Egton and saw you. Thankfully, he arrived before the police did.'

'Oh my God!' She pressed a hand to her mouth. 'The other boot. I'd forgotten about it. The man must have found it. I went back next morning and it had gone.'

Casey gave a mirthless chuckle, 'It's gone all right. I cut it up into tiny pieces and threw it into the slurry pit.'

Georgina stared hard at her father, 'After you'd paid out for the privilege?'

Casey screwed his lips up and shrugged. 'What's money against you being put in prison?'

'Who saw us?' Riley's face was grave.

'The local know-all in person, Gil Thomas.'

'How do you know it's going to stay at one payment.'

'For the simple reason Gil came to me rather than one of his other more lucrative options. He was concerned about Georgina.'

'And what about the second boot?'

'I found it. Fell over it, actually. Don't worry, that one's in the slurry as well.'

'No problem then. I forced Georgina to help me.'

'If the police accept that of course. However, I've a feeling Attewell's got some other line he's following. Have you any idea what it could be?'

Riley shook his head. 'No idea at all.'

'I have.'

Both men looked at Georgina.

'Constable Attewell was standing behind me in the chemists. I tried to buy some quinine tablets. I settled for a bottle of paracetamols and walked out.'

'Right.' Casey slapped a hand against his leg. 'I wondered why he asked me if the farm workers were ill.'

'It still doesn't prove anything against her.'

'No, but if the police arrive here and find both of you . . . '

'Or even if they find you on your own Casey. They'll assume you've tipped us off. We all need to get out of here p.d.q. And not only get out, but do it without arousing anybody's curiosity.'

'But where do we go? I've more than had it right now,' Georgina's voice was edged with exhaustion.

'As I see it, we've only one option,' Riley replied, 'my place.'

15

The Duke of Allington laid his fountain pen aside and stretched. 'We'd better call it a day. I have to change shortly. I apologise for making you work Saturday afternoon.'

Maureen smiled, 'I really don't mind.' She began to gather up the scattered papers from his desk. 'I've hung up your suit in the dressing room.'

He smiled warmly at her, 'How about gracing me with your company say, at lunch tomorrow? My tangible thanks for your hard work.'

'I'd like to very much.'

'Settled then, twelve-thirty ready for one o'clock. I look forward to it.'

Although she knew there was no hidden meaning, and the phrase was one of the Duke's standard replies, it had the effect of pinking Maureen's cheeks. 'And so do I,' she murmured and behind her words was a wealth of feeling the man was totally unaware of.

The Duke went upstairs and ran a bath. He climbed in the bath and lay back. Alex Blake would be at tonight's party. Strange that the

224

man seemed to bear such animosity when they'd both suffered loss and grief last March. This time next week he'd be all packed ready to leave for Ireland the following morning. And Saturday night might very well be his last night alive. It was a grim thought. He'd turned down all security arrangements. OK. Michael O'Malley was safely locked up in prison but his aggrieved friends weren't. Ashley took a deep breath. He could well find them gunning for him — literally.

But what was the point in making a peace gesture if it was backed up with police protection? It would simply be a sham. Still, the danger would be very real.

He reached for a towel and stepped out of the bath. There was no going back. He needed to live in peace with himself. The commitment had been made and that was an end to it. He padded into the dressing room.

Maureen had not only hung up his dinner suit, she'd laid out a clean white shirt too. It crossed his mind she'd make some man an excellent wife.

Crossing to the mirror, Ashley released the hidden catch and opened the safe door. Taking out the blue jewellery box, he cradled Belinda's gold cross and chain in his hand for a few seconds before carefully fastening it around his neck. The ironic thought occurred to him that he was going to celebrate the birthday of an elderly lady whilst his daughter had died on her eighteenth birthday before they'd had chance to celebrate.

He laid the cross tenderly against his chest and buttoned the shirt over it. Life went on certainly but sometimes it took more guts to live than to die.

★ ★ ★

Baxter slipped on a dark jacket over his black sweatshirt and slid the long handled set of keys into the pocket together with a set of car keys. He turned to Anne. 'I'm away now, love.'

'When will you be back? Tonight?'

'Maybe, maybe not.'

'I wish you'd tell me exactly what you're doing.'

'Just leave it to me, OK? Remember, I'm doing what I have to do for all of us, you, me and the baby.'

He'd left the stolen Vauxhall round the next corner. Minutes later, he'd pulled away and nosed the vehicle eastwards. In twenty minutes, he pulled into a gateway in the country lane leading to Allington Hall. Switching off, he sat for a few moments letting his eyes get used to the starlit darkness of the night. Climbing out, he locked the car. It was very quiet the only sound the gentle rustling of leaves brushing against each other in the wind.

Baxter walked silently up the lane towards the big iron gates at the entrance to Allington Hall. Ignoring them, he walked past for several yards to where a large horse chestnut straddled the boundary with the lane. Reaching up he got a grip on the rough bark and hauled himself up onto a low bough. From there it was a simple job to ease along and drop down into the grounds. Up ahead, the drive widened out into a wide semi-circle in front of the Hall.

The plans had shown the Duke's bedroom to be on the west side. Baxter skirted round carefully, noting the position of the security lights. At an oblique angle, using the cover of the shrubbery, he reached the wall in darkness.

A Virginia creeper grew in flamboyant profusion up the old bricks. Tentatively, he put up a hand and gave the nearest thick stem a tug. It bent for a few inches and then held firmly. He inched along by the wall and came to a drainpipe. It was not the modern variety and he felt satisfaction swell inside. The downpipe was iron and where the junctions occurred, these were banded by thick jutting out rims. In combination with the creeper, it would give him all the support needed to reach the first floor level.

There were several windows facing west, all with wide stone sills, and Baxter counted them until he came to the fourth, the Duke's. It was closed. The fifth one, however, was open a couple of inches. According to the plan, it should be the adjacent dressing room.

Bending down, Baxter undid the laces on his trainers and slipped them off. He tied the shoes together and hung them around his neck.

Placing his foot on the first ridge of the heavy drainpipe and pressing himself hard against it, he began to climb upwards. The worst part was negotiating the jutting stone window sills but by climbing up higher and swinging downwards, he managed to finally stand on one of the wide ledges. Pushing the window further open, he slid soundlessly through into the room.

There was only one mirror situated above a small wash-hand basin. He moved across and delicately ran his fingers around the edges. The safe catch was carefully concealed at the bottom but his questing fingertips triggered it and the mirror swung outwards revealing the tiny safe hidden behind.

Groping inside, he drew out a jewellery box. The box opened easily. But his fingers traced only the imprint of where the cross had been lying in the soft velvet. The cross and chain were missing.

Anger rose within him and he thrust his hand back inside the safe taking out the remaining items, a Cartier watch and several cufflinks. Swearing under his breath, he put them inside his jacket pocket and once more, in desperation, scrabbled around inside the empty safe. Nothing else remained.

The desperation swelled within him. If he didn't deliver the cross tonight, his safety would be on the line. And not only his, there was Anne and the baby too. A cold sweat enveloped him making him feel sick.

Running the options through his mind, Baxter came up with the only one. He'd cut and run. At the least it would give him a breathing space, maybe Riley would even turn up. It was on the cards. Riley was an ace right now. Whoever handed him over to the boss would be in good books. The only place Riley would be likely to make for would be Baxter's old address in Nottingham. No 6 Calgary Street.

It would amount to betrayal of course. For a second or two sibling loyalty vied with self-survival. To betray him would be a filthy trick. But boyhood was long past, this was the big cold world. He'd got to look out for himself now. And for once, he was one up on the opposition, he knew where to look.

With gloved hands, Baxter closed the safe door end secured the catch. It was possible the Duke might not even look in the safe until much later. Any time lapse at all added a bonus.

He climbed back through the window, partly closing it behind him. Going down the pipe was a piece of cake. Baxter squirmed his way back through the shrubbery. Then he ran until he found the horse chestnut at the boundary of the estate.

With pounding heart, he climbed out over the thick branch and dropped into the lane. Without waiting to see if any alarm had been given, Baxter raced back along the lane to the waiting Vauxhall, switched on the ignition and drove away.

He glanced at the fuel gauge as he hit top gear. Lady Luck was starting to ride after all, the gauge showed well over three quarters full.

His spirits rose, it was more than sufficient to get him to Nottingham.

★　★　★

Matthew O'Malley smiled and took the after dinner coffee Sylvia Rooney had poured. 'As ever, an excellent meal, thank you.' He stood up and walked from the dining room through to the presbytery's cosy sitting room. A peat fire burned invitingly, flickering on a pile of drying peat waiting on the hearth. A heavy spatter of rain hit the pane emphasizing the snugness of the room.

O'Malley set the coffee down and went to the window. He stood a moment looking out at the dark wet night. It was to be hoped next Saturday, and especially, the following morning, would be different. With the boat booked to carry the Duke down river from the proximity of the plane runway, a deluge on the day really would put a damper on the celebrations. But next Sunday was a week away yet.

O'Malley drew his thoughts back to the present. He had a homily to write for tomorrow first. The theme was no problem, it had presented itself to him yesterday after seeing Rosamund O'Connor in the Church. It seemed right as a lead up to next week's peace service.

But Rosamund wasn't at peace, far from it. There was a great burden on her conscience, that much was obvious. And it disturbed him in a deep uneasy way. She had said she couldn't tell him of all people. The why behind it was giving him a great deal of unrest.

He held many of the darkest secrets of his parishioners. Because they trusted his sacred position and found it intolerable to carry the weight of their own sins locked away inside, they unburdened all the distasteful, immoral secrets onto his broad shoulders. And because of his oaths, he could never speak out, never betray.

But O'Malley himself was not so fortunate. There was no-one to whom he could unburden himself. Memories of the day of the car crash that had taken the lives of Gloria and Patricia were locked away inside him. And he blamed himself totally for their deaths. If his brother Michael hadn't set up the explosive intended for the Duke of Allington, then he wouldn't have been driving like a lunatic trying to out-race time itself. It was a terrible secret to keep and the passing weeks and months rather than easing the agony, seemed only to increase it. And because he could never disclose to anyone what had really happened, the guilt fed upon itself and grew.

But the reason why Rosamund could not confess remained niggling away at him. It could only mean whatever unpleasantness she was concealing concerned him personally.

O'Malley reached for notebook and biro and wrote the heading 'Past Sins and Consequences'.

* ★ ★

Only one cobwebbed fluorescent tube struggled to light up the dusty interior of the warehouse on Dock Street.

Sean Rooney said, 'Nine thirty-three. What time do you make it, Palmer?'

'Mine says the same. Baxter should have been here now, he's had time.'

'Exactly,' Rooney's voice was hard. 'We'll give him half an hour, make it ten o'clock. If he's not here by then, he's not coming.'

Palmer took up the whisky bottle, 'Another?'

Rooney looked around the bare, cheerless warehouse and grimaced, 'Why the hell not. It's the only comfort going, so it is.'

'What's the form if Baxter doesn't show?'

'It's entirely his choice. If he's not for us . . . ' Rooney left the sentence unfinished.

'A damn good job he doesn't know the full S. P.'

Rooney said very softly, 'But he knows too much already.'

The whisky bottle rattled a little against the glass tumbler as Palmer shivered at the unmistakeable threat behind the words.

Rooney continued, 'And he's not the only one.'

Palmer started with fear. 'Why? What do you mean?'

'Seems Strachan's gone missing as well.'

Palmer, much relieved but still shaken, said, 'Not at the pub then?'

'No. Barbara rang up from the Russet Fox complaining she wasn't paid to run it on her own. Strachan left around Friday lunch and hasn't been seen since.'

'In the helicopter?'

'No, that's another sore point. Strachan drove off in the Land Rover because the helicopter had already been taken by Riley.'

'You don't say!' Palmer gaped in surprise.

'We knew Riley had slipped the net on Dartmoor, Strachan told us that much over the 'phone. What he didn't say was that Riley had made his escape in our chopper. Rumour has it down there in the sticks that the girl from the farm was forced to go with Riley.' Rooney took a gulp of whisky, 'Don't know how true it is.'

Palmer closed his mouth with an effort, still trying to assimilate the implications. 'Riley could be making for anywhere. Does he know about next Sunday?'

'Not a chance as far as we can make out.

Well, we've kept Baxter in the dark about it. O.K., he's got an inkling something's up about the Duke of Allington but that's all.'

'It will be plastered in the papers soon enough now about his peace visit to Ireland. Shouldn't think it will take Baxter long to put some of the pieces together when he reads it.'

'Have you thought what would happen if Riley and Baxter get together?'

The two men were silent considering the possible dangers. The level in the whisky bottle fell steadily as the time slipped inexorably round to ten o'clock.

Rooney slammed his glass down hard, 'That's it! There's no way Baxter will turn up now. We'd better get back and report to Blake.'

'I wouldn't like to be in Baxter's shoes,' laughed Palmer nervously, following Rooney to the door. 'Blake isn't going to take kindly to it, is he?'

'Take kindly to it?' Rooney spun round and glared at Palmer. 'After weeks and months of planning things to the finest detail and a little rat like Baxter sods up the whole thing? I'm dead sure you can say he will not be pleased.

'When Blake gets his hands on the man he'll be down on his knees screaming for a quick end.' Rooney slammed the door viciously, locked it and started down the fire escape.

Palmer closed his eyes for a second and swallowed hard before scurrying after him.

16

Riley went out the kitchen door carrying the log basket and sauntered down the garden path to the woodshed. The interminable rain had finally stopped leaving behind a dripping landscape washed clean and with a fresh wind blowing. He took a lungful of cold, clear Yorkshire air and savoured it.

The relief at being free and his own master again was sweet within him. All that was needed now was to get back amongst his beloved horses and ride winners. The jump season was already under way. But before life returned to normal, Baxter had to be contacted, warned that the police were looking for him. And the reason why he hadn't honoured the agreement to finish the prison sentence made known. He owed the man nothing further, yet he could not shake off the bonds between them. The memory of boyhood days held deep roots.

He swung open the woodshed door and filled the basket from the massive pile of logs stockpiled inside. A frisson of warm pleasure quivered through him at the thought of Georgina curled up in the big leather armchair beside the fire. It was down to glowing embers right now which was why he'd stirred himself to fetch more logs.

The cold and wet from the moor seemed to have left her cold through to her bones because she'd been shivering and sneezing ever since.

Whatever Georgina thought, he knew until he'd seen Baxter a question mark hung over them. He'd already made up his mind to go down to Nottingham later tonight. But if Georgina grew worse he'd have a hard job to leave. She'd looked after him at great risk to herself and to shirk when it was his turn was something not to be entertained.

Riley closed the woodshed door and returned to the cottage. Opening the sitting room, warmth enveloped him like a snug duvet but he could see Georgina was still very pale and going across he took her hands. They felt coldly moist.

'Ridiculous, isn't it?' She smiled wanly at him. 'All this gorgeous heat and I'm still out there, or as good as. Ilkley Moor certainly knows how to leave its mark.'

'I know your house has central heating, but there's nothing like a good old fashioned log fire for upping the temperature.' Riley placed two good sized logs on the glowing coals. 'I'd hoped you might thaw out here at my place.'

'Please, Jack, I'm in no way complaining. A fire like this is absolute luxury. And if I wasn't feeling so bloody awful, I'd be revelling in it.'

'So, you're admitting feeling rough?'

She pulled a face, 'Guess I am.'

Riley frowned. 'I wish to goodness your father had stayed on now instead of getting back to the farm.'

'But he saw us both safely here, away from my house, surely that was enough?'

'It would have been,' Riley conceded, 'except for the problem that I've got to go and leave you.'

She regarded him steadily without speaking, but the one word her eyes were saying made him feel like a traitor.

'Yes it's Baxter, I can't help it. I've got to see him, sort this lousy mess out. There's a feeling inside, oh, I can't explain it, but something is very wrong. Pressure is being put on somewhere down the line, what I don't know, but it's there. I can practically smell it.'

Still she didn't speak and he went on, 'If Baxter's back home, O.K. it shouldn't take long. But I have to know what's going on, try and persuade him to give himself up to the police. It would probably be the safest thing he could do in any case.'

'Maybe I shouldn't say this,' Georgina said,

239

dropping her gaze as she spoke, 'I really don't want you to go, I'll miss you.'

Her words seemed to send a blaze of light through the room as the same spark within him flared high in response. With great difficulty he held down the surge of emotion her words had ignited. 'I promise I won't be gone long. You'll be safe here. The police don't know I exist so they won't come looking. Nobody else knows you're here either. All you have to do is rest and try to keep warm.'

'Are you going straight away?'

'No. I'll cook us a meal and make you a bed up in here.'

Georgina began to protest and Riley cut her short. 'Look, if I didn't have to go, I wouldn't, believe me. You really need looking after. There's a camp bed upstairs, I'll bring it down and you can get some sleep.'

'There's no point my arguing then, is there?'

'None at all.'

★   ★   ★

Strachan shifted uncomfortably in the rickety chair. He'd sat watching through the dingy net curtain for most of the twenty-four hours since he'd taken the room at The Black Swan.

He desperately needed a break and a beer.

He went downstairs, ordered a pint and took it over to a vacant seat near the door. What if Riley didn't turn up and he was left upstairs in the dreary room watching an empty house? Moodily, he took a gulp from the misted glass.

As he set it down, the street door opened and a clean-shaven, dark haired man walked in.

It was so unexpected that Strachan choked on the mouthful of beer. The newcomer turned and saw him. Fear flickered across his thin face and he headed back for the door.

Still coughing, Strachan jumped to his feet and stepped out in front. 'Hold it, Baxter. You and me, we're going upstairs to my room for a chat.'

'Like hell,' Baxter tried to push past him.

Strachan dropped his hand into his jacket pocket and jammed the barrel of the Walther hard into the man's side. 'Upstairs, now.'

For a moment Baxter hesitated and the gun scraped painfully along his ribs. 'Now, Baxter.'

They went up to the first floor. 'Second door and put both hands high, flat against it.' Strachan unlocked the door and roughly thrust the man inside.

'Right, let's have it, what're you doing here?'

'My bloody business.'

Strachan put the palm of his left hand against the man's chest and propelled him backwards. The backs of Baxter's knees hit the edge of the narrow bed and he sat down suddenly. Strachan stood straddle legged in front, the gun trained steadily at Baxter's chest.

'O.K. I'm making it my business. Why are you here?'

Baxter glared at him, 'Why don't you ask the boss?'

'Blake?' Strachan narrowed his eyes.

'If that's his name, yes.'

Realizing he'd given information away, Strachan said angrily, 'Let's stop messing about. Did Blake send you?'

'No', Baxter said sullenly, 'he thinks I'm still at the house on Janes Street at Holmington.'

'Whose house?'

'No. 25 of course, the one he put me and Anne in.'

'Why are you down here?'

'I couldn't find the soddin' thing, could I? And they wanted it handed over tonight.'

'Thing? What thing?'

'The Duke of Allington's cross and chain.

It should have been in the wall safe and it wasn't. I got the safe open all right. But what happens? The cross wasn't there, was it? So what am I supposed to do? Ask for Union back up?' Baxter slumped and put his head in his hands. 'They'll carve me up if I don't produce it.'

'So you did a runner instead, eh?'

'I need some more time. I can have another bash later.'

Strachan changed tack, 'And Riley? Where's he then?'

'How the hell should I know, I'm not his keeper.'

'But he'll be looking for you, bound to be.'

'Well I'm staying here, I can lay low for a few days then maybe try again next Saturday night.'

Strachan laughed nastily. 'You won't even be in England next Saturday night. You'll be over in the emerald isle.'

Baxter stiffened warily, 'Will I now?'

'You don't think Blake will leave it right to the last minute before he has you in position, do you?'

Baxter took a chance, 'Blake's not told me when I get sent over.'

'Well, take it from me, he's sending you over on Saturday. You'll need to suss out the Church layout. See whereabouts the Duke'll be standing. No good turning up for the service with a gun instead of a prayer book unless you know.'

Baxter drew a long ragged breath, 'If I'm down to waste him, why the hell does Blake get me on stealing this Duke's cross and chain, it doesn't make sense.'

'Sure it does.' Strachan sneered, 'never heard of psychological warfare? Blake wants this bigwig's security shaken. Not safe even in his own home, etc. Nothing like your own patch being infiltrated to frazzle the nerves.'

'If that's the reason, I'm in the clear then,' Baxter grabbed pathetically at the straw, 'See, I've nicked these.' He took the sets of cufflinks and the expensive watch from an inside pocket. 'I took them from Allington's safe tonight. Worth a hell of a lot more than a cross and chain they are.'

'You stupid sod.' Strachan said. 'No idea at all have you? The cross and chain belonged to the Duke's daughter. The whole idea was to leave everything else and just take that.' He sneered at Baxter, 'Blake's going to be really mad when I tell him how you've cocked up his plans.'

'You wouldn't drop me in it,' Baxter licked dry lips, emotions swinging from deep fear to flimsy hope and back again.

Strachan gave him a hard stare, 'There is

something you could do, something I want which you've got.'

'Come on, then,' Baxter was all eagerness now, 'Tell me, I'll give it to you if you keep quiet about this to Blake.'

'I want Riley's home address.'

Baxter swallowed. 'I don't know about that. He's sort of family, y'see.'

'Either you tell me where Riley lives or I tell Blake you stole the watch and stuff out of the safe.'

Baxter thought quickly, Riley was certain to look for him at 6 Calgary Street so it was odds on he wouldn't be at his home address at Ilkley. If anything it would be doing Riley a favour to point Strachan in the opposite direction.

Baxter looked at Strachan, saw the uncompromising ruthlessness in the man's eyes and decided, 'OK.' he said, 'I'll tell you.'

★   ★   ★

When Rooney returned home from the warehouse, Blake's car was already parked up. He went in. 'How come you're back so soon?'

'By going to the party, I've found out something important.'

'Oh yes,' Rooney flung himself down in an armchair, 'like what?'

'Like I know that Baxter didn't give you the cross and chain tonight.'

A slow smile spread over Rooney's face, 'Sure, and it saves me admitting it. So, you cunning old devil, how come you know?'

'Simple, my son, because it was around the Duke of Allington's neck.'

'He was wearing it?'

'Yes. Quite a turn up that. It seems the Duke sets a lot more store by it than we'd thought.'

'Must do.'

Blake chuckled, 'I guess I owe the waiter one.'

'How come?'

'My shoe chanced to come across in front of the man when he was carrying a tray with Avocado dip. Unfortunately, his Lordship just happened to be standing in the line of fire. Right down the silk shirt, of course, probably ruined it, too.'

'Had to strip off, then?' Rooney was laughing. 'Privately, I hope. Not in front of Lady Crewton, surely?'

'Well, I needed the bathroom too, didn't I? With all the drinks being plied on the guests, it was a natural thing to do.' Both men were laughing now.

'So,' Rooney grew serious, 'what gives now?'

'I take it Baxter didn't show?'

'No.'

Blake nodded, 'Predictable, you see. He'll be back in Nottingham by now.'

'So what do we do?'

'Do, my son? We go get him.' He stood up, 'Here you are,' he flicked the Mercedes keys into Rooney's lap. 'With all the liquor I've taken on board tonight, you're driving.'

★ ★ ★

The Duke of Allington waited until George had driven through the gates of Roster Hall and then shrugged off his dark jacket. The wet silk shirt clung unpleasantly to his bare chest. He let it drop in a sticky, damp heap onto the floor of the car.

As they reached Allington Hall, he put the jacket back on and tucked the gold cross solicitously inside.

'Round the back I think, George.'

'Very good, sir.'

Ashley got out at the kitchen door. 'Dispose of the shirt, please, George.'

The chauffeur's lips twitched faintly, 'Of course, sir.'

'I'd like you to collect Miss Kingston in time for lunch, tomorrow.'

'Yes, sir, goodnight sir.'

After a short hot shower to remove the unpleasant viscid residue from his chest, Ashley went to his dressing room.

He opened the wall safe and took out the jewellery box. He laid the cross tenderly on the velvet and replaced the box. As he withdrew his hand it brushed the side of the safe. Frowning, he felt around but the safe was quite empty. The Cartier watch and sets of cufflinks were missing.

Ashley's face hardened as he took the jewellery box out again. From the security aspect, it was pointless to leave it in now. If he hadn't been wearing the gold cross and chain tonight, assuredly it would have been stolen.

But the risks of breaking into Allington Hall for a watch and cufflinks weren't justified. So what had the thief been after? His thoughts switched to Lady Crewton's party. Obviously, the intruder must have been aware of his movements tonight and had utilized his absence to risk breaking and entering. But it was odd he'd been the one to have the dip tipped over his shirt. Almost as if someone at the party had been checking on the whereabouts of Belinda's cross.

He pulled himself up sharply; he was allowing his imagination to run away with him. If it hadn't been for the peace visit to Ireland scheduled for next Sunday, he supposed he wouldn't have been so sensitive.

All the same, he reopened the jewellery box and fastened the cross carefully round his neck. It was the only safe place. Then he dialled the police.

★ ★ ★

Riley unfolded the camp bed and set it up on one side of the sitting room. He'd brought down a pile of blankets and a couple of pillows.

'Anyone would think I was a helpless invalid,' Georgina protested.

'Prevention, girl, I don't want you getting any worse. It's entirely selfish. I don't want the job of looking after you.'

'Says you.'

'And I suppose you didn't look after me at all when I was down with malaria.'

'Not a lot.'

'Of course not. I mean, trekking across the moor on horseback just to bring me something to lower my temperature, that's not putting yourself out one little bit.'

'Oh shut up,' she smiled at him.

He deftly made up the bed, piling a load of blankets on top. 'There, I reckon when you're tucked up under the covers with the fire built up, you'll last until I get back.'

'You're spoiling me.'

'Give over. It's the first time I've had chance to spoil a female. You don't want to debar me that pleasure, do you?'

'Put like that, what can I say?'

'Nothing. Just enjoy it.' Riley put another log on the fire and the flames danced up blue and gold. 'If you want to get into bed, I'm just off into the kitchen to fix some food for both of us.' He went through the door.

'Jack,' the girl called his name softly.

Riley stopped and put his head round the door. 'Short of something?'

'Oh yes, you can definitely say that,' she whispered, her face softening as she looked at him. 'The same thing most people are short of. Maybe I'll tell you what it is one day.'

The atmosphere changed perceptibly, became charged with held emotions. Jack, standing smiling at her, was unaware how much of his feelings were transparently clear to the girl through the warmth shining from his eyes.

'I just wanted to say thank you. I appreciate it,' she said in a low voice. 'It's been a long time since a man took pleasure in doing things for me.'

'Then it's time some man did.'

They remained holding each other's gaze, silent now, aware of being on the brink of something momentous, both thrilling and

250

frightening at the same time.

In the fireplace, the log slipped and settled, sending up a shower of bright orange sparks. It burst the magic bubble which held them and Riley said thickly, 'Must get the food fixed.'

Whilst he'd gone, Georgina undressed and put on a spare pair of Riley's pyjamas. Despite the warmth of the fire, shivers still ran the length of her body and she was feeling peculiarly light-headed and weak. By the time Jack brought in hot minestrone soup, Georgina had climbed into bed and gratefully stretched out aching limbs.

'Any warmer?' he enquired, putting the tray on top of the covers.

'Yes,' she lied.

They sat, dipping spoons in the sustaining soup, enjoying each other's presence and watching the flames flickering warmly in the hearth. It was very peaceful, the stillness effectively enhanced by the sonorous tones of the grandfather clock ticking away in the corner.

'Hmmm, lovely,' Georgina finished her soup.

Riley gathered up the tray. 'Next course.'

'I don't know if I can manage anything else.'

''Course you can.' He disappeared into the kitchen and returned with two plates of grilled fish with vegetables.

'Smells marvellous.'

They both tucked in and when the meal was over, Riley left Georgina to slide under the covers whilst he cleared up the kitchen.

Afterwards, looking round the door to check the fire, he caught his breath. The girl was fast asleep, auburn hair loose about her face and for the first time he noticed her long thick eyelashes. She was as beautiful asleep as when awake and with gut jerking certainty, Riley realized he was totally lost. He had fallen hopelessly in love with her.

Sitting down on the carpet beside the bed, he gently took one slim hand in his, a rush of tenderness flooding him. Totally, blissfully content now, warmed by the open fire, he leaned back and closed his eyes. Nottingham could wait awhile.

17

Strachan smiled with cold eyes at Baxter. 'That's Riley's address.'

'Yes, what are you going to do?' Baxter shifted uneasily.

'You mean, what are *we* going to do?' Strachan jerked the Walther's barrel sideways towards the door, 'Move.'

'Where are we going?'

'Keep asking questions and you'll get an answer you don't like,' snapped Strachan. They went along the corridor and down the stairs. Just before they entered the bar, Strachan said, 'One wrong move and I waste you, got it?'

Baxter nodded and kept moving. Strachan went up to the barmaid and passed over the room key and some notes.

The two men left the pub, walked up the street, turned at the junction and continued until Strachan indicated the entrance to the Victoria Centre car park.

'This it?' Baxter gestured at the Land Rover, taking in the almost bald tyres and dilapidated upholstery.

'What were you expecting? A Rolls?'

Strachan unlocked the door. 'Now clam up and stay that way.'

Driving out of the car park he headed north driving several miles before suddenly slowing down and pulling in at the kerbside. He switched on his mobile phone, 'Stay put, I'm making a call to Blake.'

The call went on to answer phone.

Caught off guard, he babbled, 'It's me, Strachan. I've got an address for you. No. 25 Janes Street, Holmington, no, no, wait, that's Baxter's. It's Riley's I meant . . . ' He gave Riley's address in Ilkley and cut the connection.

'Where are we headed?' Baxter asked nervously.

'I told you to clam up,' Strachan snarled. He pulled away, picked up speed and began eating up the miles to Yorkshire.

★　★　★

The baby girl had finally gone to sleep. Anne Baxter felt pretty exhausted, too. She put the kettle on the gas stove to boil and slipped a couple of slices of bread under the grill. Quite suddenly she was starving.

Buttering up the toast, she wondered, for perhaps the thousandth time, what the first baby would have been like. And the big question — had it been a boy or girl?

The miscarriage had happened so soon in the pregnancy that it had been impossible to say. Anne rescued the spluttering kettle and made a mug of tea. Looking back now, it had happened for the best.

Clint never mentioned the lost infant. But it didn't stop her wondering. At times like this when he was away, the pain of loss came creeping back.

Anne went through to the sitting room and switched on the television.

The film finished at eleven forty-five. Anne went upstairs to check and found the baby fast asleep. She crept quietly back downstairs and curled up sleepily on the settee.

The next thing she knew it was two o'clock and upstairs the wails of hunger were strident and demanding. As she fled upstairs to feed her daughter, Anne realized with a sense of deep unease that her husband hadn't come home.

★   ★   ★

The grandfather clock struck ten o'clock. Riley awoke, he was still holding Georgina's hand.

The fire had settled down to a mass of glowing orange-red embers now and he placed a thick log in the centre and arranged the coals around it, building it high at the back. With luck, Georgina might sleep for several hours. He placed the fireguard in front of the fire for safety and switched off the main light leaving only the standard lamp shedding a soft golden glow.

The urge to abandon the chase, leave Baxter to whatever the future held, rose up strongly within him. He was all sorts of a fool to be leaving the security of the snug cottage to drive through the dark night to Nottingham to face an unknown and possibly hostile situation on arrival.

For a second or two he wavered, looking down at the sleeping girl, knowing they had been brought together not as a chance circumstance but because destiny was rolling and their meeting was a meant thing. But if the future was written, then it also spelled out he must face Baxter and clear the dead wood before any solid new growth was possible for the future.

Out in the garage the Porsche's engine fired immediately. Resolutely, he drove away from the cottage. Being a jockey held certain advantages not least the ability to drive long distances at fast speed. He settled in the driving seat, if there were no hold-ups on the A1, he could be in Nottingham in less than two hours.

Rooney shot a quick look sideways at his father-in-law asleep in the passenger seat. 'Blake . . . Blake, wake-up. We're not far off Nottingham.' Blake awoke, instantly alert.

'You made good time, son.'

'No sense in messing about, eh?'

'None at all.'

'I don't see why we had to come,' grunted Rooney sourly, only too aware of the amount of whisky he'd downed whilst at the warehouse. It boiled down to risking being picked up by the police for drunk driving or risking Blake's wrath if he'd admitted being over the limit. No contest. 'Couldn't Palmer have collected him?'

'Look, son. I've told you before, when you get to be the boss you can give the orders. Palmer's fine for routine jobs but he has no finesse.'

'You what?' Rooney snorted in derision.

'Finesse. The kid glove that conceals the iron fist. Palmer doesn't possess any. Just imagine if he mishandled Baxter on this one. What happens? I'll fill you in. Baxter's had a taste of the rough stuff once before from Palmer. If he thinks he's in for some more, is it likely he'll come meekly? Of course not, the very reason he's scarpered in the first place is to avoid G.B.H. So, faced with Palmer what does Baxter do? He takes off again. And this time, we have no idea where the rabbit will run. No, this is one job, I'm doing personally.'

Rooney shrugged, trying hard to conceal the burning irritation he felt. Right now, he had as much chance of becoming boss whilst Blake was still alive as being born for the second time. The whisky had taken the brake off his usual icy cold self-control — and he was just sober enough to acknowledge the fact.

Knowing the effect drink had upon him, he had not yet made up his mind whether or not he was going to hit the bottle the following Sunday, the 29th. He had, however, long since decided that, although Blake's orders were for Baxter's hand to be on the gun inside the Church, if there was the slightest chance, he wanted the satisfaction of revenging Patricia's death himself. He knew if he drank that day, he'd have the courage to defy Blake. But it was a two edged thing, there would be only one chance, one shot, it had to find its target. With a quantity of whisky under his belt the chances of a straight aim were lowered.

His thoughts were interrupted as he negotiated the Nottingham ring road concentrating on taking the correct junction leading onto Mansfield Road. Finding it, he let the Mercedes purr sweetly down into Nottingham itself.

Blake said quietly, 'OK, son. Now we need a left hand turn onto Huntingdon Street.'

'Right'.

'Take it steady,' continued Blake, 'Calgary Street is somewhere in this hotchpotch but I don't fancy parking up and walking around at this time of night.'

'No more do I.'

The Mercedes motored gently in and out the connecting streets until Blake said with satisfaction, 'There it is, on your right.' They cruised passed and noted the absence of any lights or drawn curtains.

'Looks deserted.'

'I wonder just where the police are, son, because don't forget, they'll be wanting Baxter just as much as we do.'

'That's true enough.'

'Once more round the block, keep driving, don't stop.'

Rooney nosed the big car round the maze of narrow streets. He was about to turn into Calgary Street for the second time when Blake said, 'Up ahead, going under the street light, see him?'

'Don't I just!'

'Is it Baxter?'

'Well if it isn't, it's his double.'

'Let's find out shall we?'

The car drew level with the thin, dark haired man. He swung round as he heard the car's engine. With elation, Rooney said, 'It is him!'

'OK, stop the car.'

Rooney braked. Blake slipped quickly from the car. He fell into step with the man who had continued walking down the street.

'Heading home, Baxter?'

Riley stopped, realising he'd been mistaken for Baxter. He looked at Blake. 'Why shouldn't I?' he said, deciding to play along.

'Because I want you to come back to Yorkshire and finish the job for me.'

'And if I don't want to?'

'Don't be a fool, Baxter, I know you've backed off because you couldn't find the Duke's cross and chain.'

'Do you?'

'Sure. I was at Lady Crewton's party, too. The Duke was wearing the damned thing so there was no way you could have lifted it from his safe tonight.'

Riley said nothing. He was learning a great deal from this masquerade and he intended to let the game run for as long as he could. 'I did try,' he said, deliberately making his voice sulky.

'Course you did,' Blake clapped a chummy hand on his shoulder.

'Anyway, there's no need for you to stay in Nottingham now, absolutely nothing for you at all here. Come on, come back with us. There's Anne and the baby waiting in Holmington.'

'Suppose you're right,' Riley muttered grudgingly, hiding his elation at finding out at least part of Baxter's address.

Blake smiled expansively, 'You've got a lot going for you after next week.'

'Have I?'

'Oh yes. I've something fixed up that will line your pockets very nicely. A job worth at least £50,000.'

'What sort of a job?'

'We don't discuss these sorts of matters on street corners. Shall we get into the car?'

Riley nodded and allowed Blake to open the rear door of the Mercedes, which had crawled along beside them.

'Where are you taking me?'

'Don't ask awkward questions. When we've briefed you, you can go back home to Anne for a few days. We shan't need you until next Saturday. You might as well get some R. & R. and be on the ball ready to do a good job on Sunday morning.'

Whilst Blake had been speaking, Riley felt

himself being scrutinized by Rooney. Lifting his eyes, he met the man's narrowed, questioning gaze with a sardonic half-smile. That particular facial expression was typically characteristic of Baxter. With an inward sigh of relief, he saw the frown of suspicion leave Rooney's face. He decided to press his advantage.

'So I could take Anne away for a few days holiday then, if you don't need me?'

'Provided you don't try to go overseas,' Rooney sniggered. 'You haven't got a passport, remember.'

'Fortunately, you won't need one for Ireland,' said Blake. Both men looked at each other and laughed.

'Dead right, Blake,' said Rooney.

Riley said nothing, simply filed the snippets away with the others. If he could continue to bluff it out for the rest of the journey, he was pretty certain Blake would give him the details of this special job. It was obvious now Baxter himself had no idea what the job involved. However, the question of just where Baxter was right now remained a mystery but Riley was content to let the ball keep rolling and see where it led.

★ ★ ★

The Land Rover with Strachan at the wheel motored on.

Baxter lit up another cigarette from the butt of his first one.

Strachan, a non-smoker, flung an angry look at him. 'For God's sake. Do you have to smoke to that extent?'

'Did I ask you to buy the fags?'

Furiously, Strachan thrust his right foot down hard on the accelerator. 'We'll be bloody suffocated if you keep it up all the way to Yorkshire.'

'Just drive and mind your own business.'

Strachan glared at him, 'Cut it out . . . ' he began.

There was a report like a gunshot and the front nearside tyre burst. The vehicle swung crazily from side to side and Strachan hauled desperately at the wheel. Totally out of control the Land Rover hit the central barrier, bounced back across the carriageway and over the grass verge. Ploughing through a hawthorn hedge, it careered across a field and smashed into an oak tree.

Strachan stood no chance. He took the full force of the impact and died instantly.

Baxter, protecting his face and head with his arms, escaped with bruises, and flung himself from the vehicle. The lighted cigarette lay on the seat where it had fallen. In seconds the battered upholstery was smouldering and by the time Baxter had slipped back through the hedge onto the grass verge it had begun to blaze.

Unaware of the fire, Baxter seized his chance to cross the dual carriageway and jog-trotted back until he reached a junction. Hearing a lorry approaching, he desperately jerked a thumb. Amazingly, the engine changed its roar as it overtook him and began to slow down. Baxter put a spurt on and ran to the side of the cab as it pulled up.

The lorry driver leaned across and opened the door. 'Where do you want to be, mate?'

'You going anywhere near Nottingham?'

'I am that, grab a seat.'

'Thanks a lot.' Baxter swung himself up and closed the cab door.

In seconds the lorry had turned the next bend and was thundering along on the way to Nottingham. The driver cocked his head sideways.

'Got any fags going spare?'

Baxter fished in his pocket, trying to conceal the shakiness that was overtaking him as shock began to make itself felt. 'Never without them.'

He took one out himself and handed the driver the packet. 'You keep them, I can get some more.'

'Right.' The driver took them eagerly.

'Now I know why you gave me a lift.'

Both men were unaware that a quarter of a mile away, the inside of the Land Rover was burning fiercely and already the body of Strachan was engulfed in flames. Then with a great roar, the petrol tank exploded turning the Land Rover into a fireball. Flames licked up in great tongues at the rough bark of the oak tree. Clouds of black acrid smoke billowed into the night sky and the lower twigs and branches of the tree caught fire and blazed up unchecked, the flames hungrily devouring as they surged upwards.

18

Riley learned little else of value on the journey back to Yorkshire. Rooney concentrated on his driving and Blake went to sleep.

Uppermost in Riley's mind was Georgina's safety. He had an unpleasant sixth sense that he would find her worse rather than better. And even if she were reasonably all right physically, just what risks would she be running simply by being with him?

It might be better if he could move her somewhere farther out of town. But what was he going to use for transport? The Porsche was parked up in Nottingham. He shrugged the thought away and concentrated on just where he could take Georgina that would be totally safe.

Rooney had already swung the Merc west just before Harrogate when Riley remembered Frank Talbot. A second cousin and a great friend, he had an isolated cottage surrounded by moors up country at Grassington. Smugness ran through him. In October it would be deserted except for grouse shooting parties. Georgina would be absolutely safe there.

He became aware the big car was slowing down. Rooney climbed out and opened the rear door.

'Out.'

Riley climbed out warily.

'Turn your back, Baxter.'

'Why?' Riley deliberately put a whine to his voice.

Rooney didn't bother to answer but caught hold of his shoulder and spun him round. A scarf was wound around his eyes, pulled very tight and securely knotted at the back. 'Now get back in.' Rooney thrust him roughly back into the car and slammed the door.

The blindfold had taken Riley completely by surprise and he couldn't see even a chink of light either through it or at the sides. He was reduced now to listening for any unusual noises that might give him a clue as to the direction they were taking.

They were certainly heading west, about six or seven miles out of Harrogate. But after only a couple of miles, Riley heard the gears change down. The car was being driven over gravel now, probably the drive leading to a building. The Merc turned sharply right and stopped.

Both front doors opened and closed and then the rear door opened and Rooney's hand seized his shoulder, 'Let's have you out.'

'Where are we?' Riley said in a petulant tone.

Blake's voice said, 'Never mind, just walk. Go up two steps through the doorway and keep going.'

Riley followed the instructions.

'In front of you there's a flight of stairs, go right up and turn to your left.' Riley once again complied and found himself pushed through a door.

Riley heard a deep menacing growl and his heart lurched as he felt the cold, questing nose of a large dog as it sniffed his bare hand.

'All right, Max,' Blake said and the cold nose was withdrawn.

Riley took a deep breath, 'What about this blindfold?'

'I shan't keep you above five minutes. You will do exactly what I say because you have no option. If you don't, I shall simply turn you over to the police. You are a wanted criminal.'

'No, please.' Riley let just the right amount of fear creep into his voice. 'I'll do what you want. Just tell me what job it is.'

'It's straight forward enough.' Blake's voice held a note of satisfaction. 'You will go to Ireland next Saturday. Once there you'll visit Kileverton church and check the layout inside ready for the next morning.'

'Just what do you want me to do in a church?'

'You will shoot a man, and you will shoot to kill.'

Riley felt his stomach turn to ice. 'I'm no killer!'

'That's not what I've been told.'

'What the hell do you mean?'

'A little bird sang me a song about a night security guard you gunned down because he came between you and a safe that needed blowing.'

Riley frantically racked his brains. Whilst he knew about Baxter's track record, this was the first time he'd heard anything about a murder.

Blake, taking Riley's silence as an admission laughed softly. 'You were highly recommended. I'm quite sure you'll do a good job.' His voice became brisk. 'We'll supply a gun and arrange to get you over to Ireland. In fact, Baxter, you might be interested to know Rooney and I will be part of the congregation at the peace service next Sunday.'

'I don't seem to have any choice.'

'You don't.'

'Whose the man I've got to waste?'

'It happens to be the Duke of Allington.'

'Flying high, aren't you?'

'He's only flesh, blood and bones like any

other man. With a bullet in his heart, he'll die just the same.'

Despite the revulsion and shock he was feeling, Riley knew if there was to be any chance of saving the Duke, he desperately needed to fit together all the pieces. 'What the hell has this Duke ever done at you?'

'Let's just say, if it hadn't been for him, I'd still have a wife and daughter living with me instead of in the churchyard.'

The grate of hatred in the man's voice came across strongly. The implacable, savagery underlying the words was almost tangible.

A coldness settled over the room, malevolent and intense. The Alsatian picked up the negative vibrations and whined anxiously. Riley felt the coldness run along his spine and shivered, 'A vendetta?'

'If you like.'

'And what do I get out of it?'

Blake's voice was flat, emotionless, 'You get £50,000.'

Riley allowed a few seconds to elapse. 'Done.' Despite the appalling knowledge of the Duke's intended assassination, he felt at last he knew most of the picture and the only way to avoid the catastrophe was to involve himself as deeply as possible.

Blake moved across to the desk. 'I'll take

this one message off the machine. Then we'll drive you back.'

The machine clicked and Strachan's voice came into the room giving Baxter's address. Riley memorised it as the elation ripped through him. But then in horror heard his own address in Ilkley given out.

'How very interesting!' Blake said with deep satisfaction.

'Well, well,' Rooney said gleefully, 'just down the road you might say.'

'Certainly. Very considerate.'

'Do we go and get him now?' There was no mistaking the predatory tone in his voice.

Riley froze in apprehension. If the men left him here, they would find Georgina alone and vulnerable at Melling Cottage and heaven only knew what they'd do to make her talk about his own whereabouts. He felt sweat, coldly unpleasant, run down between his shoulder blades.

Blake snorted, 'After a night with no sleep? Like hell we do. Riley will keep for a few hours, or at least until we've had some shut-eye, and my Sunday lunch.'

'I could go,' Rooney's voice was impulsively eager.

'I think not.' The ring of finality in Blake's words reassured Riley.

'We'll drop Baxter off then get some sleep.'

And he added perceptibly, 'You'll be considerably more sober by then.' His words irritated Rooney immeasurably.

'If you thought I'd had a few, why tell me to drive?'

'Because, son,' Blake's voice was clipped, 'I needed a definite I.D on Baxter. You forget, I've never seen him before.' Animosity suddenly flared between the two men.

Rooney said angrily, 'I could have lost my licence tonight.'

'Possibly, but you see, son, I'm prepared to take any risks to nail Allington's proud Duke.'

'You're a grade A1 bastard, Blake.'

'And I'm not going to argue with you there'

'So,' Rooney was breathing heavily now, 'what next?'

Blake moved across the room and dropped a hand on Riley's shoulder. 'Right now we escort Baxter back.'

★ ★ ★

The truck driver turned to Baxter, 'Nearest I'm going to Nottingham, mate.'

'Out here? This is barely the ring road.'

'Sorry. If you want Nottingham, this is where you get out.'

'Bloody hell!'

'You could try thumbing.'

'Bloody Hobsons,' said Baxter sourly. He opened the cab door and jumped down. The truck drove off.

Cursing, Baxter turned up his jacket collar and began the long trek to Nottingham. Although he kept an optimistic thumb out, he didn't expect any vehicle to stop and he wasn't disappointed.

Gritting his teeth, Baxter ploughed on to Nottingham.

Finding a 'phone box, he staggered inside, leaning against the glass. He'd change for only one call. Anne would have to wait. He dialled Riley's home number. Shaking with fatigue, Baxter heard the double rings peal away into silence.

* * *

At Melling Cottage, Georgina was dreaming. She was walking down the aisle of Paxton Church, her arm linked with Dave's, her new husband.

The beautiful delicate perfume of the freesias and white rosebuds she was carrying drifted up with a sweetness and purity encapsulating the whole ceremony. Looking up, she found Dave smiling at her, the softness in his eyes made her heart turn over with love for him.

Now they were moving out of the Church door, the brilliance of the sunshine outside making her blink after the darkness of the sacred interior and the pealing of the bells rolled out over the surrounding Churchyard and the village beyond.

The ringing of the bells went on and on . . . and on . . . and on . . .

Georgina woke up with a start. And still the bells rang. She lay confused, wondering where she was. Everything seemed to swim in and out.

Touching her left hand, she could feel no wedding ring. 'Dave,' she cried out feebly in panic, 'Dave.' But there was no reply, only the ringing of the bells.

A burst of clarity came to her. There was no Church, no Dave, no bells . . . Just a telephone ringing — a continuous, melancholy sound.

Only two people knew she was here, her father and Jack Riley. She tottered over to the telephone, just as the ringing stopped.

★   ★   ★

Rooney drove the Mercedes right up to the front of 25 Janes Street, Holmington and switched off the engine.

'OK, Baxter,' Blake said, 'out you get.'

'What, with this blindfold on?' Riley reached up a tentative hand and twitched at the scarf. His hand was smacked down.

'Leave it!' The authority was back in Blake's voice.

He felt his arm grasped and he was propelled firmly forward. One of the men knocked on a door. He heard footsteps and the door was opened.

'Who is it?'

'It's all right, Mrs Baxter,' Blake said, 'we've brought your husband home.'

'Oh! Please come in.'

Riley felt Blake take his arm and lead him into the house. The girl bit back an exclamation of alarm. 'What's happened? Why is he blindfolded?'

'Just a precaution.' Blake began to undo the scarf.

Riley's heart beat faster. He prayed the girl wouldn't give him away when she saw it wasn't Baxter. The scarf dropped from his face and he found himself looking straight into Anne Baxter's startled blue eyes.

'Hello, love,' said Riley, 'sorry you were taken by surprise, you know, with me being blindfolded.'

'Yes, It . . . er . . . it did make you look different, Clint.'

He felt his heart leap in relief. Anne wasn't going to give him away.

'You've got until next Saturday, O.K.?' Blake said. 'We'll be back to pick you up here at three o'clock. Be ready.' He went out followed by Rooney.

Through the window, Riley watched the car drive away then turned to the girl, 'Well, that gives us a breathing space.'

'Do I get an explanation, Jack?' Anne Baxter stared at him, her eyes hard and unfathomable.

'Course you do, girl,' Riley reached for her hand. 'I owe you one for covering for me.'

'Yes, but where is Clint? Is he all right?'

'I'm sorry, Anne, I've not seen him since I went to Princetown. I've absolutely no idea where he is.'

'He went out to do a job, what, I don't know.'

'What time did you expect him back?'

'I'm to expect him when he comes through the door.'

'So, what are you worrying for? Clint can take care of himself.'

'You think so? Look what's happened. Those two charmers obviously took you for my Clint. Tell me, Jack, just what is going on?'

'Clint was supposed to do some sort of job for Blake, the boss of the outfit, but the job backfired. Clint took off to Nottingham.'

Anne's eyes flashed,' Clint wouldn't leave me.'

'Steady, girl, I'm not saying he's run off and left you. He was trying to save his skin. Blake went to Nottingham to pick Clint up. But I'm afraid . . .'

' . . . he picked you up instead.' Anne nodded her head. 'It figures. You're as alike as natural born twins.'

'Exactly.' And for once I'm glad. Because Blake mistook me for Clint, he's come across with all the details for a big one laid on for next Sunday.'

'Just what sort of a job?'

'Something very nasty.'

'Being iffy goes without saying, I suppose, knowing Clint.'

'An assassination.'

'Oh my God!' The colour drained from her cheeks. 'You can't mean it, Jack. Surely Clint hasn't sunk so low?'

'I think this is the first time Clint's been propositioned to kill for money. Whether he would . . . ' Riley shrugged his shoulders.

'Be honest, Jack, does Clint have a choice?'

He looked at her with sympathy, 'Possibly not. When he comes back, ask him straight out.'

'I will, believe me.'

'A man's life depends on how we handle the situation.'

'Couldn't we just tell the police?'

'We've got to find Clint first. Don't forget, the police are looking for him now I've broken out.'

Tears filled her eyes, 'What a hell of a mess.'

He held out his arms to her. 'It seems to me we've been in a hell of a mess together before.'

Anne clung tightly to him. 'You don't need to remind me,' she sobbed.

'That will haunt me for the rest of my life.'

He stroked her hair gently, 'Steady now, girl. It will work out, somehow. I don't know how but it will, everything does in the end.' He squeezed her hand and went to the door. 'I'll ring you sometime tomorrow, all right? In the meantime, we've got until Saturday before the heavy mob turn up.'

19

Riley, after leaving Anne, picked up a taxi in Holmington. For a few hours at least Georgina would still be safe at Melling Cottage but after that, there was not the slightest doubt Blake and Rooney would come calling.

He alighted from the taxi on the outskirts of Ilkley having no intention of leaving a hot trail behind him. The night was pitch black, unrelieved by even starshine.

He jogged along the grass verge and the piercingly cold wind cut straight through his jacket chilling him to the marrow. And Grassington would be even colder. The problem of how he was to move Georgina up there without transport occupied his thoughts all the way to Melling Cottage.

As he let himself in through the kitchen door, he heard the telephone ringing. But by the time he'd entered the sitting room the phone stopped. Georgina stood near the bed swaying unsteadily. He was by her side instantly, arms going round her. 'All right, girl, I'm back.' He picked her up and laid her down on the bed.

The phone began to ring again.

'Clint! Where the hell are you?' Listening intently, Riley said, 'Sounds like you had a night of it, too. Anyway, before this call runs out, give me the call box number.' He wrote it down, 'O.K. Put the 'phone down, I'll ring you back.'

Going over to Georgina, he tucked the bedclothes around her. 'I'm not asking how you are. You look pretty awful.'

'I love you, too,' she whispered, eyes glassily over-bright, 'but I'm so glad you're back.'

Placing a palm against her forehead, he grunted. 'Hmmm, thought so. You're running a really good fever. I'll return this call then see to you.' She nodded and closed her eyes.

Riley dialled Nottingham. Baxter told him about Strachan giving the address of Melling Cottage to Blake. 'It's O.K., Clint, you had no choice. Water under the bridge now. But I'm expecting Blake and his sidekick here in a few hours time. Now listen, you're stuck in Nottingham and I'm desperate to get my car back. I've left it parked in Joe Barker's pub, you know, The Cat and Fiddle, just off Mansfield Road? He's a mate. I'll tell him you're collecting the keys. I filled up as I came down so there's plenty of juice in the tank. Are you sure you're fit to drive? OK. See you in a couple of hours.'

He cut the connection then rang Joe Barker and gave permission for the Porsche's keys to be passed to Clint. Finally, he put the 'phone down and went over to the girl's bedside.

'It rang before, Jack. I couldn't reach it in time.'

'Don't fret, girl. Clint tried to reach me earlier to give me a warning but in fact there was no need.'

★   ★   ★

'What warning?' Georgina asked drowsily, trying to keep awake and losing ground all the time.

Riley kneeled down at the side of the bed. 'Basically, we're going to have a couple of visitors in a few hours from now. But before they turn up, you and I will be miles away.'

'But where will we go?' Georgina's eyes opened and she looked apprehensively at Riley.

'You are not to worry about a thing. Leave it with me. I've been thinking about the best thing to do all the way up the A1. There's one place that's perfect, if the owner doesn't mind. And he's not likely to. He's a sort of second cousin, name of Frank, a vet actually.'

'How far is it?'

'Not that far, about fourteen miles up

country. He's got an isolated cottage a couple of miles north of Grassington. You'll be quite safe there.'

'By myself?'

'No, I'll be staying up there too, well, if you want me.'

She smiled weakly, cold sweat standing out in tiny drops on her forehead. 'I want you.'

He squeezed her hand gently, 'And I want you.'

'That's all right then,' she murmured and drifted off into sleep.

He stared down at the helpless girl feeling an overwhelming surge of protective love rise within him. No way would he subject her to any danger. She had ingeniously improvised on Egton Hill when he had been as helpless as she was now. She had brought him down off the moor to the safety of the farmhouse. Now it was his chance to repay the favour.

In the grate the fire burned lower and lower and still the girl slept. Riley eventually rose stiffly to his feet. If he didn't make the fire up it would be out. But nothing could put out the inner glow he was feeling, a contented sureness.

Georgina was the woman he'd been unconsciously waiting for, seeking for, and now he'd found her. Preordained circumstances had led her to find him. The only thing he was concerned about now was her safety.

Looking at his watch, he found that Baxter would soon be here. If he packed a suitcase now and had a quick meal, they could set off in the Porsche immediately.

Baxter would need a lift back to Holmington, of course, but afterwards, a whole week stretched before Georgina and himself. A week in which they could get to know one another, and what mattered to each of them.

Riley went into the kitchen and cooked himself an omelette. He rinsed the dishes and made a strong black coffee laced it with honey and returned to the sitting room.

The fire had burned up now, the golden flames dancing. With just the standard lamp lit and the firelight, it was a snug, inviting, cosy room. It was a great pity they would both have to leave so soon. He had thought Georgina's safety had been a cinch staying here but already life had taken an unforeseen twist. It was a case of flowing with the stream not trying to battle against it.

Riley sat down in the armchair, sighed and let his weary muscles relax. For so long he had been living a bachelor life, free of the burden of having to think about or consider another person's feelings, needs.

But it had also been a case of sitting behind life's curtain waiting for it to rise so that the play could begin. Now, quite unexpectedly, the curtain had risen. Life or destiny, whichever had thrown him head first into a situation where at the very least, three people's lives were very much in his hands. The Duke of Allington, of course, albeit unknown to him, would be depending on the outcome next Sunday morning. And then there was Clint Baxter, who had sometimes seemed more like a twin brother than a cousin, he also needed to rely on the skilful handling of the highly dangerous situation. Lastly, there was Georgina's safety and the possibility of a shared future.

Riley stirred uneasily in his chair and drank the rest of the hot coffee. A lot depended on him now, too much, far too much. He heard the sound of the Porsche's engine pulling in at the front of the cottage. Baxter had excelled himself, he must have had his foot down hard most of the way from Nottingham.

Riley opened the front door, 'That was a damn quick journey.'

'You can say that again. Any whisky going? I'm all in.' Baxter slumped against the doorframe with exhaustion.

Riley put an arm around his waist and helped him into a chair. 'I reckon there's half a bottle.'

Baxter slumped over the kitchen table, resting his head on folded arms.

Riley came back with the whisky. 'It's more comfortable in the sitting room.'

Baxter stumbled after him.

'Don't make a racket,' Riley put a warning hand on his shoulder, 'I've got a sick girl in here.'

Baxter stood, rocking slightly, 'In bed as well, looks interesting.'

'Don't let your imagination get out of hand,' Riley said dryly. 'And sit down before you fall down.' He pushed Baxter into an armchair by the fire.

Baxter swallowed the rest of the whisky in one go. 'Any more where this came from?'

'You might as well have the bottle and pour your own.'

'Thanks, Jack, you're a mate.'

'Not half as much as you think.'

'Why, what d'you mean?' He filled the tumbler to within a quarter of an inch of the top.

Riley looked at him steadily, 'I think you'll need most of that when I've told you.'

'Get it off your chest then. Just what's eating you?'

So Riley told him, the whole sordid story. Baxter listened growing whiter all the time. 'But what I want to hear,' Riley continued remorselessly, 'is your side of what happened to the Irish security guard. Did you kill him?'

'OK, OK,' Baxter gulped the whisky savagely, 'Yeah, I took a pot at him, silly bugger, coming for me like he did.'

'A pot shot? Come on, we're both members of the Marksmen Club. If you took a shot at him there was no way you'd miss.'

'I had no choice.'

Riley shook his head in disgust. 'Now you know why Blake's had you recommended. You didn't give a toss did you? You took a man's life. And you're not losing sleep, it doesn't get to you does it?'

'It was him or me,' Baxter said sullenly, lowering the level in the tumbler.

'So you'd kill the Duke in cold blood, too?'

'Looks like I'm over a barrel. If I don't, Blake will get me.'

'You could always give yourself up to the police.'

'Like bloody hell!'

'Well, that's it then,' Riley sighed heavily, 'looks like it's up to me.'

Baxter narrowed his eyes suspiciously. 'First you take my rap, now you're staking yourself out. Why?'

'Because if I don't, a man's going to die.

You've already admitted you'll go along with Blake's orders.'

'I've got to look out for my own skin, haven't I?'

'Yes, but in the end you'll have to live with it.' At the sound of Georgina's voice, both men swung round. 'Oh, It may not trouble you at the moment, but one day it will catch up. Once the past is written it can't be erased.'

'I'll take my chances,' Baxter said sourly and lifted the glass to his lips.

Georgina raised herself on an elbow and glared at him. 'Do you have to drink that foul stuff?'

'What's it to you?' Baxter snarled back at her.

'OK. Let's break it up.' Riley rose from his chair. 'I'll drive you back home.'

'I'm ready right now.' Baxter drained the whisky and slammed the empty glass down on the coffee table. 'I'll tell you one thing, Jack, your booze is sound but I don't rate your taste in women.'

'That's enough. Save your comments if they're not good ones.' Riley held open the door and Baxter went out. 'You'll have to excuse him, Georgina. I'll run him home. Stay in bed until I get back.' She nodded tiredly and lay back.

★ ★ ★

Frank Talbot, Grassington's local vet, was asleep.

The cottage seemed wrapped in somnolence, the only signs of life on the surrounding hills being the slow movement of a sheep or two cropping the rough grass. It was very, very quiet, too early yet for even the peal of bells to carry on the still air from the nearest Church over a mile away just the other side of Grassington.

Drift, the huge St. Bernard, was lying on a rug by the front door, back to the slowly warming radiator. He was snoring gently.

The hands of the clock reached seven and the alarm went off. Frank rolled over, flung out an arm and smacked the button down. The clangour stopped. He yawned and sat up.

His flight to Malta left Leeds airport at noon. Seven glorious days — the first break he'd had all year. The only drawback was taking Drift to the kennels. But it couldn't be avoided. He climbed out of bed and padded downstairs in bare feet.

Drift opened one eye, the warmth from the radiator had penetrated his thick coat and he was reluctant to move.

'Lazy old devil,' Frank rubbed a bare toe up and down behind the dog's ear. Drift sighed with pleasure closed his eye and thumped a heavy tail languidly against the rug.

Talbot went into the kitchen and flicked on the electric kettle for some coffee. He twitched back the curtains and glanced out of the window. He was about to reach for the coffee jar when he noticed a Porsche coming up the winding lane.

He watched the car until it drew up at the cottage. A man got out, tall, thin, black-haired — Jack Riley. Frank was about to reach for two coffee mugs when he saw a second person in the Porsche. She was lying back in the passenger seat. It had to be a woman, her hair tumbled over her shoulders in a long auburn mane. But she wasn't moving.

There was a tap on the back door and Riley came into the kitchen.

'Jack, good to see you.' Frank slapped him on the shoulder.

'Likewise. Glad we found you home.'

'Only just, a seat on the noon flight to Malta has my name on it.'

'Of all the luck . . .' a frown creased Riley's forehead.

'Problems?'

'Yes. Most definitely. In the form of one sick female in need of t.l.c. and shelter.'

'You were hoping to stay here?'

'I thought you might take pity on two strays, yes.'

'Well, you're very welcome to the shelter, but I'm afraid it will be up to you to provide the t.l.c. for the lady.'

'You don't mind?'

'Put it this way, if you're my house guests for a week, you could do me a great favour. You are staying a week, possibly?' Riley nodded. 'Fair enough. That means I don't have to drag my oversized hearthrug of a dog to the kennels.'

'We'll be glad to look after Drift for you, no sweat.'

Talbot smiled widely, 'You've made my day. I can go off now and enjoy my holiday.'

'Just one thing,' Riley hesitated, 'you won't mention to anybody about us being here, will you?'

'Like that is it?'

'Yes, I'm afraid it's very much like that.'

'Married is she, the girl?'

'I think so,' Riley said looking guilty, 'but I don't really know.'

Talbot was laughing out loud now. 'Then I should find out, you could find the irate husband after you.'

'It's not like that,' Riley protested.

'No?'

'No!'

Talbot held up both hands, 'O.K. I believe you. But if it's platonic now, by the time you two have spent a week of seclusion here . . . '

Despite himself Riley began to smile.

Talbot continued, 'I mean, let's face it, you'd have one hell of a job proving it wouldn't you?'

'That, Frank, is the least of my problems.'

'Well, what are you waiting for? Go and fetch the mystery lady. She's not terribly ill I take it?'

'A good chill certainly, and a temperature.'

'If you like to change the sheets on my bed, she could have that. At least it's aired, should be, I only fell out of it ten minutes ago.'

'Thanks,' Riley gripped Talbot's shoulder, 'I owe you.'

Talbot grinned, 'Go get the lady.'

★ ★ ★

Rosamund O'Connor slammed the brakes on and the Land Rover skidded to a halt at the side of the churchyard wall. She scrambled out. It was bad luck the mare's leg had swollen again overnight. Unfortunately, being Sunday, the Ballykenny Stud stable lads were down to half strength and she'd had to wait for the vet.

She pulled open the heavy oak door, the

swell of sound from the organ filling her ears. She swiftly genuflected and slipped into the nearest pew. Only on one face was there a smile of welcome recognition. That person was Sylvia Rooney, Father O'Malley's house-keeper. Rosamund gratefully smiled back.

The organ died away and the service continued. Rosamund found herself wondering what the following Sunday morning service would bring. It seemed like a bad dream, knowing she was deeply involved in the planning of a man's murder. If only there was a way out, she'd take it.

Fervently, with eyes closed, she prayed for God to guide her.

But her attention was suddenly brought back sharply by the Priest's chosen theme for his homily — 'Past sins and consequences.' Guilt coloured her cheeks bright red. Father O'Malley's words could have been written with her in mind.

'And we shall all have to pay for our sins.'

The final words made her shudder. She looked across the Church at him and his eyes met her own.

She took a deep breath and rose to leave.

'Hello to you, Rosamund.' Sylvia Rooney drew level with the last pew. 'A thought provoking homily of the Father's wouldn't you say?'

'I would, Sylvia, yes.'

'Indeed it is to be hoped it will stay in people's minds when they're tempted in future.'

'I'm sure it will.' Rosamund edged passed.

Sylvia continued, 'He is a shining light for the people of Kileverton. Keeping them all on the straight path.'

Rosamund having now reached the Church door was stung by the woman's words. She spun round, 'But what about the sins we have already committed? What can he do about those?'

Sylvia, caught momentarily off-guard, sought desperately for the answer. Then relieved she said, 'But he has told you, in his homily.' And she quoted triumphantly, 'In the end, we shall all have to pay for our sins.'

20

Anne Baxter, washing up the Sunday lunch dishes, was still recovering from the shock of seeing Jack Riley when she'd expected it to be Clint. It had been obvious Jack had needed her to cover for him so she had played along. Jack had been so much more than a comforting tower of strength three years ago when Clint had been sent down for burglary. When the two men had come home later, all became clear.

But the thought of next Sunday made her physically ill. Clint was a stupid fool to have got involved and if it weren't for Jack's intervention, she'd be screaming up the curtains right now. But Jack would handle it, she was sure of it.

At that moment a heavy knocking sounded on the front door.

She opened it and her heart leapt in fright as she saw it was the two men who had blindfolded Riley. They shouldered passed her into the kitchen.

'Where is he?' The elder one asked abruptly.

Anne looked from one to the other, eyes

wide with fear. 'Where's who?'

'Your husband, you stupid woman.'

Anne thought of Clint lying vulnerably asleep upstairs. 'He went out, after lunch, to the pub.'

'Which pub?'

'He didn't say.'

'So, when do you expect him back?'

'I don't know, he makes his own rules. Doesn't bother telling me.'

The two men exchanged glances. The older one said, 'Do you know Jack Riley?'

Trying to contain the rising hysteria within, Anne nodded, 'Yes.'

'Lives in Ilkley, doesn't he? At Melling cottage?'

'Yes.'

'We've just discovered the cottage is locked, empty. We wanted a few words with him.'

'But he's not there.'

Sean Rooney took a couple of steps forward and thrust his face towards her, 'And how do you know that?'

'Because he . . . he sent me a card,' she improvised frantically, 'from Ireland. He's gone over for the racing.'

'Has he now?' Blake said softly. 'This card, where is it?'

'I showed it to Clint this morning and then

295

threw it away onto the fire.'

'How convenient,' Rooney sneered.

Blake ignored his son-in-law's comment. 'Did Riley say when he'd be back?'

'He thought at least a week, possibly ten days.'

The men looked at each other. Rooney shrugged his shoulders, 'Won't matter then, will it?' Blake inclined his head in agreement.

He turned to Anne, 'Just tell that husband of yours, we'll pick him up, Saturday, three o'clock, OK?'

Anne swallowed hard, 'I'll tell him.'

'And he'd better be ready,' Rooney said viciously, 'because if he's not . . . God help him. And you can tell him that as well.'

★ ★ ★

Riley, one hand almost buried in the St. Bernard's dense coat as he held onto the leather collar, lifted his other hand in farewell. Talbot paused before he opened the taxi door.

'If I didn't know your ability to handle a firearm, I'd never have agreed to this. But for goodness sake, Jack, be sensible, don't take any chances. Why not let the Irish police deal with it.'

'And ruin the Duke's grand gesture? No

the plane came in low over the private airstrip adjacent to the Ballykenny Stud farm. The plane landed smoothly, taxied to the far end of the runway and stopped.

They climbed out. Morgan, the pilot, said, 'Mr Blake suggested a return flight about twelve noon, does that sound all right?'

'No, it does not. I've another call to make whilst I'm over. You can make it one thirty, so you can.'

Morgan sucked in his bottom lip wryly, 'I've a client coming for a flying lesson at one o'clock.'

'Tough,' Rooney hooked a finger in the loop of the collar and swung the Puffa jacket over his shoulder. 'Without Blake's backing, your business is no business.'

Morgan shrugged, 'Whatever you say.'

'You have cancelled all bookings after two on Saturday for the following twenty four hours?'

'Yes, and lost out on a packet. Weekends are the main earners in this game.'

'How sad,' sneered Rooney. 'Just remember who bought the plane in the first place. The punters come second to Blake's use of it.'

'Without punters I don't get paid.'

'You shouldn't have been a bad boy and strayed off the straight and narrow when you flew for British Midland. With your track record, who the bloody hell is going to give you a job?' Morgan didn't reply.

Rooney strode away to the complex of buildings and stables that formed the Ballykenny Stud. He pushed open the office door and went in.

Rosamund O'Connor was sitting behind the desk. She was still a good looking woman for her age but the signs of tension showed in the weary lines around her eyes. Her ashtray was overflowing with cigarette butts. 'Problems, Rosamund?'

'Just the roof repairs that you've come about.' She leaned forwards and lit a cigarette, taking a long pull and exhaling very slowly.

'Looks to me,' said Rooney sagely, 'as though you could have a big problem on your mind.'

'Well you should stop looking at me,' she said tartly, 'and go and look at the foaling area roof. Now that is a problem.'

Rooney rose to his feet, 'Come on. Sure and you can show me exactly what's happened?'

She took down her coat from a hook behind the door, 'At least it's stopped raining. That's one blessing, I suppose.'

''Are you hoping for more, blessings, I mean?'

'Oh I'm hoping all right, like the rest of us, but the trouble is, I'm not finding any.'

They walked down the yard and over into a large airy building. It was obvious immediately what damage the rain had caused. In one part the roof had sagged and the timbers were saturated with moisture. Rooney walked around inside and tested the roof at intervals. There were several other wet patches. He turned to Rosamund, 'Pointless patching it up again. I'll tell Blake it needs stripping off, all support timbers and chipboard renewing and the whole roof refelting.'

'It'll need to be done soon, at any rate, before the foaling begins. That means before the last part of December in case we're unlucky enough to have some early ones.'

They walked back to the office and Rosamund boiled up the kettle and made two coffees. 'So, you're going straight back to the mainland, now?'

'No, I think I'll pay a visit to another lady first.' Rooney took a gulp of the hot drink.

Rosamund smiled slightly, 'Business or pleasure?'

'Business, of course. What else?'

She inclined her head, 'As you say, Sean, what else?'

He hurriedly finished the drink and stood up, 'Get two or three quotes from some local builders and let Blake have them, OK?'

'Will do. Thanks for coming over.'

'Any chance I could borrow a vehicle for a couple of hours?'

'To be sure, help yourself,' she pushed the Land Rover keys across the desk. 'It's parked up by the feed room. I don't need it until tonight.'

'Oh, what I have to do won't take long.' Rooney picked up the keys and walked off across the yard.

He drove straight to Clonmore. It was a lap of the Gods job whether Magda Casey would see him or not. But he had a gut feeling about the outcome.

He slowed the Land Rover and drove carefully down the lane, pulling up at the cottage.

Mary Casey opened the door to his knock. An appetising smell of cooking drifted towards him.

'Smells good,' Rooney smiled, 'home cooking takes a lot of beating. My name's Rooney, Sean Rooney.'

'Good day to you, Mr. Rooney, I'm Mrs. Casey. What would you be wanting?'

'To see Magda Casey, if it's possible.'

'It's a reading you'll be wanting, is it?'

'I would that.'

Mary screwed up her lips 'I can't say she

will, Magda is her own woman, she pleases herself.'

'Could I see her, ask her?'

'To be sure, you can come in and ask.' She held the door open and Rooney stepped inside. 'Someone to see you, Magda. A Mr Sean Rooney.'

The old woman in the chair beside the hearth, turned slowly. Rooney went forward and held out his right hand. 'It's pleased I am to meet you.' Magda held it briefly, looking searchingly into his face.

'You'll be wanting a reading.'

'Please. You gave one to my father-in-law a while back.'

'And now you want one . . . ' she sighed.

'It's important, a life and death matter.'

Magda nodded her head very slowly, 'It often is.'

Rooney fished in his pocket and held out the small white card he had taken from behind the photograph on Blake's desk. 'Can you tell me who wrote this?'

The old woman's fingers closed over it and she took several deep breaths. Closing her eyes, she began to rock gently back and forth. One minute, two minutes, went by in silence. Then softly, she started speaking, 'Love . . . and death, they are both present.' She continued to breathe deeply. 'I can see a grave and flowers, a line of flowers.'

Rooney leaned forward eagerly as if to speak but Mary Casey placed a warning hand on his sleeve, shaking her head reprovingly.

Magda carried on speaking in a low voice, 'More flowers are being placed, scarlet . . . bright scarlet, they show up so clearly against his black robes. This card lay with them. There is a great grief, regret . . . but the love vibration is so very strong.' Magda paused, her eyes remained closed, frowning now in disapproval, 'but the love is not just spiritual . . . it is love of long ago, yet it flowers still today.' She was silent for a moment, 'I see the crumpled red bonnet of a car . . . her car. He is there too, mourning, with love, but also with guilt. The woman is now in spirit, she was sent over so swiftly by the crash. No time for suffering.' There was a long pause, 'it is fading, slowly fading.' A smile crossed her face, 'No wait, they are all there now where there was one, I see three.'

Rooney lunged forward and grabbed the old woman's arm shaking it, 'Tell me, tell me what you see! 'My three in one' — what does it mean?'

Magda's eyes flew open and she gave a cry of fright.

'Mr Rooney, please. What do you think you're doing?' Mary Casey bustled forward.

'Take your hands off my mother-in-law.' She placed a protective arm around the old woman's shoulders. 'Don't you know better than to do that?' she flared up at Rooney. 'Never, never disturb the sitter, it is very dangerous. Please go.'

Rooney stooped and picked up the card from where it had fallen onto the rug by Magda's feet. 'I'm sorry, I didn't mean to alarm her. But I must know what the phrase means.'

'Tip the bottle, Mary,' Magda shakily clutched her daughter-in-law's arm. 'I need a glass.'

'Won't you tell me what it means?' pleaded Rooney.

Mary ignored him and patted the old woman's thin, blue-veined hand, 'Don't distress yourself, Mother. I'll bring you one.'

'For God's sake, won't one of you give me a break?'

Magda lifted her head and looked at him. She gave a harsh laugh. 'I could tell you but I won't. Leave this house, you will have to seek the answer yourself.'

Mary put a glass of Jameson's into her hand. Taking a deep drink Magda added, as Rooney started for the door, 'One thing I will tell you, before the week is out you will know the answer. And you will wish you'd never asked.'

21

Georgina Casey slowly opened her eyes as the door opened and Riley looked in.

'Feeling better?'

'A bit,' she said but was surprised to hear how weak her voice sounded.

There was a snuffling at the side of the bed and a large brown and white head appeared, dark eyes soulful and sympathetic. A wet pink tongue caressed her cheek.

Georgina smiled and looked across at Riley, 'Instinct, I suppose, trying to revive me.'

'Maybe he's mistaken the white sheets for a snowdrift,' agreed Riley.

'How long have I been languishing? What day is it?'

'Tuesday.'

'What happened to Sunday and Monday?'

'Lost forever. Anyway, I'm off downstairs to fix breakfast.'

Georgina closed her eyes. Their needs were now reversed.

Riley came back with a tray. 'Eggs topped with grilled bacon and stacks of toast and honey to follow. Sound all right?'

'Sounds perfect.'

They ate together in companionable silence for a few minutes.

Then she lifted her gaze, met his eyes, saw the warmth shining from them and felt the chemistry. It sparked between them, holding, bonding, electrifying. With difficulty, she broke eye contact. 'What's on the agenda?'

'Getting you better for a start.'

'And then?'

'We relax and enjoy ourselves, until Saturday.'

'And what happens on Saturday?'

'All hell breaks loose.'

'Go on.'

'I think we'll leave the gory details until you're feeling a bit better.'

Georgina finished breakfast and smothered a yawn. 'You're right, I'm bushed. How can I be when I've spent two days in bed?'

'Easy when you're getting over an infection.'

'Is that what I've had?'

'Frank reckoned so. Maybe from swallowing some of that water you fell into on likley Moor.'

'Whose Frank?'

'The chap whose bed you're sleeping in. He's a good sort, distant relative of mine.'

'So where is he now?'

307

'Soaking the sun up in Malta.'

'But we move out Saturday?'

'Correction. I move out Saturday. You stay put.'

'Now look here . . . ' she began.

Riley grinned. 'You won't be on your own. Your dad's coming up from Devon to stay with you.'

'In case anything should happen to you?' she said astutely.

'Well, yes, if you put it like that.'

She took a deep breath, 'I don't want to risk losing you.'

The atmosphere between them quivered in the silence following her words.

Riley looked steadily at her, 'You won't lose me,' he said thickly.

'I didn't think I would the first time, but I lost Dave.'

'Your dad told me Dave was your husband.'

'Was, yes,' she said in low voice.

'Want to tell me?'

'I guess I've a lot bottled up inside. After it happened, I sort of clammed up. Grew a shell, if you like, to protect the softness inside. You know what I mean?'

'Do I!' he said with feeling.

She smiled briefly, 'I suppose most people do. I certainly did.'

'So, break down the shell, let it out. You have to in the end if you want to go forward.'

'I've never met the right person to tell,' she hesitated, 'not until now.'

Riley put a hand over hers. 'Tell me if it feels right, in your own time.'

'I married Dave four years ago, at Paxton Church. He was a fireman and came from Skipton. I met him whilst he was on holiday in Devon. Cutting it short, we bought the cottage in Skipton and after the wedding we went back up north to live.'

'You were happy?'

She opened her eyes, 'Very.'

He nodded.

'Nothing lasts, though, does it?' she added.

'Depends. It does sometimes, if you work at it. But I suppose you have to want it badly enough to start with.'

'I wanted Dave badly enough.'

'But it didn't work out?'

'He was killed.'

Riley gripped her hand.

'It was last year. He'd gone to work and been sent out on a job, a factory fire. Part of the roof collapsed. He never returned.'

'Terrible for you. The shock must have been devastating.'

'Yes, it was. There was a post mortem and he was found to be drunk, or almost.'

'At work?'

'Yes, at work. Apparently Dave used to call at the local pub at lunchtime. He was having an affair with the barmaid, Janice her name was. I never knew about it of course, until afterwards. Too late then.'

'Do you know why? There must have been a reason when he had a wife like you.'

'I think it was because I couldn't have children. When we found out it hit him hard, he was very fond of children, you see.'

'And you? How do you feel about it?'

Tears welled up in her eyes. 'How the bloody hell do you think I feel?'

And then his arms went around her and she clung to him sobbing.

Cradling her gently, he rocked her as though she were a baby herself.

★   ★   ★

Sean Rooney arrived back too late to catch Blake who had gone away on business until Thursday.

Rooney swore forcibly. Magda Casey's refusal to level with him over the meaning of the phrase 'three in one' had irked him to the extreme. It had been his intention to confront Blake immediately on returning to find out.

He lifted the photograph of Gloria and

Patricia from the desk. Releasing the catch at the back of tile frame, he took out the photograph. The four words 'My three in one' were written in Blake's handwriting. The old woman had said before the week was out he would know what it meant. But right now it remained as elusive as ever.

Rooney replaced the photograph and the white card and fastened the frame. Turning it over, he stared at the picture of the two women.

In five days from now, he promised them, they would be avenged.

★　★　★

On the Wednesday morning, Georgina had improved considerably and Riley had no qualms at leaving her. From Grassington, he headed the Porsche towards Harrogate. Passing Bolton Abbey, he turned onto the A59 and put his toe down hard. Fifteen minutes later found him pulling in through the gates of Allington Hall.

He drove the car round to the rear and left it near the outbuildings. Walking round to the front, he rang the bell.

A smartly dressed woman opened the door. 'Mr Riley?'

'Yes, I'm Riley.'

She smiled, 'Do come in. Your appointment's eleven o'clock.'

Riley stepped into the hall, 'I'm obliged to the Duke for seeing me.'

'But I believe it's in the Duke's own interest. Isn't that correct?'

'Too right it is.'

She smiled again. 'Please follow me. I'll show you straight through.'

Riley followed her down the hall and through a door on the right. The Duke smiled and stood up. 'It's Mr Riley, isn't it?'

'Yes, your Grace.'

They shook hands, and the Duke motioned him to a chair. 'Do have a seat, Mr. Riley.'

'Thank you.'

The door closed with a discreet click as Maureen left them alone.

'Now Mr. Riley, you said on the telephone it was very necessary I see you.'

'And it is,' Riley leaned forward, 'Sir, your life is at risk.'

The Duke smiled, 'All life is a risk.'

'I agree. But we're talking specifically.'

'Do I take it you are referring to my Irish visit?'

'I am.'

'Then I want to know.'

At the end of Riley's brief but concise account of Blake's intentions for the Sunday morning, the Duke, his expression grave now, said, 'You're in it up to your neck, man. But that's not why you've come to see me is it? There's more you haven't told me.'

'Yes, there's more. I've worked out what I'm going to do. That is, if you still wish to go to Ireland.'

'I intend to.'

Riley sighed, 'I thought you would.'

'So? Let's hear what you have in mind.'

Riley told him. The Duke listened intently as Riley outlined his plan.

'It could work,' the Duke said slowly, 'Yes, I'll go along with it. It would need split second timing, of course.' His eyebrows drew together and he looked hard at Riley, 'and a great deal of nerve on your part.'

'As I see it, your Grace, it's the only way of saving your life, if you insist on going and without any security whatsoever.'

'Which I do. No point doing otherwise.'

'Oh I agree, it would be a waste of time to have an armed police escort on a peace mission.'

'But what happens, after my intended assassination?'

'Simple, really very simple,' Riley smiled grimly, 'I shoot Blake and Rooney.'

★ ★ ★

Rooney was sitting at Blake's desk when the door opened and Blake walked in.

'Everything ticking over?'

'You could say so.'

'Good. Well, I want you to ring your mother in a while and check Sunday's visit is still going ahead.'

'Will do.' Rooney flicked three quotes across the desk. 'These are for a new roof at Ballykenny Stud.'

'You authorised a complete re-roofing?'

'It was needed.'

'And what kept you? I was expecting you back before I went up north.'

Rooney darted a glance at him, 'You're not going to believe this.'

'Try me.'

'I paid a visit to Magda Casey.'

'The devil you did!'

'Yes, I did . . . and I took something with me.' Rooney leaned across the desk and picked up the photograph of Gloria and Patricia. Suddenly there was tension in the air that hadn't been there before.

'Well?' Blake stiffened.

In reply, Rooney, released the catch at the back of the frame and took out the small white card and handed it to his father-in-law. Blake's face froze.

'You showed this to Magda?'

Rooney nodded.

'And what did she say?' Blake's voice was low, cautious.

'She saw the cemetery, on the day of the funeral.'

'Keep talking.'

'This card was with the scarlet wreath. You did find it there, didn't you?' Rooney's face was twisted with pain now. 'Why didn't you tell me?'

'What's to tell? It was meant for Gloria, not Patricia.'

'But it's tied in with the explosion, isn't it?'

'All I know, Sean, is it was from a man, someone Gloria knew years ago. Obviously he's still carrying a torch. Or would be, if she were still alive.' He buried his face in his hands. 'I don't know any more than that, and God, it's enough.'

'Well I do, Magda saw this man.'

Slowly Blake raised his head. With a softly menacing note in his voice he said, 'You'd better tell me what Magda said. Think back, tell me every single word she said, just as she said it.'

Rooney recounted everything that had been said except for the last couple of minutes.

'And that's all, you've forgotten nothing?'

'That's all.'

'Not much to go on really,' Blake grunted.

'It means nothing to me,' Rooney said. 'But I thought it might tell you more.'

'I wish it did.'

'Well, now I've told you everything, you can level with me.'

'About what?'

'About this.' Rooney took the photograph out of the frame and turned it over. 'These four words.'

'I don't know.'

'Oh don't come it, Blake.' Rooney rasped, 'It's your bloody handwriting.'

There was silence. Blake rose to his feet. 'I'd vowed to myself never to tell you, Sean. Can't we just leave it?'

'Not this side of hell.'

Blake's shoulders dropped, 'Then you'd better prepare yourself for a shock.'

'I'm listening.'

'The photograph shows Gloria and Patricia but the words, 'My three in one' refer to the unknown, the unseen. What you didn't know was that when Patricia died, so did your first child, and my first grandchild. You see, son, Patricia was three months pregnant.'

22

Late on the Friday evening, Georgina put down the empty coffee cup and stretched out her bare toes towards the crackling fire. 'That meal finishes off the most enjoyable day I've had in the last year.'

Riley leaned forward and pushed a log further into the fire. 'Two horses, the Yorkshire Dales and all the free fresh air you can breathe, it's not exactly every girl's idea of the perfect day.'

'Possibly not, but the company couldn't be faulted.'

Riley placed his hand over hers and squeezed it. 'It's been a day I'll remember as well. That's if I get through this weekend.'

'I want to know what's happening tomorrow. You said when I was better you'd tell me.'

'If I'd told you earlier, you wouldn't have enjoyed today. Neither would I. And I wanted us to have some time together that we could hold as a memory.'

'You sound as though you're going before the firing squad.'

Riley smiled twistedly, 'You've got it the

wrong way round, girl. I am the firing squad.'

With her eyes wide with incredulity, which rapidly turned to horror, Georgina listened as Riley told her of the Duke's visit to Kileverton church in Ireland and the assassination plan for Sunday morning.

'You must be mad,' she gasped, 'they'll kill you!'

'It's possible, yes. But if I don't, then the Duke will certainly die.'

'But if he knows of the danger, it's surely up to him to back off.'

'I agree. But at some point in his life every man has to face a tough decision and go through with it. Even if it means the finish of him. If not, he can't go on living in peace with himself. No-one can run away from themselves.'

'It could mean your life, not just the Duke's.'

'Well, fate or destiny, whatever, has placed me in this situation. It's up to me now how I play it.'

'And you've already made up your mind, haven't you?'

'Of course.'

'But you've given me today.'

'Yes, I'd hoped we could enjoy a day or two together before I left. Life hasn't been a cake-walk for me either.'

Georgina gently eased him down onto the settee, placing his head in her lap. 'Want to tell me?'

'Confess before the gallows?' He closed his eyes. 'Yes, you're the only person I could tell, we've grown pretty close this week. Close enough for me to want to spend a lot more of my life with you.' He opened his eyes and looked at her. 'If you want to, after hearing what I'm going to say.'

'You'd better say it and find out, hadn't you?'

'OK. Baxter's mother and mine were twins. We two boys were practically identical. We even became blood brothers.'

'So, what caused the rift? A girl?' Georgina put in perceptively.

Riley opened one eye, grinned ruefully and said, 'Not daft are you?'

'I try not to be.'

'Doesn't work though, does it? I mean, look where you are right now, here with me.'

She patted his hair gently, 'Go on with your revelations.'

'Yes, we both fell for the same girl. She went out with me first, for about a year.'

'What happened?'

'I had a few falls that cost me rides. It was

a bad season and I was short of cash. My temper ran a little short, I guess.'

'And Baxter had plenty of money?'

'You could say that. Dirty money, though. He'd discovered a talent for crime. Anyway, she took up with Baxter.'

'Did it lead anywhere?'

'Oh yes, they married a year later.' He laughed shortly. 'I was best man, actually. Well, I'd accepted things. She preferred him so ... We lost touch. I was racing in Ireland quite a lot. Then one evening three years ago Anne rang in an awful lather, Baxter had been given a prison sentence. She begged me to go and see her. I should never have gone. But, mug that I am, I did.'

'What happened?'

'The inevitable.'

Georgina wrinkled her forehead, 'I don't follow.'

'I turn up on the doorstep, Anne lets me in. We sit on the settee and she pours out all the sorry tale about the mess Baxter has got himself in. There she is crying on my shoulder.'

'So was I a few days ago.'

'But we didn't go any further. Anne and I did. It started out harmlessly but ended up with us making love. I'm not excusing myself, but we were both looking for comfort.'

'Obviously you found it.'

'Please,' Riley pulled himself upright, 'don't be like that.'

'Like what?'

'Distant, cold.'

'How do you expect me to be? It hurts.'

'Why?'

'Why do you think? You make love to another woman and ask me why.'

'Tell me,' Riley said very softly, 'I want to hear you say it.'

Georgina took a deep breath, 'Because, I love you.'

'You may change your mind. There's something I've not told you yet.'

'Whatever it is, it won't change how I feel.'

'Don't be too sure, it's pretty heavy.'

'So, tell me, get it off your chest.'

'I kept away and didn't hear from Anne for several months. When she did ring, it gutted me completely. Anne was expecting my child.'

Georgina winced, 'Go on, she whispered.

'Anne let Baxter think it was his.'

'But the child's yours! You can't give up your own flesh and blood. Don't you want it?'

Riley said in a low voice, 'Anne miscarried, she lost the baby.'

Georgina gripped his hand tightly, 'So

that's why you felt you owed Baxter?'

'Yes.'

He bent his head and very gently, kissed her lips. 'I love you, Georgina, marry me?'

'Why is life so cruel, Jack?' Tears filled her eyes. 'You lose a baby, before you even know it's on the way, and now . . . you fall for me . . . ' she stopped unable to go on.

Holding her close, he prompted, 'And?'

'Oh, Jack, don't you see the irony? If you marry me you'll lose the chance of having any children. You've forgotten, I told you, I can't have children, I'm barren.'

'My darling, I haven't forgotten. But you've not given me an answer.'

Brushing the tears from her cheeks, she choked, 'You know the answer. I love you. Yes, I will marry you.'

He made to kiss her but she held up a hand. 'On one condition.'

'Anything,' His voice was thick with emotion.

'I want you to love me now, Jack.'

'What, right now, here?'

'I want to belong to you,' she said urgently, 'now, tonight.'

Riley looked deeply into her eyes. 'Because of tomorrow?'

She nodded. 'You know how dangerous it is. And I want you . . . '

Her words stopped abruptly as he kissed her hard, his lips demanding and hungry. 'By God, I want you too.'

Laying her gently back onto the cushions, he switched off the light. The cosy room became filled with soft shadows as the firelight flickered and danced. He lay down beside Georgina, their faces only inches apart, and the fire's glow was reflected in her eyes.

In the morning the fire had gone cold, its glow gone. But the man and the girl still lay warmly entwined and in the girl's eyes the glow remained.

★   ★   ★

Blake lay in bed unable to sleep on the Friday night. After Thursday's showdown with Rooney he'd not seen his son-in-law. By admitting he'd known since before the funeral of Patricia's pregnancy, it had driven a wedge between them. But the rift was not all that prevented Blake from sleeping.

A couple of years after he and Gloria were wed she'd told him of a previous love affair. Gloria had come in with a newspaper. 'Would you believe', she'd said, 'after we split up, Matthew became a priest.' She'd tapped the paper with an immaculate scarlet nail,

'There's a piece in here about him.'

'Who?' Blake had asked.

'Matthew, Matthew O'Malley.'

'Is he still history?'

'Silly boy. Of course.'

'Then I'm not interested.'

That was what he'd said at the time and meant it.

Now a good twenty-seven years later, it was filling his mind and losing him sleep. Blake mulled over Magda Casey's words. Another piece of jigsaw now clicked into place. Etched vividly in his mind was a picture of a black robed figure carrying a red wreath and he knew it was O'Malley.

He'd unlocked one of the drawers in the desk that had not been opened for months and taken out all the press cuttings covering the explosion last March. One article in the Irish Press covered the trial of Michael O'Malley, subsequently sentenced and now serving time, whose brother had been mentioned for media interest because he happened to be a priest. He'd been named as Matthew O'Malley from Kileverton, in Ireland.

However much Blake had shunned the thought of Gloria having had a previous lover, fate had now decided they would meet face to face on Sunday morning.

It was very early on Saturday morning when the telephone rang in the presbytery. Matthew O'Malley hurried to answer it. He'd been checking over yet again the details for the following morning.

The timing was crucial. First, the hired car to collect the Duke as soon as his private plane landed, transport him to the landing stage and see him safely on board the boat for the trip down the river into Kileverton itself. And finally, the short walk to the church.

Inside all was in readiness, spotlessly clean with stained glass and brasses gleaming. Masses of flowers already filled the church, their glowing vibrant colours spreading around the walls and shading towards the pulpit where a large display of pure white lilies took pride of place, setting the tone for the peace service itself.

O'Malley lifted the telephone receiver. It was Sean Rooney. It was the first time he had ever spoken to his natural-born son. Sweat beaded his forehead and he struggled to keep his voice even.

'It's unfortunate, Sylvia is still asleep in bed. Could I be of any help?'

Rooney asked if the Duke's visit was still

scheduled to take place in the morning.

'But of course, it's his Grace's intention to attend.' The line went very quiet then Rooney's voice came through asking who was speaking. 'Father O'Malley,' he replied. There was a click and the line went dead.

With a shaking hand, O'Malley put down the 'phone and slumped in his chair.

Sylvia came in carrying a tray of coffee. 'Good morning, Matthew.'

'Very kind,' he murmured, his mind far away wondering just why Sean Rooney needed to check on the peace visit at such an early hour.

'Are you all right, Matthew?' Sylvia handed him a cup.

He looked up at her his brows furrowing, 'Did you tell Sean about the Duke's visit?'

'Hmm,' she nodded, 'I did that.'

'Long ago or quite recently?'

'The very day we received the confirmation from his Grace.'

'I've just taken a call from Sean. He was checking that the visit is still on for tomorrow morning.'

She stared at him, 'But why should he do that, and at this time of a morning?'

O'Malley's face was grave. An awful fear started low down in his stomach and he suddenly felt very cold. Taking a long drink, he felt the coffee burn the back of his throat but it didn't warm him one little bit.

'Why should he?' she repeated.

He looked bleakly at her. 'That, Sylvia,' he said, 'is what I would like to know.'

23

Riley and Georgina awoke together on the Saturday morning. The room was still cosily warm. Georgina felt the strong masculine body entwined with her own and lifted a hand to gently stroke Riley's face. 'It wasn't just a beautiful dream then, was it?' she whispered.

He didn't answer, simply slid his arm around her and held her tightly against him, covering her face with small, soft kisses. The intervening hours of sleep might never have existed as they continued love-making from the previous night. Time did not exist as they loved one another in what seemed to be a spiritual dimension far removed from the earth plane.

The grandfather clock striking nine brought reality back into the room.

'It can't be that time, surely?' Georgina sat up quickly pushing back her long, tangled auburn hair. 'Didn't you say Dad's due this morning?'

'It is and I did.' Riley rolled off the settee and disappeared towards the bathroom.

'I'll fix some tea and toast,' Georgina took

herself off to the kitchen.

Fifteen minutes later, with the fire hastily laid and lit, they were sitting eating toast when Casey walked up the path. At his knock, Drift, sitting on the hearthrug, gave a token woof without taking his eyes from the food. Georgina jumped up and let Casey in.

'Dad, lovely to see you,' she gave him a kiss, 'smelt the tea, did you?'

'I could certainly do with one,' Casey slipped off his coat and sat down. 'With the look of my daughter, you've done a good job, Riley.'

'Time and nature I think are the pair to thank,' Riley pushed the sugar bowl across the table. 'I'm relieved to see you, I can go over to Ireland without wondering if she'll be all right.'

'Of course I'll be all right. Anyway, I'm pleased to see Dad.'

Casey took a gulp of tea, 'It's nice to know you're wanted.' The close bond between the two of them was obvious. Riley wondered what Casey would think when he told him they were to be wed.

Casey turned to him. 'What gives about this fool's game you're going on?'

'Good description. It just about sums it up,' Riley agreed. 'I'll drive to Holmington, make sure Baxter's out of the way before Blake and Rooney turn up.'

'Will Anne Baxter be there?'

'Yes,' he hesitated, 'she'll be looking after their baby.'

Georgina looked steadily back at him, 'Of course, I forgot, that's what started all this, Baxter wanting to get out of prison to be there for their first baby.'

Riley shook his head, 'No, it started a long time before. A lifetime ago.'

'When do you leave for Ireland?' Casey poured himself another cup.

'As far as I know it's three o'clock.'

'Where will you be staying over there?'

'That I don't know. I'm in Blake's hands all the way down the line once we leave England. The church sits on the bank of the River Liffey in Kileverton. The Duke will be taken down river by boat on the Sunday morning.'

'What time will you get back?' Georgina asked.

'At the earliest possible moment.' Their eyes met, and exchanged warmth.

Casey was suddenly, shrewdly, aware of the chemistry between them discreetly dropped his eyes. 'Well, whatever time you get back will be fine, just come back in one piece.'

★　★　★

O'Malley's hand was shaking as he dialled Allington Hall.

The Duke himself answered.

'O'Malley here, Anthony, from Kileverton. I must speak to you.'

'You sound upset, Matthew. What's wrong?'

'Tomorrow's peace gesture. Call it off, while there's still time.'

'Sounds like you've developed cold feet.'

'No, I'm pretty certain there will be . . . an incident.'

'What you're saying is that someone is planning an assassination attempt?'

'Yes. It's almost sure to happen.'

'Calm yourself, Matthew. In fact, I'm already aware of this, incident, as you delicately call it.'

'Oh, it's not just a possibility, I know who's behind it.'

The Duke sighed, 'It's Blake and Rooney, isn't it, the two men who lost their wives when I lost Belinda?'

'I'm very much afraid it is. How did you find out?'

'Jack Riley, told me. Some might call him a fool, I prefer to call him one of God's own.'

'But Blake and Rooney mean business.'

'Yes, I expect they do.'

'Then be sensible, call off the visit.'

'If I did that, Matthew, I should never have peace of mind again, never be able to live with myself.'

A long silence hung between them.

Finally O'Malley said in a low voice, 'Would you listen to me, Anthony? I can't live with myself either. I need to confess, to let out the rottenness.'

'My dear chap, you of all people? What could you possibly confess to?'

'Two very great burdens, sins, really. But right now I'm referring to the heavier one. And believe me, Anthony, the weight of it is bringing me to my knees. It's bad and getting worse.'

'Then I think you should unburden yourself and tell me. Even if I can't help, confession is good for the soul, don't they say? So, go ahead, confess.'

'It wasn't the explosion that killed those two women. It was because of my frantic driving that day. I'd had a tip off that my brother, Michael, had planted an explosive. It was intended for you, you know.'

'I'd already come to that conclusion.'

'I was driving like a maniac, trying to reach you at Allington Hall to warn you. And because of me another vehicle had to swerve. It was a Yaris with the two women, Gloria and Patricia inside. There was nowhere for it to go. It ploughed into a tree inside the grounds and a second later, the explosive went off. There was absolutely no hope of anybody getting out alive. At that moment I realized I was only human. I might wear a dog-collar but underneath, I'm as weak as anyone else. I crawled away — literally. I don't think I got above first gear for miles. Nobody ever knew. I've kept it to myself all these long months.'

'It's high time you released it, Matthew. Good heavens, man, you've kept all that bottled up inside, it's a wonder you haven't cracked up.'

'Well, it's out now.'

'One is yes, and that's bad enough, but you said there were two.'

'The second one I've carried the weight of for many years but this situation has now brought it home to me very forcibly. It concerns another person, I can't confess without betraying them. I would like to unburden myself but I cannot.'

'As you wish. But I'm facing my burden, Matthew, before it gets too big and crushes me.'

'So you're still going ahead tomorrow?'

'Yes. I'll see you when my plane lands.'

'Then all I can do is pray for you.'

'Whilst you're about it, Matthew, try saying one for yourself as well.'

'I might just do that.'

★　★　★

333

Anne Baxter opened the door. 'Thank God, you've come, Jack.'

'I said I would.'

'Yes, I know but I'm still very relieved to see you.'

'Clint home?'

'Yes, keeping a low profile.'

'It is still all on, for tomorrow?' She looked at him anxiously.

'I take it you haven't heard from Blake to the contrary?'

'Not a word.'

'Then we assume it is and he'll be here at three o'clock.'

Baxter emerged from the living room. 'Good to see you, Jack. I knew I could count on you.'

'Did you now?'

'We go back a long way.'

'It's a great pity you didn't think about that when you left me sweating it out in Dartmoor.'

'Anne and the baby needed me.' Baxter deliberately attacked Riley's Achilles' heel.

'OK. We'll agree to drop it.' Riley ran a hand through his hair, betraying just a hint of the tension inside. 'When Blake turns up, I want you well out of the way. It will blow everything if he gets a smell that I'm not you.'

'Don't worry, I'll keep my head down.'

'How will we find out what's happened, Jack, you know, after the Duke's visit?' Anne Baxter put an anxious hand on his arm.

'If I don't make it back by Sunday night, at the latest, then Clint will have to take you and the baby and get out before Blake comes calling.'

Anne hastily scribbled on the telephone pad and tore off the top page. 'Here's our 'phone number. If you get chance . . . '

He closed his fingers over it and nodded, thrusting it into his trouser pocket.

'I'm banking on you stitching it all up,' said Baxter.

'I bet you are.' Riley gave Baxter a withering look. 'If you shot the Duke it would be ironic, the son finishing off the father's job.'

'It's not my bloody fault Michael O'Malley's my father.'

Anne, seeing the relationship between them deteriorating, hastily tried to defuse the situation. 'Could you chaps eat any lunch?'

Riley swung round to her. 'Good idea. Might as well have some food I don't know when I'll have the chance to eat later. In fact,' he gave a wry smile, 'I might not even be around later.'

* * *

It was just a couple of minutes to three when a black car pulled up outside.

Anne gave Riley a terrified glance, 'It's them, oh God, they've come!'

He gripped her arm, 'I'm counting on you. Don't go to pieces, I need your back up.'

She bit hard on a lower lip. 'I'll do my best.'

'Good girl, I know you will.'

There was a single hard knock on the door. Riley jerked his head, 'Off you go, let the devil and all his works in.'

Immediately he was admitted, Blake strode through into the living room. 'Ready are we, Baxter?'

'Yes.'

'Have you packed some gear?' Rooney snapped.

'Sure, my holdall's behind the kitchen door.'

'Get it, we're leaving straight away.'

Riley walked into the kitchen and picked up the holdall.

Rooney thrust out an impatient hand and gave him a shove, 'Come on, we haven't got all day.'

'Hang on,' Riley walked up to the girl and put an arm around her, 'a man's entitled to kiss his wife goodbye, isn't he?' He gave Anne a prolonged loving kiss to which she responded.

Rooney jerked the door open angrily, 'You're bloody lucky you've got a wife to kiss. Bear that in mind in case you've any ideas about double crossing us.'

'Leave her out of this.' Riley's voice hardened. 'I'm doing the job for you. Let's leave it at that.'

The three men left the house and went out to the car. Riley was hustled into the back and it drove rapidly away.

Anne Baxter broke down and began to sob. The door to the stairs opened cautiously and Baxter appeared.

'Gone have they?'

Incapable of speaking, she simply nodded.

★　★　★

Blake drove straight to the private airfield. The Piper was already out on the tarmac with Morgan waiting for them. Blake drove the car inside the empty hangar, the three men got out and he locked up.

Riley, with Blake and Rooney on either side of him, found himself propelled swiftly along the tarmac and into the plane. In minutes the plane was gathering speed down the runway. Riley felt his stomach turn over as the aircraft took off. It was too late now to have second thoughts; in about an hour they'd be landing in Ireland.

There was a taut silence, no-one spoke and the tension grew with every mile they flew.

When they reached the Irish coastline, Blake said, 'Myself and Rooney are booked into an hotel for the night.'

Without removing his gaze from the window where he was covertly watching the two men's reflections, Riley said, 'What about me?'

'You get yourself into the Church without being seen and stay there.'

'What, all night?'

'All night.'

'What if anybody sees me?'

'For your wife's sake, they'd better not.' Rooney's voice was like a razor.

Riley held back a biting retort. 'And Sunday, what then?'

'You take out the Duke, permanently. It's a private service so pick your moment. But you'd better not miss.'

'Oh, don't worry, I won't miss.' Riley smiled grimly, 'whoever I aim at, I hit.'

'Just make sure you do.'

'Oh I will, believe it.'

The Piper began to lose height and Riley saw a private landing strip ahead. The plane came in low and with the slightest of bumps, the tyres hit tarmac.

Blake led the way across to the rear entrance of the Ballykenny Stud. Behind them, the Piper swung round and roared away. It took off, climbing steadily, a black outline against the pale blue sky and Riley watched it go with a sinking feeling in his stomach. The last link with England was gone, he was well and truly on his own now.

'Come on,' Rooney shoved him roughly, 'what are you waiting for? Waving him goodbye?'

They went down the stable yard, past the loose boxes into the foaling area. Inside, at the far end a wall of straw bales had been erected. An old jacket was nailed up at the right height for use as target practice. Blake opened a wall cabinet and took out a Walther and several clips of ammunition.

He turned to Riley, 'Get the feel of it, use whatever ammo you need. There's plenty to go at. Rooney and I will be over in the office for two or three hours. When you're ready we'll send out for a meal to keep you going.'

'And then?'

'We'll drop you off in Kileverton and you make your way to the church. At nine o'clock the priest locks it so you have to be inside by then.'

'And after that?'

Blake laughed shortly, 'You're on your own.'

24

Georgina stood staring unseeingly out of the cottage window, the beauty of the countryside around Grassington was totally lost upon her.

Peter Casey went over and put an arm around her shoulders. 'Riley's a damn fool, of course.'

'Oh, Dad,' she crumpled against him, 'What if he doesn't come back?'

'It's a dangerous game, no doubt of it.'

'The waiting's going to be awful.'

'No, it isn't.' Casey gave his daughter a quick hug. 'You see, my love, you and I will be over in Ireland as well.'

Georgina looked at him in amazement. 'What do you mean, we'll be in Ireland?'

'Exactly that. We're flying out tomorrow in the Duke of Allington's private plane.' He smiled as her mouth dropped open. 'I've met the Duke at the races. Don't forget, he's a Steward of the Jockey Club. I telephoned him last night and explained that we desperately needed to be there.'

'And he agreed?'

'Apparently Riley spoke with him earlier in the week. He impressed the Duke no end.

When I told him that you and Riley were practically engaged, he agreed immediately.'

'Dad!'

'OK.' Casey put both hands in the air. 'But it's obvious you and Riley are in love. Anyway, the plane takes off at eight o'clock.'

★　★　★

It was very dark. A few sparsely dotted stars pin-pricked the black sky above Co. Kildare. A high wind filled the night with strange sounds and shook the tops of the trees edging Kileverton churchyard.

Riley stumbled against a gravestone, taking some skin from his knee and grazing a hand. His watch read almost nine o'clock.

The black bulk of the church was only relieved by a light burning at the far end. Cautiously, avoiding the erratically placed gravestones, Riley made his way towards it. Just as he reached the porch, the heavy oak door creaked noisily and swung open. A priest stepped through. Both men halted, startled.

'Who are you, my son?' Father O'Malley recovered himself quickly, leaning forward trying to see Riley's face.

'You first, Father, if you don't mind.'

'I'm Father O'Malley.'

'Father Matthew O'Malley?'

'That is correct.'

'My name is Jack Riley, sometimes mistaken for my cousin, Clint Baxter.'

The priest caught his breath, 'Is that so? Well now, and just whose side are you on, my son?'

'Yours. Father. But tomorrow morning, I'm posing as Baxter.'

'Haaaa . . . ' the priest exhaled lengthily, 'and afterwards . . . ?'

'I'll be Jack Riley, jockey.'

''Tis a jockey you are then?'

'Yes, Father, a jump jockey.'

'Hmm,' O'Malley rubbed a hand across his chin, 'and what stakes will you be running in tomorrow morning, my son?'

'Assuming I haven't seized up after a night lying on a church pew, it's got to be Life's Handicap Stakes.'

O'Malley chuckled. 'Come with me. We will walk alongside the trees as far as the presbytery. I'm sure we can find you something softer than a wooden pew to lie on tonight.'

★　★　★

At first light on Sunday morning, O'Malley took the Church keys and motioned Riley to

342

follow him. Their footsteps were muffled by the mulch of wet leaves under the trees. 'Everything is quiet, people are still sleeping,' said the priest.

'Yes,' agreed Riley and he patted a headstone, 'silent as the grave.'

O'Malley looked at him under lowered eyebrows, 'Your levity does not fool me, my son.'

'Perhaps it's meant to fool me instead.'

O'Malley gripped him by the shoulder. 'Remember, God is on our side, He is invincible.'

The priest opened up the Church and the perfume of hundreds of flowers filled their nostrils. 'I think the best place to hide you would be in the sacristy. The Duke will arrive at eleven o'clock so there are several hours to go.'

'Don't worry, Father,' Riley smiled a little twistedly, 'I shall probably need several hours for all the things I have to say.'

'Say? To whom, my son?'

Riley pointed his index finger upwards, 'The Boss.'

*   *   *

The waters of the River Liffey creamed smoothly past the bows of the Pride of

343

Kileverton. Her trim lines were decorated with bunting and at each end flags flew gaily in the breeze.

Anthony Ashley, Duke of Allington, stood with one hand on the polished brass rail. Casey and Georgina were also aboard. They respected his need for quietness and walked back to the stern. Peter Casey put a reassuring hand on his daughter's arm. 'Won't be long now, love.'

She gave him a brief smile, 'I wish I were clairvoyant and had a crystal ball.'

At her words, Peter was instantly transported back to Magda's cottage, holding his mother's hands as they listened to the old woman's words, 'A river winding through emerald fields . . . beautiful flowers inside the church . . . lilies spattered with blood, crimson on white.'

Up until now, Casey had firmly believed that Riley would pull it off and save the Duke's life. But as he remembered the fateful words, a coldness settled in his stomach. All at once, he was not sure, not sure at all.

★   ★   ★

Rooney drove the Land Rover from Bal-lykenny Stud through Kileverton and parked it as close as possible to the church gates. He turned to Blake who was sitting in the passenger seat. 'Now we wait, yes?'

'Dead right, Sean. The Duke has to go into the church first. That way everybody will be watching him, not us.'

'Let's hope Baxter's already inside.'

Above the sweet sound of church bells, a ragged cheer went up.

Rooney twisted in his seat, 'If he isn't inside now, he's too late — here comes the Duke.'

★　★　★

Inside the church, Riley heard the cheer go up from the crowd and his heart began to pound. O'Malley's timing was not far out.

It was four minutes to eleven.

★　★　★

The Duke entered the church as the last peal of bells rang out sweetly and was stilled. Late autumn sunshine slanted through the high windows bathing the interior with golden light.

The peace service began. Father O'Malley, face calmly serene, led the prayers.

Riley, obscured by a massive stone pillar, scanned the assembled congregation.

Blake and Rooney, predictably, were sitting at the rear of the church. Riley felt satisfaction rise within him. It looked as though lady luck was with him so far. He had banked on them sitting in the back pew. What he had not banked on was the middle-aged woman sitting next to Rooney and smiling proudly up at him. Riley decided from what O'Malley had told him the previous night it could be no other than Sylvia Rooney, Sean's mother.

At the front of the church sat Georgina. How she'd got here was a mystery but he felt a warm rush of love for her. He noted with relief Peter Casey was seated beside her.

The Duke himself sat right at the front, head bowed in prayer.

Riley fingered the trigger of the Walther and looked down at the second gun lying by his feet. The element of surprise would give him the precious seconds needed for reloading.

Father O'Malley left the pulpit and the Duke of Allington took his place. He made an impressive figure standing tall and motionless. In a calm controlled voice, he told of the death of his daughter, Belinda.

While the congregation listened in respectful silence, he spoke impassionedly of the need for forgiveness as a precursor of peace, lasting peace. 'If each of us could only find that forgiveness within ourselves,' he told his audience, 'it would add up to the whole and the result would be peace with ourselves, our neighbours, our country and with the world.' He urged each person to consider what it could ultimately mean — total world peace.

The Duke dropped his right hand which had been upheld throughout his speech and as his hand touched the edge of the pulpit, Riley pulled the trigger. The shot reverberated throughout the hushed church. Riley immediately dropped the Walther and snatched up the gun lying near his feet. From a crouching position, he aimed at Blake.

Standing in the pulpit, the Duke clutched at his chest, blood streaming from between his fingers. For a second or two the stunned congregation watched in horrified disbelief and then the Duke of Allington pitched forward over the edge of the pulpit, hanging like a puppet with cut strings. Blood trickled down from his chest, spattering drops of crimson onto the pure white lilies below.

When the shot rang out, Blake grabbed for his own gun. He hissed viciously at Rooney, 'It was the priest Magda saw, he used to be Gloria's lover, he killed her and Patricia.'

Rooney's face twisted up with hatred at Blake's words. 'He's mine!' he snarled and snatched at Blake's gun. Twisting it from Blake's hand he levelled it at O'Malley's back as the priest bent forward towards the Duke.

'This one's for Patricia!' he shouted.

As he did so, Riley fired at Blake, hitting him in the neck. The man slumped down in the pew, unnoticed by Rooney or his mother.

Sylvia Rooney, intent upon preventing Rooney taking aim, threw up her arm in front of her son's face. 'No! Don't do it, Sean.'

Rooney pushed her savagely to one side and aimed again.

'You can't kill him, you can't,' she screamed, 'he's your father.' Her words stayed Rooney in his tracks. He stared at his mother, stupefied disbelief on his face.

Taking his chance, Riley reloaded and fired again. Rooney rocked and went down. Sylvia dropped to her knees beside him.

Peter Casey, with Georgina close behind, raced up the aisle. 'You bloody fool, Riley,' he gasped.

Riley swung round to him a wide smile on his face. 'Give me a hand, Peter, let's get them tied up.'

'But you shot them!' Georgina clutched his arm wildly.

'So I did, but only with Frank Talbot's gun.' While he was talking, Riley deftly bound

Blake's hands behind his back. 'It's a Capchur, a tranquilliser gun. The vet uses it on deer.'

'You mean, you haven't just seen these two off?' Casey said, hope flaring in his eyes.

'Afraid not, just put them to sleep for a few minutes with a shot of Ketamine.'

The whole congregation was now on its feet, the noise deafening. Above it all rang out a clear firm voice. 'Everybody, everybody, please. In the name of God . . . I ask you all to keep calm and sit down.' Slowly the noise abated and one by one the congregation resumed their seats. O'Malley raised his voice again, 'Is everything all right at the back, Riley?'

'All under control, Father,' Riley replied as he and Casey finished tying up Rooney.

O'Malley turned towards the pulpit, 'Did you hear that, your Grace? It is all over.'

A great gasping sigh went up as the Duke of Allington slowly straightened up in the pulpit and wiped the blood from his hands with a handkerchief. 'Ladies and gentlemen, you have my abject apologies for giving you a terrible scare.'

O'Malley raised his hand for silence. 'As you can see, our honoured guest, by God's grace, is perfectly safe. The shot fired at him was a blank.'

A wave of outraged protest ran around the Church.

'Yes, I know, there is blood all over the lilies, but the blood you see is not the Duke's it came from a plastic bag concealed in his top pocket. He simply let it run out through his fingers,' the priest continued. 'It had to look authentic. If it hadn't fooled everyone else, it wouldn't have fooled the two killers at the back of this church.

'The purpose of this service was to promote peace and forgiveness. If the Duke of Allington had not gone ahead, it would have been a victory for vengeance. However, due to his bravery, we have overcome violence without violence. The two men at the rear of our church have not been harmed, merely rendered harmless.'

His words were interrupted as Sylvia Rooney ran to the front of the church, tears streaming down her face as she turned to face everybody.

'I have something to say,' her voice cracked a little but she carried on. 'This is supposed to be a service of forgiveness — then let it be so. I do not dispute his Grace is a very brave man, but I want it to be known that your priest, Father O'Malley, is a courageous man too. He knew of the danger and carried the knowledge alone.

He should not have to carry the burden of concealment about anything anymore.' She took a deep breath, 'I am grieved to have to say that one of the two men who intended harm was my own son, Sean Rooney.'

A buzz of voices began but she continued, 'Please, please, let me finish. Not only is Sean my son, but what has been unknown to anyone else until now is that Matthew O'Malley is his father.' She waited until the hubbub died down. 'Now he has been freed from the weight of concealment, I ask you all to remember the purpose of this visit by the Duke and find it in your hearts to forgive.'

The priest stood, head down, his hands hanging by his side. A sudden silence filled the church.

Slowly then, in one's and two's, the voices came . . . 'I forgive . . . I forgive . . . I forgive . . . ' until the church swelled with the sound and the words surged up like a great tide.

A much chastened Father Matthew O'Malley stepped forward and held out wide embracing arms to the whole congregation.

'Dear friends, I thank you for your forgiveness and your support,' emotion threatened to choke him but he continued with difficulty. 'It would seem our service of peace and forgiveness, which could have ended in disaster and death has turned into a victory. But the one man we must all thank for this outcome is the man who has remained out of public view at the rear of the church. Jack, please, come forward.'

Riley hesitated, suddenly finding himself looking into the smiling faces of Georgina and Casey.

'Go on,' Georgina whispered, 'he needs you. But come back, because I need you more,' and she gave him a little push.

Red-faced, Riley made his way to the front of the church. The Duke of Allington shook his hand firmly. O'Malley, smiling broadly, put an arm around Riley's shoulder. 'This, everybody, is the man we should applaud and thank,' he said. 'Without him our service would have ended in tragedy instead of in triumph. Ladies and gentlemen, Mr Jack Riley.'

Epilogue

The peace service had ended. The church was now hushed and empty.

Inside the presbytery, Jack Riley came through from the study to the sitting room. 'The Dublin police are on their way,' he announced looking round at the assembled group and particularly at Blake and Rooney who were sitting secured to hard backed chairs. 'Just in case you're wondering who I am,' he continued, 'the name's Jack Riley. Baxter is my cousin. The English police have already picked him up and by now he'll be back in Dartmoor.'

As he finished speaking, Father O'Malley moved across to the two men. He ripped the sticking plaster from Blake's mouth first and then from Rooney's. 'If you wish to talk, now is the time. We have only a few minutes.'

Blake looked at him with hatred. 'You murdered my wife.'

Father O'Malley swallowed, 'Do you think . . . do you really think it was with intent?'

'Does it make any difference?' Blake said harshly.

'Oh yes, all the difference in the world.

Murder is a premeditated act, an act of the vilest contempt and disregard for human life. I was trying to prevent the waste of an innocent life when the accident happened.'

Blake looked at him with loathing. 'And you killed her instead.'

O'Malley looked back at him. 'You forget, Gloria and I ... years ago ... we were lovers.'

'I know that.' he rasped.

'Ah, but what you don't know, my son, is that I still love her.'

The only sound in the room following his words was a tiny indrawn breath from Sylvia Rooney.

O'Malley turned to her, 'My dear, I'm sorry, it is a day for truth, as you yourself said in Church. Let us not have any more concealment.'

Sylvia drew herself up straight and said proudly, 'She may have been your lover, she may still have your love, but I bore your son.'

Rooney shouted wildly at her, 'Like hell I am.'

'It's true, Sean, Matthew is your father.'

'You're no father of mine,' Rooney spat the words at O'Malley. 'I'll never acknowledge you as my father.'

O'Malley said sadly, 'Forgiveness takes strength. It must come from within.'

Blake's gaze swung across to Sylvia. 'The one thing Gloria always wanted was a son. And it was denied her.' He laughed harshly, 'The irony of it is her lover's son married our daughter. And became her son-in-law.'

'What you're all bloody well forgetting is I lost my wife too, my Patricia,' Rooney shouted with rage. 'I lost her and I also lost my son, or it could have been my daughter . . . who the hell knows now, anyway. Yes, it's right, Patricia was pregnant when you killed her so think on that Father Bloody O'Malley. When you killed Gloria and Patricia you killed an innocent unborn child as well.'

O'Malley turned very pale and contained his emotions with great difficulty. 'We have all suffered and lost the ones we love.'

'I second that,' put in the Duke of Allington. 'I too have lost my daughter.'

'Violence is never the answer,' said the priest in a low voice. 'There are no victories for any of us. We are all losers.'

Riley moved over to the window and glanced out. 'There's a police car just arriving. It's up to them, they can take over now.' He held out a hand to Georgina. 'If you will excuse us, everyone . . . '

Leaving the presbytery, they walked hand in hand beneath the trees into the church-yard. The midday sun was bathing the church in mellow autumn sunshine and in one of the tall trees a wood pigeon cooed sleepily adding to the somnolent air of peace which had descended.

'Was it true, what you said about Baxter having been picked up by the police?'

'No,' Riley grinned, 'but those two believed it.'

'So they won't bother gunning for him?'

'Hopefully.'

'Anne Baxter must be wondering what's happened,' Georgina murmured.

'No problem,' Riley smiled at her. 'Before I 'phoned for the Dublin police from O'Malley's study, I spoke to Baxter in England. Told him the score.'

'Bet he was relieved.'

'He certainly was. I told him now he was clear of Blake's tentacles, he should do the sane thing, the only thing, and give himself up.'

'Do you think he will?' Georgina trailed a hand across one of the ancient lichen covered headstones.

'I don't know. You can only help someone so far, after that . . . '

'Life is so fragile, so impermanent,' she sighed.

Riley squeezed her hand and they walked on between the weathered old gravestones, the grasses swishing softly around their ankles. Coming to the church wall, Riley leaned against the rough bricks. 'You've got it wrong, my love,' he said. 'Life is eternal, about the only thing that is except, of course, for one other thing. Come here.' He drew her to him and looked down into her radiant face. Her sparkling eyes mirrored back the depth of his feelings for her. 'I really don't need to tell you what that is, do I?'

'Tell me anyway,' she said softly.

He stroked her cheek very gently. 'Love is eternal. Love lasts forever and always. And I love you. Will you stay with me, Georgina — forever?'

She looked steadily into his eyes. 'That decision is not in my hands,' she whispered. 'Our destiny was written aeons ago, in another time, another place. And so be it.'

Riley bent his head and she closed her eyes as he kissed her on the lips with the lightest, most tender of kisses. It was a single brief kiss, yet one which said it all.

He slipped an arm around her waist and together they walked slowly on through the quiet churchyard.

We do hope that you have enjoyed reading this large print book.

Did you know that all of our titles are available for purchase?

We publish a wide range of high quality large print books including:
Romances, Mysteries, Classics
General Fiction
Non Fiction and Westerns

Special interest titles available in large print are:
The Little Oxford Dictionary
Music Book
Song Book
Hymn Book
Service Book

Also available from us courtesy of Oxford University Press:
Young Readers' Dictionary
(large print edition)
Young Readers' Thesaurus
(large print edition)

For further information or a free brochure, please contact us at:
Ulverscroft Large Print Books Ltd.,
The Green, Bradgate Road, Anstey,
Leicester, LE7 7FU, England.
Tel: (00 44) 0116 236 4325
Fax: (00 44) 0116 234 0205

Other titles published by
The House of Ulverscroft:

PHOTO FINISH

Glenis Wilson

Black pearl smuggling and an abducted
ex-government scientist seem totally
unconnected and a million miles away
from English horse-racing — but as Jim
Crack, ex-jump jockey, now private eye,
discovers, they are not. As the attention
swings between the race-courses of
England and Malta, Jim finds himself
caught up in a web of danger, intrigue and
romance, and he is forced to confront the
dark shadows from his own past. The
suspense builds up, as twist follows twist,
into a totally unexpected, explosive climax.

BLOOD ON THE TURF

Glenis Wilson

When Jack Hunter is badly injured in a race accident, his daughter, Tal, finds herself having to take over his rides and the running of their racing stables. To keep the stables afloat, winners are required on the track; Tal is determined to get them, but someone is equally determined she will not. Ancient family skeletons are rattled from their cupboards and Tal's world is shaken apart when she discovers just who the 'someone' is.

MURDER IN MIND

J. A. O'Brien

As acting DI, Andy Lukeson had not expected to head up a high-profile murder investigation, but there he is, thrust forward into the limelight, investigating the murder of a woman whose death may be linked to a string of murders long unsolved. As he struggles to find the killer, Lukeson's fears of the case going cold haunt his every waking moment. Can he get to the heart of the matter before it's too late?

LOVE TO DEATH

Patti Battison

What happens when love goes bad — and it becomes an obsession . . . ? Ageing rocker Johnny Lee Rogers is performing a series of charity concerts in Larchborough. His biggest fan, librarian Lizzie Thornton, has won tickets to see his final show. She's convinced that Fate is bringing them together . . . and Lizzie's always wanted a December wedding. As the town basks in the hottest temperatures for decades, it will be no Summer of Love for DCI Paul Wells and his team. Lizzie, a group of travellers and a missing girl seem to have conspired to bring a time of torment, intrigue and murder.